MORE THAN A MISTRESS

LATIN MEN SERIES

DELANEY DIAMOND

GARDEN AVENUE PRESS

More Than a Mistress by Delaney Diamond

CHAPTER 1

*S*ome men enter a room and transform it. That was exactly what happened when Esteban Galiano strolled into Arturo Salvador's retirement party at the Blue Top Hotel on South Beach.

Jackie rushed over and plopped down her silver beverage tray. "He's here!" she hissed.

Sonia Kennedy paused in the process of pouring light magenta wine into glasses lined up across the shiny surface of the bar.

A gentle hum of excited whispers permeated the attendees and guests approaching Esteban, seeking his attention and halting his progress into the room. The Argentinean restaurateur oozed confidence in a dark jacket and no tie, appearing relaxed for the evening celebration.

Sonia went back to draining the last of the wine into the final glass.

"He's even more gorgeous in person," Jackie murmured.

Jackie Wen was Sonia's best friend. Tall and model thin, she looked even taller and slenderer in a torso-hugging black T-shirt and equally tight black stretch pants, her raven hair secured atop her head in a vertical ponytail.

Sonia signaled for the male and female servers standing nearby. They walked over and lifted the glasses onto their trays and moved away to circulate among the guests.

"He is handsome," Sonia agreed, as she wiped down the counter, at the same time casting a surreptitious glance in the direction of the man who had the entire room buzzing.

Intensely private, Esteban Galiano was not often photographed, despite counting celebrities and other famous people among his friends and acquaintances.

Some estimates placed the self-made man's personal wealth right at a billion dollars, while conservative estimates suggested three-quarters of a billion. No one knew for sure, but no matter the amount, he'd amassed his fortune in the past ten years, starting at the age of twenty-one.

His investments included art, hotels, and other real estate, but what he was known for, and where his passion truly lay, was in the restaurant industry. As a successful restaurateur, he had a reputation for having the Midas touch. His restaurants received rave reviews and earned both him and investors an enviable return in an industry known for its volatility.

Resting a hand on her hip, Jackie tracked his progress in the room, while Sonia pretended not to notice and restocked the glasses.

"I would love to work for him," Jackie said.

"Why would you work for him? You have a job at Azul," Sonia pointed out.

They both worked at Azul Restaurant, Jackie as a part-time hostess currently "finding" herself. She didn't need the job because her father, originally from China, was a wealthy hotelier with resorts around the world who supplemented her income from the UK. She had grown up socializing with the rich and famous and the not-so-famous. Living in Miami was a way for her to have a little fun before settling down into a life that included marrying an appropriately wealthy and well-bred man from her social circle and taking over her family's hotel empire.

Unfortunately for Sonia, business at Azul had slowed considerably in the past few months. Sluggish sales meant they didn't need two full-time sommeliers, so her hours had been cut to part-time for now.

Thankfully, one of Jackie's friends had backed out of this weekend gig at the Blue Top Hotel, and she'd recommended Sonia for the position. Between the wages and the tips she and the other bartender would split at the end of the evening, she expected to have a very good night. One that she desperately needed to keep from borrowing any more money from Jackie.

Her friend leaned across the bar. "Aside from the fact that he's probably the most important figure in the restaurant industry today, I heard he pays better than normal," she said in her very proper British accent. "You should try to get a job at his South Beach restaurant, La Cocina Patagonia. It's high-end, and I heard he wants to expand his wine collection."

"How do you find out about this stuff?"

Jackie knew everything about everyone in Miami. Sonia learned more from talking to her than watching the news.

"People tell me things," her friend said airily, waving a hand dismissively. "If he expands his wine collection, he might have to have to hire another sommelier. He has three full-time somms now."

"One wine director and three somms," Sonia said. She knew because she'd applied for a job at Galiano's flagship restaurant, known locally as Patagonia, a few weeks ago. The restaurant took up most of the ground floor of the boutique hotel above it, also named Patagonia, which he owned. His two other Miami businesses included a bakery and an Italian restaurant named Nonna, currently closed for renovations but due to reopen soon.

"You know, I heard he broke up with that model…oh, what's her name? The rather posh French one who goes by one name?" Jackie tapped her cheek.

"Noelle?"

"Yes, her. Rumor has it, he bought her a diamond necklace and had it delivered in a Rolls-Royce Phantom. Both were her breakup gifts."

"Nice breakup gifts," Sonia muttered. She didn't even own a car and couldn't imagine owning one that cost that much.

"I know. After my last breakup, all I got was a broken heart," Jackie said glumly. She pouted, fiddling with the pendant on her gold necklace.

Sonia rubbed her friend's arm.

Jackie was still recovering from a rather abrupt breakup with a boyfriend who'd accused her of being clingy. She then declared men were "heartless, soulless creatures who didn't care whose feelings they trampled on."

"I better get back out here and do the job I was hired to do." Jackie tucked the round beverage tray under her arm and stepped into the crowd.

"I'm going outside for a quick smoke." Davis, the other bartender, sidled past Sonia.

She busied herself filling orders while he was gone, chatted with guests, and poured more of the very popular wine from Arturo's own inventory, imported from his winery in Argentina. When there was a break in her duties, she took that moment to seek out Esteban.

As he was over six feet, she spotted him easily, in what looked like an intense conversation with another man. He nodded without saying a word, while the other man spoke animatedly with rapid movements of his hands.

Working for Galiano would be a great opportunity because of his restaurants' reputations, and she was certain she could do an excellent job for him as a sommelier. Attending this event might turn out to be the perfect opportunity to make a connection and follow up on the application she'd filled out weeks ago. Maybe before the night was over, she'd get that chance.

Sonia watched as Galiano grasped the arm of the other man with his large hand, said a few words, nodded, and smoothly excused himself from the conversation.

He was sexy. Overtly so. Square-jawed and brunette, with dark, brooding eyes. He traversed the room with an elegant gait, striking up conversations with the other guests. But arrogance surrounded him in an invisible cloud, evident in the hard slope of his jaw, perfect posture, and the almost bored expression on his face as he surveyed the guests with whom he paused to say a word or two.

He may give extravagant gifts, but he didn't wear his wealth in an ostentatious manner like the men and women in the room, with flashy gold rings and twenty-five-thousand-dollar purses. His wealth was undeniable in the subtleties. Like the fit of his navy jacket, tailored to his physique. He was well groomed, clean-shaven, and with his hair cut very short and hinting at a wavy texture if allowed to grow much longer. The only jewelry he did wear was a platinum watch she caught peeking out below his sleeve. She couldn't see the timepiece clearly from here but suspected he wouldn't have chosen an obvious brand, such as Rolex.

"Excuse me, what was that wine you poured for me earlier?"

Sonia's eyes veered away from Esteban to the woman standing in front of her, holding up a glass with less than an ounce of white wine at the bottom.

"It's from Arturo's personal stock in Argentina."

"White wine from Argentina?"

"Yes. You're probably more familiar with Malbec, but Argentina is becoming well known for their Torrontés. What you drank was Torrontés Riojano, which ranks second in wine exports from Argentina."

"You don't say."

Then Sonia got to do her favorite thing—share her knowledge and expertise about the wine she'd introduced to the guest. Hopefully, before the night was over, she'd have the opportunity to show off her knowledge to Esteban Galiano, too.

* * *

THE FIRST THING Esteban noticed about the bartender was her smile.

Which was interesting, since that usually wasn't the first thing he noticed about a woman. This woman had snagged his attention with the friendly smile she bestowed on every guest who approached the bar, male or female. Normally, his gaze encompassed a woman's breasts first, or her ass, or her hips, or the general shapeliness of her body—everything below her neck. Only then, after he was pleased by the visual, did he let his attention drift up to her face.

Lucky for him, this lovely creature was not only friendly, she was the type of shapely he liked. The black-on-black uniform did nothing to hide the lusciousness of her S-shaped curves. Full breasts sat atop her chest like monuments of perfection, straining against the black T-shirt. And when she temporarily moved from behind the bar, he glimpsed how the snug pants molded to her hips and thighs.

She had beautiful, golden skin and wore her hair in a short pixie—parted on one side and framing her round face. He'd already noted that she didn't wear a ring. And her lips…*maldito*. Full and painted a brilliant red that called to him. He had to speak to her before leaving tonight.

A heavy hand clapped his shoulder. "Esteban, glad you could make it! How was Buenos Aires?"

Dragging his eyes to his friend, Arturo, Esteban replied, "Excellent, as always." He returned the enthusiastic greeting with a firm handshake. "So Maria finally convinced you to retire. What did she have to do, put a gun to your head?"

Arturo chuckled, and the wrinkles in his face contracted. Wavy hair as white as fresh snow touched the collar of his shirt. "Almost. She threatened to leave me if I didn't stop working. Ever since I collapsed, she's been after me to quit."

Arturo and his wife had a strange relationship. In the thirty-plus years they'd been married, he'd never been faithful, and Maria turned a blind eye to his indiscretions. Two years ago, Arturo's so-called assistant "found" him collapsed in the bathroom of a hotel, and Esteban thought for sure Maria would leave him then. Instead, it seemed to have brought them closer together.

"What will you do with yourself now?" Esteban asked.

"I suppose I could do what men my age are supposed to do, and play with the grandchildren."

They both laughed, knowing Arturo was nothing like the typical grandfather. He liked to party, and see and be seen in the hotspots around the world. Basically, he was a twenty-five-year-old man living in a sixty-five-year-old's body.

"She's beautiful, isn't she?" Arturo inclined his head toward the bar before lifting a glass of wine to his lips.

"Yes," Esteban said evenly.

The pretty bartender stood out among the other women there, even dressed in the same black uniform as the other staff.

"I flirted a little bit with her, but there was no interest."

Even with his wife in the room, that didn't stop Arturo from making advances toward other women. At times Esteban wondered why his friend had gotten married. Why not live the unattached bachelor life, like Esteban? He never lacked companionship and didn't have to worry about thorny issues like commitment and monogamy.

"I give you my blessing to pursue her," Arturo said.

Esteban cast a sidelong glance at his friend. "I don't need your blessing."

"No, you don't." Arturo waved at a friend across the room. "I take it you're not carrying a torch for Noelle?"

"You know better than that," Esteban said dryly.

"Good. She was no good."

"Is any woman good?" Esteban asked with a cynical twist of his lips.

"My Maria," Arturo said definitively.

That was the closest Esteban had come to seeing how deeply his friend cared for his wife.

"Lucky you. You found the only woman worth marrying."

"There are others, but until you find the right one, might as well have some fun." Arturo cackled and patted Esteban's shoulder. "I'll see you later, friend." He walked away, leaving Esteban behind.

Esteban shot a glance at the bar, a slow smile lifting one corner of his mouth.

If he played his cards right, he might have some fun tonight.

CHAPTER 2

*A*rturo saw his retirement party as an opportunity to do PR for his wines, and part of Sonia's responsibility was to talk them up. She managed to sell bottle after bottle, and even an entire case to one of Arturo's business associates. As the crowd dwindled late in the evening, she found herself in the middle of a conversation with an older man by the name of Gene, and his much younger girlfriend.

The young woman's hair extended down to her butt in a long blonde weave. She barely paid attention as Sonia made suggestions about wine and food pairings, but the man, wearing thick black glasses and holding an unlit cigar between his fingers, listened attentively and asked the occasional question for clarification.

"What about Muscadet wine? Do you have any recommendations?" he asked.

"I do. If you want a little more body and complexity, I suggest you look for a Muscadet with *sur lie* on the label," Sonia replied.

"Sir Lee?"

"*Sur lie*. S-U-R L-I-E. That indicates the wine has spent extra time in contact with the yeast, and you'll find the flavor much more interesting...rich and toasty."

His eyes lit up with excitement. "Thank you so much. Times like this make me think I should hire a wine consultant." He laughed softly.

"Well, you can."

He looked at her with renewed interest. "Are you available?"

"As a matter of fact, I am. And I do parties."

"Tell me you have a card."

Sonia lifted her cards out of her pants pocket and handed two of them to Gene.

"How much do you charge?"

All of a sudden, a wave of energy rippled through the air. Her eyes angled to the left and collided with the gaze of Esteban Galiano, strolling toward them with his gaze holding steady on her. Her heart hopped and chills flickered down the length of her arms. For a moment she remained immobilized, only able to stare as he approached with a determined set to his chiseled jaw.

Taken aback, Sonia blinked rapidly and looked away. "I—ah—I… the price is um…" Goodness, she could barely talk. She swallowed. "The price per hour is negotiable, depending on the venue, the type of service you require, and the number of hours you'll need me. If you go to my website, you'll see general rates and options."

"Thank you. I'll be in touch."

The couple moved away and, taking a deep breath, Sonia turned around to face Esteban. Up close she saw he had chocolate-colored eyes and a thin upper lip resting on a plump bottom one. The strands of his black hair glimmered beneath the lights, and his pale yellow shirt, opened at the top to reveal a strong throat, looked even paler against his swarthy skin.

"Can I get you a drink, Mr. Galiano?" she asked, kicking herself for the breathlessness in her voice. She'd met plenty of attractive men before, certainly not unusual in a city like Miami, where appearances were very important for both men and women. With a diversity of cultures, at any given time, one could run into a handsome Brit, a handsome Russian, and, certainly, a handsome South American. So why did this man unnerve her so much?

"I'm not in the mood for a drink, but I am interested in knowing more about you."

"Me?"

Rounding the bar, Sonia put the barrier between them as a safety mechanism. She hadn't expected his voice to sound like that. She was accustomed to hearing Spanish accents, but it wasn't simply his accent. The smoky huskiness was very appealing. Sensual, almost as if he'd caressed her with his words.

"Yes. I've heard nothing but complimentary remarks about you all evening. You know your wines." A whisper of a smile lifted the corners of his mouth but didn't quite soften his features. His eyes were too assessing. His jaw too rigid. In fact, he made her a little uneasy. She sensed a ruthlessness beneath the polished exterior.

"I should. I'm a sommelier." His unnerving attention left her a little short of breath.

"You are? Are you certified?"

"Not yet, but I plan to be eventually." She'd already earned an introductory certificate and was studying for the next level. The coursework required a substantial investment of time and money. Both, particularly the latter, were at a premium of late.

Interest sparked in his eyes. "Tell me"—his gaze flicked to the gold nametag—"Sonia. What do you know about Argentine wines?"

She debated whether or not to mention that she'd put in an application at La Cocina Patagonia. She sensed that he was testing her, which meant he might be considering her for his restaurant. She tried not to get too excited, instead concentrating on impressing him with her knowledge.

"I know there's more to Argentina than your Malbecs, though it's what the country is best known for producing, and they're your number one wine export. But Argentina produces other varieties, including Chardonnay and Cabernet. Torrontés—a floral, tropical-tasting wine—are gaining in popularity in the U.S., and I personally enjoy a good Bonarda to change things up a bit."

The corners of his mouth quirked higher, and this time she did note a softening in his features, which created a tightening in her belly.

"You did well," he said.

"You had doubts?"

"Not at all. I'm certain you're a very talented woman."

Heat suffused her skin. A bit flustered, Sonia laughed softly and cleared her throat. "Thank you for the compliment."

"Do you have plans after you leave here?" He rested an arm atop the bar, and his voice dropped lower, a gravelly texture infusing the words. "Perhaps you could join me for drinks at Patagonia, my hotel. We could continue this conversation about wines or...other things."

"Other things?" Her spirits deflated as she realized what was happening. He wasn't interested in her knowledge or expertise. He was making a pass at her. "What other things?" Sonia asked, still holding out hope that she was wrong.

He kept his eyes on her as a knowing smile drifted over his face. "The type of things men and women talk about. If you prefer to change, I could have my driver take you home and bring you back to the hotel for us to...talk."

The slight pause and the way his eyes drifted down to her breasts before coming back up again made it clear the last thing on his mind was conversation, and she hated the way her nipples tightened under his hungry gaze. He expected her to be like everyone else—perhaps every other woman he ran into—turning cartwheels because he'd made time to speak to her. Appreciative that he'd chosen her from among all the guests in attendance. She would have been appreciative and turning cartwheels, if his interest was job-related.

Tamping down her irritation, Sonia looked him directly in the eyes. "I'm sorry, Mr. Galiano, but I'm not available later this evening."

"Tomorrow, then?"

Couldn't this guy take a hint? Of course not. He probably couldn't fathom someone had rejected his not-so-subtle offer. This was the part where she became annoyed. She could be flattered by his attention, but the truth was, he didn't even *see* her. For him, like so many men, she was a pretty face, and she couldn't complain about the insult of being reduced to tits, ass, and a pretty face without sounding like a vain bitch.

"Not tomorrow, or the day after, or any day after that," Sonia said coolly, meeting his gaze.

Take that, you arrogant ass.

One dark eyebrow lifted a fraction before settling back into place. His shoulders straightened and his face settled into an impassive expression. "I'm usually very good at reading people, but it appears I've made a mistake in this instance."

"Mistakes happen," Sonia said, disappointed she'd lost her shot at working for him.

His gaze lingered on her face. "It was a pleasure meeting you, Sonia." With a slight bow, he shoved a hand in his pocket and strolled away.

Sonia's shoulders sagged as she breathed easier. For some reason, he made her very tense.

More guests trickled out the door, and she started closing down the bar. Davis had already left, so she was alone. As she finished up, Jackie came over.

"All done?" her friend asked. Jackie lived in a swanky neighborhood in Coral Gables, but she was spending the night in Sonia's one-bedroom apartment, walking distance away on Washington Avenue.

"All done," Sonia confirmed.

They headed out the door and took the elevator to the first floor. Exiting the hotel, they started down the stairs, and right in front of them stood Esteban beside a champagne-colored Mercedes Maybach. Hanging on his arm was a lithe Asian woman with a buzz cut, wearing a figure-hugging turquoise sleeveless dress. The sight of the woman hanging on his arm initially shocked Sonia and then turned her stomach.

"Why am I not surprised he left the party with someone?" Jackie murmured.

That someone could have been Sonia.

Esteban helped the woman into the car and then walked around to the other door. Before getting in, he happened to look up and saw Sonia and Jackie.

No acknowledgment. Nothing on his face indicated they'd talked and he'd propositioned her, expecting her to be the woman he took to his hotel tonight.

And then, a slight lift at the left corner of his mouth. Not even a smile, just a small movement that suggested he was scoffing at her and her principles.

She glared at him, lifting her head a little higher in rebuttal.

Esteban slipped into the car and his driver, who'd already walked around by then, closed the door and climbed into the front seat.

Sonia and Jackie stepped down onto the sidewalk for the short walk to her apartment. Jackie chattered away, but Sonia barely listened, watching as the Maybach rolled by, the images of the occupants not discernible because of the dark tint of the windows.

She'd made the right decision. She needed a job, not a man, and she already had a boyfriend.

She wasn't jealous. Not even a teeny tiny bit.

CHAPTER 3

"*T*his is unacceptable!" Esteban thundered.

He tossed the menus onto his desk and glowered at the graphics designer. "We are months from reopening and this is what you brought me? This design is not even close to what I instructed you to create. Nonna is a fine-dining establishment, not a neighborhood diner."

The woman's cheeks reddened but she didn't respond. He didn't expect her to. He'd put up with too much of her poor performance and was at the end of his patience.

He held up a finger. "You have one more opportunity to get this right."

Quietly, she took the offending menus and headed to the door.

"You're in a mood." Oval-faced, with skin nearly as dark as a sunless sky, his assistant, Abena, strolled over from the far side of his office, where she'd made him a midmorning espresso. Originally from Ghana, she wore her hair shaved low, almost to the scalp, highlighting her stunning ebony features. She could have been a model if she weren't so short and curvy.

Esteban accepted the cup and took an appreciative sip. "Not everyone is as professional and efficient as you."

Calling Abena his assistant was a misnomer. She was more than

14

that. Her language skills—she spoke seven—proved indispensable in meetings, she supervised his administrative assistant, and managed a multitude of tasks in his personal and business life. She was his right hand, a Jane-of-all-trades. If they were married, he'd call her his rib. Except three months ago a very smart man had put an engagement ring on her finger to secure the future right to call her that.

"I need you to be charming when you meet with the investors at your two o'clock appointment."

Esteban looked up from the documents he was reviewing. "They're trying to impress *me*, not the other way around."

"We all know that you have the Midas touch when it comes to restaurants, Mr. Galiano. But these men are a prestigious investor group that represents celebrity clients. It would be good for you to be on your best behavior." Abena was the only person he tolerated talking to him like that. She managed to do so in dulcet tones, her faintly accented voice softening her words and giving them a melodious effect. "By the way, you have fifteen minutes for your appointment with Adam before the lunch meeting with your attorney."

"Dammit. Is that today?"

Esteban glanced at the clock on the desk, mentally running through the list of tasks he wanted to complete. Fortunately, he didn't have far to travel. His office was located upstairs from the restaurant. He'd commandeered an entire floor of the hotel and turned it into the seat of his East Coast offices.

"Yes." Abena removed a folder tucked under her arm and placed it in front of him. "Here's everything you need to review before the meeting."

Esteban flipped open the dossier, and she'd already marked the paragraphs he should pay close attention to with colorful arrow tabs. What would he do without this woman? He made a mental note to add to her annual bonus.

A knock sounded on the open door, and Adam Jamison walked in. A tall black male, he was approximately the same height as Esteban and commanded attention when he entered a room. He owned Premium Staffing, an international placement firm, and with his help, Esteban filled key positions in his restaurants in the States and overseas. Because Esteban was his biggest client, he often preferred to handle his requests personally instead of handing them over to one of his account managers.

"Hello, Adam, can I get you anything? Water? Coffee?" Abena asked.

"I'm fine, thanks."

"I'll leave you two alone," Abena said.

Esteban kept his eyes on the folder of information before him and didn't need to look up to know that Adam ogled Abena as she walked out the door. Not that he could blame him. The simple skirt and blouse ensemble looked striking on her shapely figure.

"She's engaged now," he reminded Adam, without looking up.

"Happily?" Adam asked, half joking, half serious. He took a seat in front of the desk.

Esteban didn't need to reply. "How is your progress on finding me a chef de cuisine?"

His current chef was leaving to open his own restaurant, and Esteban hadn't been satisfied with the first round of choices. Fortunately, he'd given Esteban ample notice, allowing him to fill the position in a timely fashion.

"My assistant emailed the CVs of three potential chefs. Have you seen those?"

"I reviewed them and I'd like to fly in the female candidate for an interview."

Adam nodded, making a note on his tablet. "I should have two more for you before the end of the week, assuming they pass the background check." He looked up. "Who will be conducting the interviews? You or the general manager?"

"Both. I want to make sure the new chef understands my vision and the food that they'll be creating." Esteban was very particular about Patagonia, much more so than with his other stateside restaurants. Patagonia was his baby, his first U.S. endeavor, and the one that had launched his success in the country. The restaurant offered a variety of South American cuisine, from Peruvian ceviche to Argentine grilled meats served with chimichurri made fresh daily.

"And that other project I asked you to work on?"

He hadn't been able to get Sonia off his mind and found out her full name from Arturo. Then he'd enlisted Adam's assistance in finding out more about her. Adam had said her name sounded familiar and, upon further research, found her information in the database. She'd applied for a position with Patagonia a few weeks ago.

Adam looked up with a curious expression, but he wasn't comfortable enough to ask the question that lurked behind his eyes. "Do you want the long version or the highlights?"

With his elbows on the chair arms, Esteban interlaced his fingers. "The highlights."

Adam double-tapped the tablet screen. "Sonia Kennedy, twenty-seven years old, finished high school in Atlanta, Georgia. No post-high-school education. Has been working in restaurants since she started waitressing in the eleventh grade. Moved to Miami a few years ago, worked as a hostess at one restaurant before getting one of two sommelier positions at Azul Restaurant. Currently holds an introductory sommelier certificate."

"So she's been at Azul how long?"

"Over a year. According to her application, the reason she's looking for work is because they cut her hours to part-time."

"She was very impressive at Arturo's party. What did she say when you told her I was interested in offering her a position as a private wine consultant?"

"Um, let's just say she wasn't interested."

"That bad?" He smiled internally. He could imagine her response.

"She seemed to think I had an ulterior motive for contacting her."

"Interesting." Esteban hid his amusement behind a stoic expression. "Thank you. I appreciate your help."

"No problem." Adam rose from the chair. "I'm sure I could find you a qualified wine consultant for your parties."

"I've found the person I want. Have a good day."

After Adam left, Esteban swiveled in his chair and released the smirk he hadn't allowed to appear in Adam's presence. Even a job offer, one she obviously needed, couldn't convince Miss Kennedy to have anything to do with him.

Patience, he silently chided himself. He was a patient man and a rich man. There was nothing he couldn't achieve with patience and money.

Her resistance only made him more determined to see her. When he did, he'd make her an offer she couldn't refuse.

* * *

SEATED in a booth near the kitchen, Sonia stifled a yawn. A few diners remained, conversation had lowered to a moderate hum, and the lights were turned low. It had been a long but productive night. All of her wine recommendations had been well received, resulting in a high-revenue night. She'd even sold a bottle of scotch for over five thousand dollars. The owner had been beside himself with glee, but it didn't change her current situation.

The landscape of the wine industry had changed over the years to include more female sommeliers. Even the Europeans were allowing more women into their wine cellars. In the States, the numbers were more impressive, and in recent years, the number of new master sommeliers that were female had outpaced the number of men, but sexism and skepticism were still rampant in a vocation where men continued to dominate, and Sonia was fairly certain that the reason she was part-time and the other sommelier was full-time was because she was female and he was male.

Pedro Loisseau, her boyfriend, sat beside her on the padded bench and rested the back of his head to the wall. The assistant pastry chef and former bad boy had found his love for creating in the kitchen surpassed his love of getting into trouble. Half Cuban and half Haitian, he wore his long, wavy hair in a single braid down his back.

"Tired?" Sonia asked.

"Yeah." There was an undertone of something else in his voice.

"What's wrong?" She touched his shoulder.

"Tired of *this*," he said. "When am I ever going to be able to do more? I'm a scientist and an artist. I have ideas for great creations, but I'm stuck making flan and *budin de pan*."

She frowned at his tone of disgust. She loved his *budin de pan*. His version was creamy, without the chunks of bread. Pedro made it even better by soaking the raisins in rum and topping off the entire dessert with a healthy dose of caramel syrup. It was a simple but decadent treat.

"You know this is only the beginning for you. You have to start somewhere."

His life before Azul was sketchy at best, but he was fortunate to get the opportunity to work at the restaurant. His restlessness stemmed from the fact that he thought he'd never be able to advance beyond an assistant's position because the restaurant owner's boyfriend also happened to be the pastry chef.

She stroked her fingers over Pedro's tattooed forearms, and he moved restlessly, withdrawing from her touch. Her hand fell to the seat.

"I've been here a long time," he muttered. "I don't want charity, just the opportunity to prove what I can do. I'm way more creative than Dan."

"You have to be patient. All good things come to those who wait." She sometimes thought it was his attitude that kept him from advancing. He was a great pastry chef, but arrogant because of it.

He glared at her. "How much longer do I have to wait? I've paid my debt to society, did my time for all the wrongs I've done, but still I'm stuck at the bottom no matter how hard I work."

She'd never heard him sound so despondent before. "Baby, stop. You're brilliant, but you've only been at this a couple of years."

"Maybe I should forget the whole thing. Go back to doing what I do best."

"*Stop.*" How could he even say that, as if he hadn't been in enough trouble in the past? He'd told her about his three-year stint and how it had broken his mother's heart. How could he even think about going back to a life of crime after all he'd put her through? "What can I do? How can I make you feel better?"

She slid a hand up his thigh. This was as much for him as for her. She was horny tonight, which she hadn't been in a long time. She didn't want to think about why, that it might have something to do with a certain Argentinean whose piercing brown eyes she hadn't been able to forget.

Pedro covered her hand with his and stared straight ahead. "Not tonight. I'm not in the mood."

She withdrew from him. They hadn't had sex in a while. Like week-old bread, their relationship had gone stale.

19

"I better get out of here." Pedro unfolded his tall, wiry body from the booth. "I'm going to hang with the fellas tonight."

"All right." She'd wanted him to come home with her, but managed to keep the disappointment out of her voice. "I'll see you later."

Silently, he watched her and then leaned down to kiss her forehead. "I'm in a mood, *ma belle*. I need to be alone tonight." Whenever he was apologetic, he used French endearments. When angry, he used Spanish ones.

"I understand." She didn't. She used to be able to cheer him up, and they used to be unable to resist making love, even after long hours at work where both had been on their feet for most of the day. "I'll see you tomorrow."

He nodded and walked toward the exit between the mostly empty tables and few diners that remained.

Sonia rested her chin in her hand. Unable to banish the face of Esteban Galiano from her mind, she indulged in the memory of him. His image was practically burned into her retinas. Why couldn't she stop thinking about him?

Because he'd had a staffing agency contact her with a phony job offer. The man was a pig, and a persistent one. Fortunately, she had plenty of experience resisting the overtures of persistent pigs.

Sighing, she stood, picked up her purse from the seat, and walked briskly out of the restaurant.

CHAPTER 4

here she is.

Seated in the back of the Maybach, Esteban watched as Sonia exited Azul Restaurant in an outfit that fit so perfectly that he damn near salivated at the sight of her. Her full breasts gently bounced as she hurried down the cement steps. The mustard-colored dress stood out in the night, hugging her full hips and ending in a swish of fabric that swirled around her knees.

"I'll be back," he said to his driver, Abel.

He exited the vehicle into the chaotic party atmosphere that was Ocean Drive at night. His vehicle blended in with the others cruising by or parked in premium spaces in front of the restaurants. He barely saw the orange Lamborghini and ignored the three young men in a Porsche convertible, bouncing their heads and rapping at the top of their lungs to music blasting on the radio.

He only had eyes for her, keeping track of her between the hordes of people milling about. A short distance from the restaurant, she stopped and removed the gold and red heels on her feet, dropping them into the oversized leather bag on her shoulder, and replaced them with a pair of burgundy ballet flats before taking off again.

The minute she saw him, she halted, eyebrows drawing down over her eyes. Her face registered recognition, then confusion, then wariness. Slowly, she approached and stopped directly in front of him, and he saw it as a good sign that she didn't walk on by.

"Good evening," he said.

"You know, some people would call this stalking."

"But you're not some people, and you know better."

"Do I, Mr. Galiano?" she asked coolly.

"You remember my name."

"How could I forget? You're one of the most important figures in the restaurant industry today."

He smiled. "I'm flattered."

"Those were my friend's words, not mine."

He took the veiled insult in stride. "Too bad. I would like to become important to you, too."

"I'm well aware, but as I told you, I'm not interested. If you came to change my mind, you've wasted your time, like you wasted your time having your friend call me with a 'job' offer." Her eyes flashed angrily at him.

"I never waste my time. Every effort brings me closer to the ultimate goal."

Sonia raised an eyebrow. Her delicious-looking body drew him in, but so did her eyes. They were almond-shaped and dark chocolate, lifted slightly in the corner, and fringed by long black lashes that gave them a dramatic, sultry look.

"And what exactly is your ultimate goal?"

"You must be tired after a long day on your feet. Perhaps we could go somewhere and sit and talk."

She looked away from him and shook her head, laughing softly. "I would never have guessed, but you're hard of hearing."

"Excuse me?"

"I thought I made it clear that I'm not interested in dinner, drinks, or any other ideas you have."

"Oh, you think this is an invitation for a date," he said.

Her brow furrowed. "Isn't it?"

"As you said, you made it clear you're not interested. My fragile ego can only take so much bruising."

Esteban waited as she studied him with skepticism in her eyes, but the corners of her mouth twitched a little.

As they stood in the middle of the sidewalk, pedestrians were forced to veer around them. He didn't move, and neither did she. Despite the animosity, he sensed that his attraction to her was not one-sided. He hadn't been mistaken when he saw her at Arturo's party. At his friend's party, there had been definite interest in her eyes, but his approach had turned her off. He would have to put in more time with this woman, but he didn't mind. He suspected she would be worth the extra effort.

Sonia bit the corner of her mouth, sinking her teeth into the plump lower lip he so desperately wanted to sink his own teeth into. "What do you want to talk about?"

"I have a business proposition for you. One that I think you'd be interested in."

"I doubt it."

"At least hear me out."

She took a deep breath, and her breasts lifted and lowered, distracting him for a moment with their luscious fullness.

"Listen, I'm not trying to be mean, ugly, or bitchy, but I'm really not interested. As you pointed out, I've had a long day and all I want to do is get home and put my feet up."

"How far away do you live?"

She stared at him, mouth firmly closed.

"I only ask because it's obvious you're walking, or you wouldn't have changed shoes. If you're walking to a location nearby, I'll walk with you."

She tugged her purse closer to her body and crossed an arm over her belly, clearly reluctant to divulge any personal information. "Over on Washington Avenue," she said finally.

"Do you mind if I walk with you?"

She shrugged. "Suit yourself."

Sonia took off, and Esteban fell into step beside her.

Casting a sidelong glance at him from beneath her lashes, she said, "I take it you're not used to hearing no."

"It's not a word I'm accustomed to hearing," Esteban confirmed.

"I figured." She laughed and brushed the hair from her brow. He preferred short hair on a woman. It didn't get in the way, and women with short hair were often uninhibited because they were free from the constraints of longer hair. The short haircut showed off the slope of her neck and exposed her profile to his hungry gaze.

"What is this great opportunity you want to discuss?" she asked.

"Right to business, I see. I like that." They briefly separated, as a couple—obviously tourists by the way they took photos of the animated nightlife on the street—walked between them. "I learned from Gene that you offer a service where you do private parties. Whenever I'm in the States, I entertain in my home from time to time and would like to hire your services as a wine consultant for those events. You impressed me the other day with your knowledge, and everyone at the party seemed pleased with your suggestions."

She eyed him suspiciously. "Don't you have sommeliers on staff at your own restaurant?"

"I do, but they stay very busy, and I prefer to keep that aspect of my business separate from the business I conduct in my home."

"There are a lot of sommeliers available in the city," she pointed out.

"Yes, but I want you."

Her gaze flitted to him before returning to the street. They turned a corner to a side street, and the difference was immediate. Much quieter and almost deserted, with only a few people trudging along ahead of them.

"I'm not interested," Sonia said flatly.

"You haven't heard the details yet. At least let me tell you more about the opportunity before you turn me down."

She stopped in the middle of the sidewalk and swung around to face him. "Okay, tell me the details. I'm listening."

"Here? In the middle of the street?" Esteban asked, as if she'd asked him to do something unbelievably ridiculous.

"Why not?"

"That's not the way that I conduct business. We should sit down and talk privately, and I'll lay out the plans, what I have to offer, and then we can negotiate from there."

She averted her eyes. With a wrinkled brow, she asked, "Is this some kind of ruse, for you to find a roundabout way to convince me to go out with you?"

He chuckled. "Have I said anything that would suggest my idea is less than professional?"

Sonia studied him, and he waited.

"Well, have I?" he prompted.

"No, you haven't," she admitted.

"You're too suspicious. I simply would like to tell you more about my proposal, if you're interested. Unless you don't need the job." He made as if to turn away.

"No, it's not that," Sonia said hastily. "I…"

"You applied for a job at Patagonia, did you not?"

She nodded. "I did."

"Well, I don't need you at Patagonia, but I could use your services in my home."

"How much did you say this position paid?"

"I prefer not to talk specifics right now. Blame my culture, but we South Americans prefer to sit down and break bread with our future business partners. Get to know each other. If all goes well, we will be working together quite often, and we should be able to get along, don't you agree?" He smiled.

"I suppose so," Sonia said slowly and cautiously.

"Good. Which means we should make time to discuss the specifics. Are you free any evening in the coming days?"

"Not until Saturday," she replied, and started walking again.

"Then why don't we plan for dinner on Saturday evening at my restaurant?" He handed her a card with his name and the restaurant details. "The number on the back is my private cell number."

She flipped over the card, stared at the number, and then tucked it into her purse. "Okay."

He heard the hesitation in her voice. "I promise I'll make it worth your time. I can be very generous."

"What time would you like to meet?"

"I'll pick you up at seven?"

"I'd rather you didn't. I'll meet you there."

He shrugged. "Very well. I hope you don't cancel on me."

"I won't."

"Seven, at La Cocina Patagonia. I look forward to seeing you again."

"We'll see."

She turned onto Washington and walked to a three-story apartment building, the sway of her hips a tantalizing motion beneath the dress. That motion would look especially seductive when she was naked and walking across the floor of his bedroom.

She went through the wrought iron gate and under the cluster of trees, looking back once she'd reached the outer door. She didn't wave or smile, simply stared at him for a brief moment before disappearing into the building.

That was easier than he'd expected.

With a private smile, Esteban started the short trek back to the main street and his waiting vehicle.

CHAPTER 5

"*H*ow do I look?"

Sonia smoothed the sides of her pixie cut and finished by teasing the top into a low lift with a rattail comb. Wrinkling her nose, she stood back and assessed her appearance. The sleeves of the lavender blouson top draped to her elbows in a loose fit, but the black slacks fit snug on her round hips.

"You look fabulous." Jackie stood in the doorway of the bathroom, sipping from a mug of coffee. "I wish I had your bum," she said forlornly. "You could set a drink on that thing."

Every now and again Jackie complained about her body and lamented that she wanted a rounder figure, but Sonia never believed her. At five ten and a size two, her friend turned heads wherever she went and loved the attention.

"Stop exaggerating, it's not that big." Sonia smoothed a hand over her hips, applied a light coat of lipstick, and popped her lips to evenly distribute the color. "Are you sure I look okay?"

The meeting with Esteban wasn't a date. She was going to discuss business, but Patagonia was a nice restaurant, and she wanted to look her best without looking like she'd tried too hard. She ignored the little voice inside her head that suggested she wanted to look her best for him, which was ridiculous. She was involved with Pedro, information she debated keeping from Esteban for now.

"What are you worried about?" Jackie sipped her coffee, her gaze trailing down Sonia's body. "Esteban Galiano will probably fire his wine director and hire you when he sees you in those trousers."

Sonia laughed and turned to take a look at the back of her outfit. Her butt did look amazing. Sighing, she said, "I have to get out of here. Wish me luck."

She breezed out the door into her bedroom and slipped on a pair of low-heeled sling-backs with a glittery design. The peep-toe front showed off her freshly painted toes. Her sparsely furnished bedroom contained a bed, an old recliner, and a heavy old dresser with a mirror above it. The three paintings grouped above her bed had been discount finds at Walmart.

"Good luck!" Jackie plopped onto the recliner in the corner of the room and flipped on the television.

"Are you spending the night?" Sonia asked.

"I'll be gone before you get back."

Sonia shook her head. "How about you stay here and I'll live in your house?"

"You'll be just as bored as I am living all alone in that big old house. Trust me."

"I'm willing to make the sacrifice." Sonia picked up her purse and rushed through the door. "See you later."

"Tah-tah," Jackie called.

Sonia took a cab, and the driver delivered her to the front of Esteban's restaurant at the far end of Ocean Drive, away from the usual hustle and bustle of nighttime activity. Before tonight, she'd done her research and learned that he'd purchased the entire building seven years ago, remodeling the hotel and converting the restaurant into a fine-dining establishment. It offered plenty of outdoor seating and private dining rooms that accommodated guests with a medium to high-end budget.

Working for a man like him could mean more doors opened up for her, but Sonia knew that wasn't why her heart fluttered nervously as she walked quickly up the steps. She still hadn't been able to reconcile her strong attraction to Esteban.

She walked through the hotel lobby to the restaurant's packed dining room. Dark wood paneling made the restaurant appear small and intimate, but she knew from the online description that it extended back for thousands of square feet. Recessed lights cast a warm halo over the diners, seated at tables and in cozy booths that could be enclosed by curtains with delicate gold beading.

The quiet elegance of the establishment caused Sonia to introduce herself in a soft voice to the maître d', an older Hispanic male in a dark suit and bold gold tie. She told him she had a meeting with Esteban.

"Ah yes, we've been expecting you, Miss Kennedy. I'm Armando." Signaling with one hand, he caught the attention of one of the waiters, who hurried over. "Cecil will escort you to the private dining room upstairs."

"Please follow me," the young man said, and ushered her through a door that led to a flight of stairs.

They entered a room situated directly in front of a large window, with a view of the Atlantic Ocean and sparkling lights in the distance.

"Mr. Galiano will be with you shortly," the waiter said, before leaving her alone and closing the door.

Sonia stood in front of the window, and before long she heard movement behind her. She hadn't even heard the door open, but there was Esteban, looking spectacular in a coal-black jacket, white shirt, and black slacks. His dark eyes remained on her as he approached.

"I'm so glad you could make it. I'd hoped you wouldn't cancel on me."

Tonight, dark hair sprinkled on his chin and jaw line gave him a more masculine appeal. She'd always been attracted to men with beards—not the lumberjack kind that was popular nowadays, but the short, barely there type, as if the man wearing it didn't have time to shave for a few days.

Her gaze drifted swiftly over his attire. Esteban was tall, easily six two, possibly six three. Though she couldn't tell for sure, he appeared to have a fit body under the clothes, and his presence dominated the dimly lit room.

The suit fit perfectly to his frame, but she wouldn't expect anything less than tailored clothing from a man of his stature. The red and blue diagonally striped tie was clipped to his shirt via a gold tie clip with a single diamond stud. Damn, this man knew how to dress and wear a suit, but she imagined he'd look just as dashing dressed casually. Just as he was mouthwateringly attractive clean-shaven or bearded.

"I promised you I'd come, and I'm very interested in your business proposition," Sonia said, ignoring the taxing press of some indefinable sensation that weighed heavy on her chest.

"Good." His eyes raked her body—a quick flicker, but noticeable. "You look lovely this evening. It's a shame I have you hidden away up here where no one can see you."

The unexpected compliment made her skin heat, and she was certain he could see the red tint on her neck.

"Thank you," Sonia murmured.

She couldn't decipher the expression on his face. Was it a smirk or simply a pleasant smile?

He held out a chair and she settled into it, inhaling the bold scent of his cologne—something citrusy, with hints of bergamot. She waited as he crossed to the other side and sat down.

"This is a lovely place you have," Sonia said.

"Have you ever eaten here before?" he asked.

"No, I haven't." She spread the white napkin across her lap, cursing inside her head at the nervous twitter of her fingers.

"Well, I can't wait to entice you with all the good food you're about to have. Everything we serve is excellent." He flashed a grin, exposing white teeth and softening his normally sharp features into an appealing expression that stole her breath.

Her attraction to him was a bit unnerving. Being in his presence created a tightening in her gut, an unexpected tension she couldn't attribute solely to nervousness about his potential business offer.

A new waiter entered, wearing the black vest, white shirt, and black slacks that made up the uniform of all the servers. His long hair was pulled back into a bunched ponytail at his nape.

"Since you've never eaten here before, do you mind if I order for us?"

She smiled briefly. "I trust your judgment."

"Good."

Esteban spoke to the young man in Spanish, and the server nodded his understanding several times. He didn't take notes, which, from working in the restaurant industry for years, Sonia knew meant he was really good at what he did. Servers who didn't take notes were often the ones asked for by name when guests arrived in a restaurant, and she wasn't at all surprised Esteban had chosen one of his best employees to serve them.

When the young man left, Esteban turned his attention to her. "So, what do you think of the view?"

Her gaze shifted to the open window. "I like it. It must be stunning during the daytime."

"This is one of our more popular rooms. It can seat up to twelve comfortably, and the wall behind you can be opened to expand the room and accommodate more seating into an even wider dining area."

"I read somewhere that Patagonia was your first U.S. venture?"

He sat back in the chair. "I see you did your homework."

"Of course."

He chuckled softly, a warm and inviting sound. She wanted to roll around in his laugh the way she did soft sheets just pulled from the dryer.

"We spent a year in renovations, remodeling and upgrading until we ended up with what you see today." He made a sweeping gesture with his hand, clearly proud of his work. "I try to capture the authenticity of the culture of the cuisine we serve, not just in the food, but in the décor. The framed textiles were handmade in Peru. Those pieces"—he pointed at two colorful impressionist paintings showing boats in a marina—"are by an Argentinean painter by the name of Benito Quinquela Martín." He said the name with reverence. The artist was obviously one of his favorites.

The waiter returned and, with a draped napkin across his forearm, displayed the label of the bottle. Esteban nodded his approval, and the young man uncorked and poured an ounce for his boss. Esteban dipped his nose into the glass and inhaled the wine's aroma. He swirled the liquid and then swallowed a drop, tossing it around his mouth before he nodded in approval.

The waiter poured her a glass and then a glass for Esteban. Sonia raised her brows in surprise as the young man disappeared from the room. The staff was well trained, right down to using the proper etiquette of serving ladies first, no matter who ordered the wine. No surprise there. Esteban had a reputation for being a perfectionist.

He continued, "Through my company Galiano Holdings, I own restaurants here in the States, South America, Canada, France, Italy, and Spain. Some serve South American cuisine, but I also own Italian restaurants, French bistros, Asian-Latin fusion restaurants, coffee houses, and am part owner of two European bakeries—one in Miami and the other in New York."

Completely enthralled, Sonia rested a chin on her hand. She'd expected to have a strictly business-centered dinner but saw the opportunity to learn more about the man so many knew very little about.

"Is it true that you once closed a restaurant because the chef didn't meet your standards?"

"Not everything you've heard about me is true, but that is true. We closed temporarily, for a week."

"That must have cost you a small fortune."

"My name and reputation are worth more than a few lost sales."

That was definitely a loaded answer, with a hidden meaning she couldn't yet decipher.

"How did you get started in the restaurant business?"

He laughed softly. "Why do I feel as if I'm the one being interviewed instead of the other way around?"

"I'm getting to know you, which is why you set up this meeting, correct?"

His eyes narrowed on her. "Correct." He took a sip of wine, and she had the distinct impression that he was stalling, as if trying to decide how much to share.

"My father was a trained chef and had what we call in Argentina a closed-door restaurant. Have you heard of this before?"

Sonia shook her head. "Never."

"They're not so popular anymore, but at one time were the only way for chefs to earn a living if they couldn't afford to open their own restaurant. It was inside our home, and included tables set up outside, as well. We could accommodate as many as thirty people at one time."

"Did your siblings help?"

"I have no siblings. It was me, my mother, and my father."

He was an only child, like her.

"How did that work? Did people walk in off the street?"

"Reservation only. My father would prepare a five-course meal, which varied from week to week. One day he cooked French, another Italian, or Argentine food might be on the menu. It all depended on his mood and the fresh ingredients available. After the guests were served, he'd sit and talk with them. It wasn't work for him. It was like having a large family over for dinner."

"Sounds like the restaurant business was in your blood." Sonia reached for her glass of water.

"Not in my blood," Esteban said, jaw hardening.

Startled, Sonia paused. A coolness had entered his eyes, and she wondered if she'd said something wrong.

"I had a choice, and I chose to follow in my father's footsteps. It was the decision that made me the happiest and continues to make me happy. There is nothing else I could imagine myself doing, despite the struggles and difficulties of the job. My father was very proud when I opened my first restaurant. It was a small café, nothing much." His mouth twisted into a wry smile. "My father worked every day until his death, seldom taking a vacation. He loved to cook. He loved to feed people."

Sonia sipped her water, choosing to remain silent. Work didn't hold the same pleasures for her, at least not lately. The uncertainty of a sporadic paycheck made her second-guess her career choice.

Esteban steepled his fingers on the table. "What about you? Do you look forward to work every day, and how did you get started?"

"I've always worked in restaurants. I had a job working at a place in Atlanta, and I stayed late one night with the owner and helped him close up. He opened a bottle of wine and we sat in his office and chatted. I was nineteen—too young to be drinking—but he asked me what I thought of it. I surprised him with my vivid description. We kept talking, he said I had a discerning palate, and asked if I'd ever considered becoming a sommelier. I'd never heard of a sommelier—didn't even know how to spell the word." She laughed softly. "Anyway, he'd piqued my interest, and I did some research. It sounded like the kind of thing I'd enjoy, and I happen to enjoy wine." She took a deep breath. There was much more to the story that she didn't need to share with

Esteban. "But lately, I've wondered if I should consider a different career."

"Why?"

"Don't get me wrong, I still love what I do, but ever since my hours were cut at Azul, I've wondered if I should do something else. As a result, I don't enjoy it like I used to."

"Hmm," Esteban said, rubbing his jaw thoughtfully. "Hopefully, I can change that."

CHAPTER 6

The food was excellent, starting with a platter of picada, served on a wood plate overflowing with a fine selection of salami, ham, and cubed cheese. Not wanting to spoil her appetite, Sonia ate a modest amount, but Esteban had no such limitations. He ate heartily and washed everything down with the delicious red wine.

When their entrees arrived, the sight and smell of the steak made Sonia's stomach dance in anticipation. She wasn't disappointed. The grilled steak was well seasoned, tender, and juicy, served with a side of basil-fried corn and chimichurri sauce. The fresh garlic and spices danced across her palate, and she emitted an involuntary moan.

"You like it?" Although the words came out as a question, they sounded more like a statement.

"Delicious," Sonia replied, around a mouthful of meat.

With a satisfied smile, Esteban sliced into his own steak, kept company on the plate by a fried lobster tail. "We haven't even gotten to the best part yet."

"And what's that?"

"Dessert."

Across the table, his eyes danced with a teasing light, and a throb of heat blossomed between Sonia's legs. Quickly, she lowered her gaze to the plate in front of her.

"That's my least favorite part of a meal," she informed him.

"Oh?"

"I don't like sweets much."

"I'm disappointed. One of the most popular items on the menu is our chocolate mousse cake. It's decadent and rich and accompanied by a healthy serving of Venezuelan gelato. It's one of my personal favorites."

Sonia wrinkled her nose. "Chocolate is my least favorite sweet. I don't see what all the fuss is about, to be honest."

He studied her from across the table. "No chocolates for you on Valentine's Day?" he said.

"A waste of time." Sonia shrugged.

"Flowers, at least?"

"Those I do enjoy."

"Let me guess. Red roses?"

A bouquet of red roses could brighten her day any time of the year. "That was easy. What woman doesn't enjoy those?"

"Not so easy. Every woman is different. Every woman has her preference. I, for example, jumped to the conclusion that you'd be a chocolate lover. Do you not like any kind of sweets?"

"Not really. Except..." She laughed. "I have a weak spot for sour gummy worms. I could eat a whole bag by myself."

"I don't think I've ever eaten one."

"Trust me, you're missing out. They're addictive."

He continued to look at her with such interest that Sonia lowered her gaze to her plate and continued to eat.

Halfway through the meal, she asked, "Is it okay for me to ask questions about the job now?"

She was feeling a slight buzz from all the Malbec they'd drunk, and a certain satisfaction from eating food that was well prepared and surpassed anything she'd eaten in a long time. No wonder his restaurant received such rave reviews.

"Certainly." Esteban poured himself more wine and topped off her glass.

"I think that's enough," she said with a little laugh, placing a restraining hand near the mouth of her glass.

"One can never have enough of a good thing," Esteban said.

Again she sensed a hidden meaning beneath the words. His eyes rested on her with such intensity that she temporarily looked away.

After clearing her throat, she asked, "What did you have in mind for the dinner parties?"

"I entertain contacts in my real estate deals, investors in my restaurants, and other business associates. Sometimes they bring their wives or a companion. I'd like to offer a unique dining experience. With your knowledge, I think I could improve my parties—make them more entertaining, and even educate my guests on the wines from my country."

"Private dinner parties with sommeliers are becoming more common." For those who could afford the luxury, receiving personalized attention from a wine expert added a sophisticated touch to any affair. "How large is your wine collection?"

"It's quite extensive," he said.

Sonia thought for a moment. "We could have a private tasting, where I explain about the different wines, educate your guests on the history and story behind the grapes, that kind of thing. We could even make a game of it, encouraging your guests to do blind taste tests. It can be a lot of fun."

She'd done several of those in the past for clients, providing wine from a local wine shop. But if Esteban's collection was as large as she suspected, she could pull from his inventory and show off his collection. It would be the kind of activity his guests would enjoy, and she'd be able to display her talents and perhaps generate more business.

"That's exactly what I'm looking for."

"How often do you entertain?" She sliced another piece of meat and slipped it into her mouth.

He slowly chewed and shrugged. "Two or three times a month. I don't anticipate needing you that often, but we can play it by ear based on our schedules."

"I'd have to see your collection at some point."

"How about tonight?" Esteban asked smoothly.

"Tonight? I hadn't planned on going to your place this evening."

"Is that a problem?"

"No, I… No, it's not." Sonia couldn't honestly think of a reason why she couldn't accept his invitation. "Should I assume I have the job?"

"I would say so, but the final decision is up to you. You should come by tonight, and if you want to ride separately, we can do that. But I'd much prefer to have you in the car with me this time."

She looked across the table at him, hesitation riding heavy on her chest. She didn't honestly have concerns about her safety, but a sixth sense cautioned she should be careful nonetheless. "I think I can trust you, and several people saw us together tonight." She softened the words with a smile, even as the hesitation swelled. "If I wind up missing, they'll at least come looking for you."

He chuckled and sat back in the chair, relaxed, idly swirling the wine glass in his hand. "You won't end up missing, I assure you. A woman like you should be on display."

That was the second time he'd made a similar remark, and Sonia shifted uneasily in her chair. "Mr. Galiano, I think I should make one thing clear. You're hiring me to be a private sommelier, correct? Nothing more?"

"Of course. Why do you ask?"

He seemed surprised, and she couldn't tell if his reaction was genuine or counterfeit.

"The comment you made about women like me deserving to be on display. That type of comment makes me wonder about your motives."

"Are you not used to hearing compliments?"

That was a difficult question to answer. If she said yes, she risked sounding conceited, but the truth was that she did get compliments a lot. Sonia knew she was an attractive woman with a shapely figure. Married men, other women's boyfriends, they had no qualms about approaching her. Over the years, she'd learned to handle the men who came onto her, and sometimes flirted with male customers at the restaurant because it ensured they'd buy more wine. At the very least, she could upsell them.

In those instances, she felt in control. She knew what she was doing. It was all part of a dance to get what she wanted. With Esteban, however, she felt at a slight disadvantage. He held all the cards. She needed to keep him happy and impress him so she could get this job.

"I do get compliments, but I don't want there to be any misunderstanding between us." She licked her lips. "You're only interested in my somm services, correct?"

"Do you offer some other type of service?" he asked. He was toying with her.

"No."

A slight smile. "Well then…"

He hadn't answered her question.

"I do have one request—two, actually," Esteban said. "We should dispense with the formality of last names. You may call me Esteban, and I hope you'll allow me to call you Sonia."

"I'm okay with that."

"Good."

"And your second request?"

"That you keep an open mind," he said.

"An open mind about the job?"

"Yes. This relationship could be mutually beneficial for both of us."

Sonia twirled her glass of wine on the tabletop. "I promise to keep an open mind," she said.

Esteban lifted his glass. "*Salud.*"

Sonia raised hers. "*Salud.*"

At the end of the meal, Esteban made a point of stopping to speak to the maître d' on the way out. He informed him that Sonia would be accompanying him to his home to take a look at his wine cellar, a conversation that was clearly to put her mind at ease, which she appreciated. Armando didn't bat an eyelid.

Esteban escorted her to his waiting vehicle, the champagne-colored Maybach she saw him get into the night of Arturo's party. As they approached, he placed a hand on her lower back in a subtle gesture, but her nerve endings tingled and sparked where he touched. The sensation disbursed everywhere and sent a tiny shiver through her body.

The driver, a middle-aged black man with toasty brown skin, wearing a black chauffeur uniform and cap, opened the door, and she settled inside. Sonia had never been inside a Maybach before. She was impressed by the plush sheepskin floor mats beneath her feet, and a series of buttons that controlled everything, from the fully reclining seats with footrests to the heated massage option.

Overwhelmed by the lavish interior, she smoothed a hand over the soft nappa leather of the seat. "This is nice." She kept her voice neutral so as not to gush.

Esteban sat on the other side of a console that separated them from each other. "A splurge, I know, but why have money if you don't buy nice things?"

Why indeed?

CHAPTER 7

They took MacArthur Causeway away from South Beach. The highway connected the mainland to the man-made islands in Biscayne Bay, one of which was Star Island, where Esteban's home was located.

Both sides of the iron gates folded inward when they arrived, revealing the splendor of the well-lit grounds and the restored 1929 Mediterranean-style home he'd fallen in love with the minute he'd seen it. The mansion had been previously owned by a pop star, and as such, he'd had to tone down the ultra-glam décor to suit his personal taste. Otherwise, it contained everything he needed, and was the favorite of his homes, even more beloved than the one he owned in Argentina.

With nine bedrooms and twelve bathrooms, the two-story house offered enough space for two families to live comfortably. Instead, the only occupants were he and his housekeeper, Delores, whose private quarters were in a wing upstairs with a separate entrance. His driver Abel lived in the guest house on the property, readily available all hours of the day and night.

Esteban watched Sonia's wide-eyed expression as they crossed the courtyard to the front door, her gaze sweeping over the expansive grounds and palm trees, whose leaves shimmied in the balmy night air.

"Wow," he heard her murmur, and wondered if she'd even realized she'd spoken.

"You flatter me with your reaction. I can't wait for you to see the inside."

"I hope I don't sound too gauche, but this place is gorgeous. I can't wait to see the inside, either."

She laughed, and the sound made the hairs on the back of his neck stand on end. She had a lovely smile and a beautiful laugh. Everything about her was beautiful, and it pleased him that she had a beautiful personality to go along with the outer package.

He entered the code at the door and flung the door wide, allowing Sonia to precede him into the interior.

"Lights on," he commanded, following close behind her, and the front foyer became bathed in the luminescent glow of the recessed bulbs.

He heard Sonia's sharp intake of air as her heels clicked on the surface of the white tile. For him, appearances were everything, and it was not only important to have a beautiful exterior—the interior of the home had to be splendid as well. This house fit the bill. It made quite an impression on anyone who walked into it for the first time.

The front hall opened into a sunken living room that dominated a third of the first floor, filled with comfortable chairs set up in various seating arrangements to facilitate conversation around coffee tables, and a round table at one end. Windows extended the full length of the room, and outside, the ninety-foot swimming pool looked like black ink. Beyond that was Biscayne Bay, reflecting the light of the full moon. Day or night, it was a spectacular view, and he didn't hide it behind curtains or blinds or any other type of obstruction.

"It's elegant but comfortable-looking," Sonia said.

"I can't take the credit. My interior designer worked closely with a host of people on this place." He took a look around, as if seeing it for the first time. "She added warmth, comfort, and style."

Sonia stepped down into the living room, and Esteban's gaze gravitated to the delicious swaying motion of her hips. Her full behind was displayed in a pair of slacks that showed off its roundness. Biting his bottom lip, he smiled to himself. He had to get this woman into bed.

"She did a good job. Your home is beautiful."

"She understood me and my needs. I like to collect beautiful things. Paintings, sculptures—"

"Women?" She arched a brow, a playful gleam filling her eyes.

She was flirting with him.

Esteban smiled slowly. "No, not women."

"No? You have somewhat of a reputation."

"I admit I like beautiful women, their softness and curves, and it's fascinating that they're the result of God making a mistake."

"You should be careful what you say." She sounded appalled. "A mistake?"

"Yes, a mistake. God created man, and then he realized he could do better. Then he created woman." He flashed his most dangerous grin, the one that could make a nun drop her panties.

Sonia took a tremulous breath. "Hmm, good answer," she said, but her voice sounded steady.

She pointed at one of the paintings on the wall, and then her eyes narrowed as she looked at the others in the room. "These are like the prints at your restaurant. Are these also works by Benito Quinquela Martín?"

"They are."

She walked over to one for closer inspection and then glanced at him. "It's an original."

Esteban stepped down into the living room and went to stand beside her. He inhaled the sweet scent of her perfume—a flowery fragrance that had teased his nostrils all night.

"I had to outbid a particularly persistent opponent at an auction for that one."

"But you managed."

"I always win," he said.

She watched him from the corner of her eye. "Is that the reason you were determined to have this piece? To win?"

"I greatly admire his work. Martín was from the La Boca neighborhood, and as you can see, his work paid homage to the port and its workers. He lived in that neighborhood until he died."

"How old was he?"

"They think eighty-six."

"They think?"

"He was an orphan, and the nuns who found him didn't know his real birth date, so they gave him one." Esteban swiveled away from her, suddenly anxious to change the topic.

"That's why you like his work so much," she said quietly.

He turned to face her again, agitated by her comment. "Excuse me?"

"You're an orphan, too. That's why back at the restaurant you didn't like when I said you had the restaurant industry in your blood."

He shoved his hands into his pockets as the area between his shoulder blades grew tight. He stared out the window at the night, his jaw clenched so hard he couldn't speak at first. She'd surprised him by getting so close to the truth. "My mother wanted me. My father did not. My mother died when I was three, and I was put in an orphanage."

The words came out in a clipped monotone. He couldn't remember the woman who had given him life, but was grateful for the photographs of her in his possession. His father, dead now, had never shown any interest in Esteban.

"We have something in common," Sonia said softly.

His head swiveled back to her.

She shrugged. "My mother died when I was young—older than you, though. I was eight. Her brother took me in and raised me. Uncle Rowell loves me as much as he does his own daughter. One day, I hope to pay him back for his generosity."

"An older couple who couldn't have children adopted me when I was six. They're both gone now." His shoulders relaxed at the commonalities between them.

They looked at each other, and a silent understanding developed as they experienced a moment of shared pain.

Straightening, Esteban dismissed the sadness that threatened to overtake him. "You're here to see my wine collection. Follow me."

The cellar had been installed near the kitchen in a temperature-controlled room, hundreds of bottles protected behind a door made of tempered glass. Distressed walls met wood and stainless steel wine racks that climbed to the ceiling, custom-built to accommodate a collection that boasted vintage from around the world. On **the** back wall there was a ladder and a mahogany humidor that kept Esteban's cigar collection in excellent condition, and in the middle of the floor, a stainless steel tasting table showcased a collection of recently imported Torronté bottles on the lower shelf.

He watched Sonia move along the wall, eyes scanning the labels, and finally lifting a bottle to admire it. She replaced it and picked up another one.

"Musigny 2003. Would you share this with your guests, or is it only for personal consumption?"

"That depends."

"On what?"

"On the person, and the guests." He took the bottle from her and picked up the corkscrew.

"What are you doing? You're not going to open it, are you?"

"I am. This is wine you drink to celebrate."

"Celebrate what?" she asked, eyes wide.

He removed the cork. "Working together. Isn't that cause for celebration?"

"It is, but that's also a forty-five-hundred-dollar bottle of wine. There are cheaper ways to celebrate."

"I have two more on the shelf."

She followed his line of sight. "Of course you do."

Esteban poured them each a glass and set the bottle on the table. "Cheers. To new endeavors."

"To new endeavors."

They clinked their glasses together.

Sonia inhaled the fragrant bouquet and then swallowed a mouthful, closing her eyes. "Oh, that's incredible," she breathed.

"It's a pleasure talking to you," he said.

"And why is that?"

"You appreciate the same things I do. It's not often I run across a woman like you—one with whom I have a lot in common. We can talk about the restaurant business, and I don't have to work so hard to explain everything to you."

"Hmm, I know what you mean. It's hard to get friends to understand the intricacies of the work I do. They think I sit around and drink wine all day. Although…" She looked at her glass and laughed. "You're not quite what I expected."

"No?"

"I thought you were an arrogant ass."

"Maybe I am an arrogant ass, and I'm playing nice to get what I want."

She hesitated in lifting the glass to her lips, watching him closely.

He drained the wine from his glass, never taking his eyes from her. She tilted the glass to her lips, averting her eyes to the shelves again.

"Have you ever been to France?" he asked.

"No." She still didn't look at him, studying the variety of vintage on the shelves.

"You should see France. I'd love to take you one day."

Swinging her head in his direction, she asked, "Are you always so generous to your employees?"

"Only the ones I take a special liking to."

She set down her glass. "I think it's time that I leave."

"So soon?"

"It's late."

It wasn't.

Esteban placed a wine stopper in the bottle, and they exited the room.

"I have to fly back to Argentina for a few days, but I'll be in touch when I get back," he said, escorting her to the door.

"Thank you. I look forward to hearing from you."

They walked out to the car, and Abel, who had remained in the front seat, hopped out to open the door.

Esteban caught her hand before she had a chance to slide in. He dusted two kisses along the inside of her wrist, noting the sudden surge of her pulse beneath his lips and the way her lashes lowered in response.

"*Buenas noches*," he whispered, before releasing her.

Without a word, she hurried into the car and Abel shut the door.

Esteban watched until they disappeared through the gates.

* * *

IN THE BACK of the Maybach, Sonia didn't want to dwell on Esteban, but she couldn't help it. His lips had touched the inside of her wrist instead of the back of her hand and lingered inappropriately long. The simple touch had inflamed her skin and awakened a craving for more —more kisses, more touching. She was out of her depth with him.

She pressed a hand over her rapidly beating heart. She'd enjoyed herself and him too much. He'd been a gentleman, but no matter how much he said this was purely about business, it was obvious he wanted her. If she were completely honest, she wanted him, too, which made this relationship a dangerous proposition. Several times she caught herself flirting with him, an absolute no-no.

As the vehicle rolled down the causeway, she looked out the window at the twinkling lights of the approaching skyline. Before too long she would be back at her small one-bedroom, a huge difference from the grand home she'd recently left. You could literally drop her entire apartment into his living room and still have room to spare.

Being wined and dined by a charming man was definitely seductive, and it became clear how women could get caught up in being arm candy for a man like Esteban. The luxury car, grand home, and fine dining were all very enticing.

But she had principles and was too smart to get seduced into such a lifestyle.

She just had to keep reminding herself of that.

CHAPTER 8

*S*onia stepped out of the shower and rubbed lotion all over her body. Once she'd finished, she left the bathroom. Pedro was sitting on her bed.

"What do you want to do today? I thought maybe we could go to brunch. We haven't done that in a while."

He had a rare Sunday off, so they'd decided to spend it together, and brunch was something they used to do when they started dating, but hadn't done in a long time. She looked forward to sitting together and chatting over a nice meal. He'd become less outgoing—at least, less outgoing with her—and wanted to spend all his time with his male friends.

She opened the drawer and pulled out a pair of panties and a black-and-white short-sleeved romper. Since Pedro remained silent, she looked over her shoulder as she discarded the damp towel to the recliner. His gaze flicked over her naked body, but there wasn't much of a reaction, which reminded her they hadn't had sex in a while. She couldn't even remember the last time.

"What's wrong?" she asked.

Sonia pulled the underwear up over her hips. They were deep blue, cotton, and comfortable. No point in putting on anything sexy, since Pedro didn't seem interested. His dissatisfaction with work had put a damper on their sex life, and the only time he reached for her was when he seemed overwhelmed by his biological urges. At that point, she felt like little more than a tool for release.

Why were they even bothering anymore? Had they already outgrown each other after little more than a year?

"There's something waiting for you in the living room. You had a delivery," he said in a taut voice.

Sonia frowned at him over her shoulder. "I didn't order anything recently."

"It's obvious you didn't order it, but it was ordered for you."

She snapped her bra in place. Pedro's face was cemented into very serious lines.

Wiggling the romper up over her hips, she stuck her hands through the short sleeves. After quickly finger-combing the curls in her hair in the full-length mirror, she went into the living room with Pedro practically breathing down her neck, he was so close behind her.

In the doorway, she pulled up short, her mouth falling open when she saw the gorgeous bouquet of red roses. The huge display sat on the coffee table between the two loveseats. There must have been four dozen of them—vibrant, blood red, and filling a crystal vase.

"Did you…?"

"Not me," Pedro said, arms crossed over his chest.

Sonia walked slowly over to the flowers, removed the card, and read the note.

Thank you for last night and the pleasure of your company. I'll call you when I'm back in town. Esteban.

The words suggested intimacy. She could almost hear the low rumble of his voice, the Spanish-accented tone making the words sound as sensual and seductive as a love poem. Heat filled her stomach, and Sonia almost lifted the note to her nose, as if the scent of his cologne—that brash, bold scent of citrus and spice—would be on it.

"Who is Esteban?"

She jumped. Pedro was looking over her shoulder. She'd been so taken with the message and the flowers that she'd temporarily forgotten she wasn't alone.

"The guy I mentioned I had the meeting with last night. He owns Patagonia hotel and restaurant."

"That's who you had dinner with? I don't think you mentioned it."

"I did." *But you never pay attention to anything I say.*

"Mhmm."

Something strange was happening. She looked at Pedro with critical eyes. She'd appreciated his physique in the past, but now his lean, wiry build appeared slight compared to Esteban's broader frame. And he was a big man, an inch or so taller than Esteban. Yet compared to Esteban, he came up short.

"He certainly seemed interested in you. Tracked you down to offer you a job, and now sent you four dozen roses. He really likes you, huh?" He glanced at the flowers and looked at her again, narrowing his eyes.

"He likes my work."

"Is that what he's referring to in that note? Sounds more personal than business. Why would he need to call you when he's back in the country?"

"Because he wants me to work for him. That's what this is all about, Pedro." Sonia set the card on the table and was about to walk into the kitchen, when Pedro caught her arm.

He studied her face. "You like this guy?"

"What?" She laughed, a guilty flush heating her skin. "What kind of question is that? This is business."

"He's rich."

"I don't care about money. You know that."

"Everybody cares about money, Sonia."

"Fine, I care about money, like everyone else. But people care about it to different degrees. It doesn't rule my life."

She yanked away her arm, annoyed at his suggestion that Esteban's wealth impressed her. And so what if it did? Anyone would be impressed by the lifestyle he lived with a driver, a housekeeper, jetting back and forth between continents, and a multimillion-dollar home on the water.

Pedro followed behind her and stood on the opposite side of the counter as she went into the refrigerator for a bottle of water. "We both know, looking the way you do, you can have any man you want."

"Stop it." Conversations like that embarrassed her and reduced her to nothing but body parts.

"You think he doesn't want to sleep with you? If so, you're a fool." He spoke with firm conviction. "Are you telling me he never made a pass at you?"

"You're making a big deal out of nothing." Despite not wanting her physically lately, Pedro had a jealous streak. She had to allay his concerns.

"Answer the question." He walked around the counter. "This rich guy sent you a bunch of flowers that must cost a small fortune, and never made a pass at you? As beautiful as you are? As sexy. You know you're sexy, *mami*. So come on, I'm supposed to believe he didn't notice, and you went to dinner with him and stopped by his house last night?"

Swallowing water gave Sonia a few seconds to come to a decision about her answer. She didn't want to upset Pedro, but she didn't want to lie, either. Still, she couldn't risk him making a big deal out of her business relationship with Esteban, because that was all it was—a business relationship. Yes, she was attracted to him, but who wouldn't be? He was an attractive man.

A strong chin, dark eyes that could be warm one minute and coolly assessing the other. Lips that looked kissable and soft, and a voice that was in and of itself a carnal delight. She was only human, after all. But this was business and business only. So why stir the pot when there was nothing to worry about?

"Not every man wants to take me to bed." She immediately diverted her gaze to the drapes across the room.

Pedro harrumphed and stepped closer. He placed both hands on her hips, and for the first time in a long time, she didn't welcome contact with him. His touch felt foreign, and she tensed, backing up until she touched the refrigerator. But Pedro didn't notice. He followed, and smiled down at her.

"I'd hate to have to fight this bastard." He kissed her, his mouth gliding gently over hers. "You still want to go to brunch?" He tugged her bottom lip between his teeth.

Sonia ducked her head and laughed, gently pushing him away. "I can't talk if you're kissing me." Better able to breathe with the distance between them, Sonia answered, "Yes, I'd still like to go to brunch."

"Cool. Let me change and then we'll head out." He kissed her again

51

and walked around the counter. He lived in the building across the street.

At the door, he said, "Hey, you think Mr. Argentina would be interested in my résumé? Maybe you could hand it to him next time he's in town, see if he has any openings at one of his restaurants or the bakery."

Sonia couldn't believe his one-eighty. One minute he wanted to fight the guy, the next he wanted a favor. One minute he seemed on the verge of telling her not to see Esteban again, now he was encouraging her to talk to him because it benefited him.

"His name is Esteban Galiano, and I'll see what I can do when I attend the first party," she promised.

"*Gracias, ma belle.*" He sent an air kiss and smile her way before disappearing out the door.

After he left, Sonia went over to the flowers and dipped her nose in the bouquet, inhaling the fragrance of the blooms. She picked up the card and read it again.

Thank you for last night and the pleasure of your company. I'll call you when I'm back in town. Esteban.

It disturbed her greatly how much she looked forward to that call.

CHAPTER 9

"*H*ow late are you working tonight?" Sonia smoothed matte lipstick, a maroon color, onto her lips.

"That's what you wearing?" Pedro asked behind her, standing at the door with his arms crossed over his white chef's jacket. He'd come by before his evening shift at Azul.

"What's wrong with what I have on? It's a black turtleneck and a white skirt." True, the outfit showed off her curves, but she couldn't help the way the clothes fit.

For the past few days, the weather had been unusually cool and windy for the end of January. Disgruntled tourists huddled in sweaters and windbreakers, complaining the low temperatures had spoiled their trip.

"It doesn't leave much to the imagination. Are you going to work or going on a date?" Pedro asked sourly.

Their gazes met in the mirror.

"Don't start. You know why I'm doing this. Working for Esteban is a great opportunity, and I need the money."

"Esteban? You're on a first-name basis now?"

"He suggested we use first names." She fastened a gold-plated bracelet on her wrist, not bothering to ask for Pedro's assistance, and he didn't offer to help. "I'm going to make sure he looks at your résumé. Do you still want me to do that or not?"

There was no guarantee, but Pedro worked hard and was good at his job. All he needed was the right contacts.

"You know I want you to give him my résumé. I just don't understand why you have to dress like that."

"I'm not wearing anything I wouldn't wear with you."

"That's the problem," he muttered darkly.

Sonia didn't want to argue. She needed to get to the house early enough to choose the wines to accompany the meal Delores and the chef had prepared.

"You're being ridiculous. I could literally wear this outfit to church, but I'm not going to stand here and argue with you because I need to go." She stepped to the door, thinking he'd move out of the way, but he remained firmly in place.

"I want you to do well, but something about this whole setup bothers me. How many parties can one guy have?"

She refrained from sighing and calmly said, "He entertains business associates at his house when he's in town."

"I've seen pictures of him. He's rich, good-looking, and I'm jealous, okay?"

She couldn't believe they were having the same argument weeks later.

"Jealous of what? It's not as if I'll be alone with him. There will be nine, count them, *nine* other people there tonight, listening to me go on and on about wine."

"And you do go on and on," he said with a teasing smile.

His comment stung a little. Whenever she wanted someone to help her with location and topography drills of wines around the world, she always asked Jackie. They worked in the same industry, but Pedro never showed much interest in her work.

At least he was loosening up a little bit. "Stop worrying. It's a job. That's it."

His smile broadened. "You're a good woman, you know that? You're so supportive, and I promise, I'll make it all up to you one day."

"I'm sure you will," Sonia said.

"How are you getting to this guy's house? Need me to call a taxi for you?" Pedro slid out of the way.

"He's sending a car. It should be waiting for me downstairs." Sonia slipped on her shoes and checked her appearance in the mirror one last time. She wanted to look her best—to make a good impression on the guests, of course.

Pedro eyed her. "I'll walk you down."

Outside, the Maybach idled on the street, and the minute they walked out, Abel exited the vehicle and opened the back door.

Behind her, Pedro cursed. Before she could walk through the gate, he stretched an arm in front of Sonia and halted her steps. "Wait a damn minute. That's your ride?"

"It's a car," Sonia said, but deep down knew that wasn't quite true. It was an experience, and she hadn't expected such royal treatment.

Pedro glared at the vehicle, a deep frown arrowing down above his nose.

"This guy is pulling out all the stops." His heated gaze switched to her. "He's paying a nice piece of cash for these parties, sending you a ridiculous amount of flowers that I certainly couldn't afford, and now he's making sure that you travel in style."

"He's rich. He likes to flaunt it." Sonia pushed open the gate.

"Good evening, Miss Kennedy," Abel said, white teeth flashing against his brown skin.

"Hello, Abel."

Pedro followed, eyes widening with incredulity. "You two know each other already?"

"We met when I went to Esteban's house to take a look at his wine collection," Sonia explained.

"So you rode in this car before?" The words barely made it past Pedro's rigid lips.

"Yes."

"Huh."

Sonia couldn't delay any longer. Abel was waiting. "I'll see you later."

She smiled at the driver, but before she could climb into the car, Pedro took her by the arm and hauled her into a tight embrace, kissing her hard on the mouth. Stunned, she froze, not even kissing him back. He'd never done anything like that before.

When he withdrew, she stared at him. Abel, meanwhile, politely looked off in the distance.

"Wh-what was that?" Sonia asked, pressing her fingers to her lips.

"Thought you needed it."

"I needed it, or did you?"

"Maybe we both did, as a reminder."

He'd been territorial in the past, but this behavior was too much. "When I get back, we need to talk, because I don't know what that was, and I don't appreciate it."

A muscle flicked in his jaw and his eyes flitted to Abel before they returned to her face.

"I'll see you later," Sonia said. She slid into the interior of the car, and practically melted into the soft leather.

Pedro remained on the sidewalk as the vehicle pulled away. The heads of a man and woman on bikes swiveled in the direction of the car as they eased along the road.

Staring out the window, Sonia clenched her fist in her lap. She was angry, but not at Pedro. She was angry at herself for the conflicting emotions that plagued her. Angry that she was looking forward to seeing Esteban, while annoyed that Pedro—her boyfriend—had kissed her.

Halfway to Esteban's home, her cell phone chirped, alerting her to a message. She looked down and read the note from Pedro.

Sorry for being such a jealous ass. Forgive me?

She answered quickly before she had a chance to think too long. *Yes.*

We'll do something nice next week. When I don't have work kicking my ass.

Sonia stared at the choppy water as they crossed over the bay. In a few minutes, they'd arrive at Esteban's.

She wasn't angry anymore. Now she just felt like shit.

* * *

Esteban's housekeeper, Delores, greeted Sonia when she arrived. She was a meaty woman with gray-streaked hair held in a bun, but a smooth, unlined face.

He was still getting ready, so both women set to work preparing for the guests. Sonia chose several wines for the tasting, which would take place pre-dinner. For the multicourse meal, she picked a red, with a rich, earthy flavor she thought would go well with the meat dish, and a white for the fish course.

When Esteban came out, he was scrumptious in a pale blue button-down shirt and dark slacks. Sonia averted her eyes and gestured toward the table. "Well, what do you think?"

"Lovely. Surpassed my expectations."

Pleased, she turned to look at him again, but he wasn't looking at the table. His eyes were on her, his hot gaze tracing the curve of her behind in the figure-hugging skirt.

A soft blush crept into her cheeks.

Esteban walked closer but stopped a few feet away. "It's unfortunate you're not accustomed to hearing compliments."

Sonia clutched the back of one of the dining chairs as his gaze practically caressed her, sliding from her face down over her body.

Her heart raced. She told herself she hated the way he looked at her, but a little voice inside whispered, *Liar*.

Guilt deepened the heat in her cheeks.

"You clearly don't hear compliments enough, or you'd be used to them."

"I get compliments, but I'm not used to receiving those kinds of compliments from men I work with."

"I find that hard to believe. I think…" He gave a knowing smile. "I think maybe you are not used to liking to hear those things from a man you work with."

She didn't have a comeback to the surprisingly accurate words. Luckily, the doorbell rang at that moment, and she was freed from the snare of his gaze.

The first guests had arrived, and she was finally able to breathe easier.

The couple included a Russian commercial designer by the name of Ivana, who looked to be in her late forties. She was tall and fair-haired, and an air of authority hovered around her even as she gave Esteban two air kisses. Her husband Craig was American, and closer to Esteban's age. Everything about him seemed casual, from the disarming smile to the khakis and pullover shirt he wore.

By the time the other guests arrived, Sonia had completely relaxed. The group congregated in the spacious living room for the hors d'oeuvres portion of the evening, and she went on autopilot, mingling with the guests, chatting and explaining the vintage in their glasses. She explained the region where the grapes were grown, and pointed out the different flavors in each.

Dinner took place in the formal dining room and was served by other members of Esteban's staff, under Delores's supervision.

As far as Sonia was concerned, the night was a smashing success. She received plenty of compliments and liked knowing she'd educated the guests on a subject she was passionate about. After the last person left, she remained in the kitchen, corking the last of the wine that remained. Nearby, Delores and the two staff members, a male and female, cleaned up the kitchen and washed dishes.

Esteban entered the room. "That went well," he said quietly to Sonia.

"I agree. It was…exciting." She clasped her hands in front of her.

"I can tell. You're glowing."

She laughed. "This is what I love to do. Well, I'll be on my way, unless you need something else?"

Esteban went to the far side of the kitchen, where a desk was set up in a cubbyhole with a computer and paperwork in neat stacks on top of it. He opened one of the desk drawers and removed an envelope. Handing it over to Sonia, he said, "I hope we can continue doing business together."

"I hope so, too."

He walked her out to the car and saw her into it.

"Good night, Sonia."

"Good night."

On the way home, Sonia removed the check from the envelope and gasped at the amount. She blinked, staring at it for a long time before calling Esteban. He answered on the first ring.

"There's been a mistake. You overpaid me."

"No, I didn't."

"The amount on the check is double my normal fee."

"I know."

"If you know, then…why did you do that?"

"Because you deserve it."

Her stomach tightened as the words hung on the air between them. "Esteban—"

"Good night, Sonia. I look forward to seeing you again."

He disconnected the call before she could reply.

What would she have said even if she'd had the chance to reply?

She let out a tremulous breath.

What could she have said, except that she looked forward to seeing him again, too?

CHAPTER 10

"What are your plans tonight?" Sonia asked Jackie as they jogged back from a run along the beach. They'd had a good workout. The afternoon air was cool and dry, and instead of feeling tired, Sonia was energized.

"Same as last Valentine's Day. Nothing. What about you?"

"Pedro and I agreed not to buy gifts this year."

"Wasn't that your agreement last year?" Jackie asked.

After they banked the corner, their strides automatically slowed to a walk, like they always did in that location.

"We did, but we're both so broke we decided to skip this year, too." She put some of the money she'd earned at Esteban's party back into replenishing her savings and repaid Jackie a portion of what she owed her.

Jackie snorted. "Sounds like that was Pedro's idea, and it's the most ridiculous thing I've ever heard."

Sonia shrugged. "He doesn't think about things the same way we do. He's a man, you know."

"Not all men are like that," Jackie said.

"He's been having a hard time because he's trying to find a position that challenges him and a restaurant that recognizes his talent. You have to admit that he's a very talented pastry chef."

"I agree, but at the same time, we're not talking about his talents as a chef—we're talking about what kind of boyfriend he is. Whether or not he likes celebrating Valentine's Day is irrelevant. He should be willing to celebrate for you."

"Valentine's Day is not that big of a deal to me."

"Oh, bollocks. That's what you say, but wouldn't it be nice if he surprised you with a box of chocolates or a bunch of flowers?"

"You'd make a terrible boyfriend. You know I don't eat chocolate."

"Oh right. Flowers, then—red roses, of course."

"If he ever did something like that, I'd wonder what was wrong, because he's not that kind of guy. He's not spontaneous and doesn't adhere to the restrictions and requirements that come with days like Valentine's Day that force men into performing in these roles."

"Ha."

Sonia shoved her friend.

They neared the apartment building, and Jackie slowed to a stop.

"You're not coming in?" Sonia asked.

"No. I'm going home to wallow in self-pity that I'm single yet another Valentine's Day."

"Why don't we wallow in self-pity together? I'll pop open a bottle of wine and we can order a pizza."

"And then what am I supposed to do when Pedro comes by? No, thanks."

"It's Valentine's night. He'll probably be at the restaurant all night working."

"Why aren't you working?"

"They said they didn't need me." If they didn't need her on such a busy night, she was fairly certain they'd be letting her go soon.

"Pedro may not celebrate Valentine's Day, but I'm pretty sure he doesn't want to see me here when he arrives. And to be honest, I don't want to be here when he does, because I don't want to see the two of you doing kissy face while I pretend it's no big deal all by my lone-some. Two's company, and three is a crowd. I love you, but I'd rather go home, thank you very much."

"You do realize you're the worst friend ever?" Sonia asked, softening the words with a smile.

"So you've told me on numerous occasions." Jackie blew her a kiss and sauntered to the red Aston Martin parked at the curb. "Tah-tah, love."

With a heavy sigh, Sonia turned on her heels and ran up the stairs to her apartment. She stripped off her clothes and jumped into the shower.

She didn't mention it to Jackie, but she was a little disappointed at Pedro's suggestion that they not exchange gifts. She'd started thinking he might be seeing someone else and was running out of excuses for his indifferent behavior.

As she stepped out of the shower, a knock sounded on the door. She wasn't expecting anyone, and Pedro had his own key and wasn't expected to come by until much later tonight.

"Just a minute," she called out.

She donned a comfy robe and padded into the living room. Peering out the peephole, she saw a deliveryman in the hall, holding a square red box with white ribbon, and a bouquet of flowers.

Sonia opened the door. "Can I help you?"

"Sonia Kennedy?" the young man asked.

"That's me." She smiled.

Pedro had tricked her. Just when she was about to give up on him, he did something so romantic, so surprising, when moments ago she had been thinking about how he lacked spontaneity.

"Here you go." The young man was smiling too.

"Thank you so much." Sonia buried her nose in the roses.

"There's more," the man said.

"More? What do you mean?"

"More flowers. Stay right there."

Stunned, Sonia remained in the doorway, and within minutes, the young man returned carrying two more bouquets. Her mouth fell open. "Are you serious? This isn't a mistake? All of these are for me?"

"Yes, ma'am."

She laughed giddily. "Let's go inside."

She led the way and set the first of the bouquets on the counter that separated the kitchen from the living room. The deliveryman set the other two beside them.

"Do you need me to sign something?" Sonia asked.

"Oh, I'm not finished. There's more." He grinned even broader, as if he was enjoying this interlude, and walked out of the apartment.

Wait a minute…

Sonia stared at the empty doorway he'd disappeared through. These gifts were not from Pedro. Sure, it was romantic, but also very extravagant. He couldn't possibly afford to get her multiple bouquets of flowers—red roses, no less—on Valentine's Day of all dates.

When the young man returned, he came back with two more bouquets.

"Please tell me this is the last one," she said.

"No, ma'am. There's one more, and I'll be right back."

He returned with the last bouquet. While the others were two dozen roses each, this one contained what looked like forty-eight. It was huge and beautiful, and the arrangement with white peonies interspersed among the ruby petals presented a lovely contrast.

"Somebody really loves you," the young man said, extending the clipboard to her.

She laughed shakily. "I don't know if that's necessarily true." She scribbled her signature.

"Happy Valentine's Day." He left and shut the door on his way out.

Sonia stared at the arrangements, overwhelmed and flattered, but also worried. Pedro did not buy her dozens of roses, and when he saw the arrangements, he would be pissed.

She found the card on the last bouquet and flipped it open. *Happy Valentine's Day. Esteban.*

Unfortunately, the doorbell rang at that moment, and then she heard the key in the door. Pedro walked in, took one look at all the flowers and his smile froze, then disintegrated.

He slammed the door. "What the hell is all this?"

"It's a gift," she said.

"From who?" His nostrils flared.

"Esteban."

He walked over and looked at the arrangements. "What is it with you and this guy? He obviously has a thing for you, and don't tell me that he doesn't." His jaw hardened into a rigid line.

"You're overreacting," she said, which was the exact wrong thing to say.

"And how would you feel if I received gifts from some woman? Would you be totally fine with that?"

"No, but..."

"But what, Sonia?"

"What do you care? You don't show any interest in me at all. Do you even still want to be with me?"

"What the fuck kinda shit is that to say to me, *mami*? We're in this together, right?" When she didn't answer, he laughed. "Oh, I get it. You got this rich motherfucker sweating you now, so all of a sudden, I'm shit?"

"That's not what I'm saying. But you don't act like you're *in this*, like you say."

"What's that?" he asked sharply.

His gaze was directed past her, and she followed his line of sight to the gift-wrapped box.

Her stomach dipped. "I don't know what that is."

"Well, I guess whatever it is it's going to be better than what I was going to do. I was gonna take you out to dinner tonight as a surprise. They fired me from Azul."

"What!"

"Yeah. The pastry chef didn't appreciate me questioning his tactics, so they got rid of me."

"Baby, I'm sorry." She reached for him, but he brushed her off.

"I came by thinking we could at least have a good night together, something to make me feel better after the shitty night I had. I even stopped and picked up a box of chocolates."

He extended it to her.

"Thanks," Sonia murmured, taking it.

He laughed bitterly. "You don't even look like you want it. I guess a box of chocolates don't compare to five hundred thousand fucking roses and whatever is in that box. Why don't you open it?"

Sonia swallowed.

"Go on, open it. I can't get any more upset than I already am." He crossed his arms.

Reluctantly, Sonia set down the box of chocolates and picked up the gift Esteban had sent over. Slowly, she opened the package, and a bag of sour gummy worm candy sat inside. Unable to help herself, she smiled.

"What is that?" Pedro asked.

"Sour candy." She lifted out the bag and held it up for him to see.

"He gave you a cheap bag of candy for Valentine's Day? Who gives sour gummy worms on Valentine's Day?" He laughed. "You did okay with the flowers, but that was a dopey, cheap move with the candy. Who is this guy?" He shook his head, laughing even harder.

Sonia glared at him. "Sour gummy worms are my favorite candy."

Pedro stopped laughing. "I knew that."

"I hate chocolate."

"I knew that," Pedro said.

"No, you didn't."

He sighed heavily and rubbed a hand over his hair. "So, do you want to go to dinner or not? I'll go home and take a shower, and we could—"

"You know what, I'm gonna pass on dinner. I wasn't expecting you until much later, and right now, I'm tired. I'm going to pour myself a glass of wine and go to bed."

"So that's it? That's how we're going to spend Valentine's Day?"

"You didn't care about the day anyway, right? It's a stupid holiday created by 'the man' to get our hard-earned money, so what difference does it make?"

A muscle in his jaw flexed, nostrils flaring as he tried to keep his temper under control. He muttered something in Spanish and then said, "Fine. If that's the way you want it. If you change your mind, I'll be at home. Or maybe not. Maybe I'll find someone who wants my company." He marched toward the door.

"Maybe I'll find someone who wants mine," Sonia shot back.

He froze, hands fisting on either side of his hips. Tension swelled in the room as the silence stretched between them.

Without turning around to face her, Pedro asked, "Are you fucking him?"

The shocking question sent her mind reeling into previously uncharted territory. She imagined her and Esteban naked, his intense eyes staring down into hers as he pinned her beneath him. His body thrusting into hers, his cologne filling her nostrils and staining her skin with its scent.

She closed her eyes and shook her head to erase the erotic image. "No," she said huskily.

"Would you tell me if you were?"

"Yes."

He finished walking to the door and slammed it on the way out.

Sonia really needed the comfort of a drink now. She poured a generous glass of wine and settled on the sofa. Flipping on the TV to a news channel, she curled her legs beneath her.

A few minutes later, she admitted to herself that she wasn't paying attention to the newscast, and picked up her phone. She took a fortifying swallow of wine and then sent a quick text, thanking Esteban for his generosity in sending the flowers and candy.

Minutes later, he responded.

Don't thank me. You deserve it.

She stared at the words for a long time.

What was he doing to her? Making her want, making her ache, against her better judgment.

She closed her eyes and imagined herself beneath Esteban again, and the flesh between her legs pulsed with desire. The shame of guilt washed over her.

Are you fucking him? Pedro had asked.

No.

But she wanted to.

CHAPTER 11

Sonia finished checking inventory in Esteban's wine room. A few days ago he'd called her from the West Coast to find out if she was available to work a last-minute cocktail party for two couples at his home. She'd considered telling him she was busy, but in the end accepted the offer.

She and Pedro had barely spoken since their Valentine's Day tiff, and when she told him she'd be going to Esteban's tonight, all he said was, "Enjoy yourself."

Stretching her arms overhead, she took one last glance at the room to make sure everything was in place, and then turned out the light.

Nearby she heard the sound of softly playing music. The Spanish tune flowed through the speakers, the distinctive strum of a guitar heightening the sexy, contemporary beat. Walking into the bright, open kitchen, she found Esteban in front of the grill side of the massive gas range.

"I finished the inventory." She stood at the stone counter of one of two islands, watching him work.

He glanced over his shoulder. "Have a seat. I'm almost finished."

"I was going to head out," Sonia said.

"Not before you taste this food. Besides, you didn't eat anything tonight."

"I was busy with the guests."

And she didn't have much of an appetite, uninterested in the heavy hors d'oeuvres Delores had prepared. She was too worried about her relationship with Pedro and knew they needed to talk, but didn't have the courage to confront the disintegration of their relationship—or her strong attraction to the man standing before her.

He looked at home in the kitchen without a jacket—relaxed, and very sexy with the sleeves of his dress shirt rolled up to right below his elbows. Beneath the material, his muscles rippled, and his back and shoulders appeared broader as they tapered down to a narrow waist and a very nice-looking ass.

"All the more reason why you should have a seat and let me feed you."

The smell of cooking meat perfumed the air, and what little resistance she'd convinced herself she needed crumbled under the strain of hunger.

Sonia sat on one of the stools and watched him work. She'd never seen this side of him. He moved easily through the kitchen, obviously having done this many times before. "I didn't know you could cook."

"There are a lot of things you don't know about me," Esteban said enigmatically.

"I can't argue with that." Sonia rested her chin in her hand and watched him turn the asparagus with metal tongs. "So tell me something I don't know."

He flipped the meat, and the flames below flared up as the juices fell onto them.

"I started in the kitchen because of my father." A faint smile softened his profile.

"You worked with him in the closed-door restaurant," she guessed.

He nodded. "Most days. Whenever I could. He taught me everything I know about food and taking care of the customer." He left the stove and poured a glass of Malbec from the bottle on the counter, then slid it over to her.

"Thank you. *Salud*." Sonia swirled the wine in the glass and then tasted it. Berry flavors and nuanced notes of chocolate and cocoa powder were abundant in this particular vintage.

"My father loved his job and taught classes on cooking and wine.

My mother and I helped wherever he needed us. It was truly a family business."

"They must have been very proud of you and your success."

"They were." She heard the mixture of pain and affection in his voice.

Esteban plated the steaks alongside the grilled asparagus and set the two dishes on the stone countertop of the island. Next, he deposited chimichurri in glass *mise en place* bowl between them.

Sonia inhaled deeply. The food smelled divine. "So you do this often, cook yourself a late night meal?"

"This isn't late. Americans eat dinner too early. This is around the time I normally eat in Buenos Aires."

"At this hour? It's after ten o'clock!"

He nodded, smiling.

"Well, I guess I'm on Buenos Aires time, and I don't regret it." Sonia sliced the tender cut of meat, perfectly cooked to medium rare.

"You should never regret anything that's pleasurable," Esteban said.

She looked up at him. "You have an answer for everything, don't you?"

"Not everything." He sipped his wine, keeping an eye on her.

"I'm shocked. And what don't you have an answer for?"

"You." The response came immediately, as if he'd been waiting for her to ask the question.

Sonia laughed. "I didn't know I was a question."

"You're a question." His eyes narrowed a little. "A big question I've been trying to figure out for a while. Do you want to know what the question is?"

"I'm not sure I do."

"I'll tell you anyway. I didn't make a good impression on you the first night we met, and since then I've been trying to figure out how to convince you to give in to the attraction between us."

She laughed louder this time. "My, my, what makes you think I'm attracted to you?"

He didn't smile. "Don't pretend. We're attracted to each other, and I think we should explore the chemistry between us."

Sonia placed a morsel of meat into her mouth, and it practically melted on her tongue. The seasonings and chargrilled taste were exceptional. "Mmmm. You did a good job."

He chuckled and spooned a dollop of chimichurri sauce onto her plate. "I appreciate the compliment, and since you obviously want to change the subject, that's what we'll do. So tell me something about you."

Sonia shrugged. "There's not much to tell. I'm an only child, and both of my parents are dead. I was raised in Atlanta by my uncle. The end."

"There is more to that story," Esteban said. He wasn't eating. He sat with both elbows on the stone top, and the powder-blue shirt wrinkled around his muscular arms.

"Nothing you want to hear, believe me."

Sonia felt in no position to share the sorrowful details about her parents. They were often described as an eye-catching pair, her mother with cinnamon-brown skin and her father with a paler complexion from his mixed-race heritage. From all accounts, they'd loved each other when they met and lived a charmed life, attending parties and in general enjoying a young, carefree existence. They split when her father's drug use became unsupportable. In the end, cancer stole her mother, and drugs stole her father.

"Is this music from Argentina?" she asked, hoping to change the subject again. Although she was curious about him, she did not welcome questions about her private life.

Esteban nodded. "The song you're listening to is '*Adiós Nonino.*' What do you think?"

"It's good." She swayed a little to the melancholy tune. She heard violins, flutes, and an accordion.

Esteban smiled. "You really do like it," he said.

"I like all kinds of music. Country, rock 'n roll, reggae, and neo soul."

"With such eclectic tastes, you can't possibly have a favorite artist."

She giggled. "I do have a lot of favorites," she admitted. "But if I had to narrow down my choice to one, I'd pick Jill Scott."

"Jill Scott," he said slowly. "The name is vaguely familiar."

"She sings and acts, but started her career as a spoken-word artist.

Which makes sense. Her songs are like poetry. She makes me...*feel*. I would love to meet her and pick her brain."

Esteban looked at her so intently, she felt exposed. Dipping her gaze to the plate, she speared an asparagus with her fork.

"How is the food?" Esteban asked after a few minutes of silence.

"The food is good. Excellent, I should say."

Esteban's eyes narrowed slightly. "And the company?"

"The company is good, too."

"Not excellent?"

Sonia swallowed, the tiny quiver that so often plagued her belly when she was near him making its presence known. "Yes, excellent." She continued eating.

The conversation lightened when Esteban told her about his weakness for cars, particularly sports cars. "I have ten at my home in Argentina."

Sonia lifted her eyebrows in surprise. "How can one man drive ten cars?"

"He can't, but like I told you before, I like to collect beautiful things." He spoke without regret or defensiveness.

"How many do you have here?"

"I limit myself in the States and only keep four vehicles."

"Only four?" Sonia asked with an arched brow.

"Yes, only," he said, amusement filling his eyes. "My limo, the Maybach, a Porsche, and I recently purchased a Maserati." He sliced an asparagus in half. "Your turn to share."

"I don't have enough cars to fill a dealership. I don't want to bore you."

"You won't."

"What do you want to know?"

"Tell me something about your career."

Sonia took a deep breath. "Well, I want to earn my certification as a sommelier. I earned an introductory certificate over a year ago, which means I have less than a year to take and pass the next-level exam, or I have to start over. Azul cut my hours, so I certainly have more time on my hands to study." She spent a lot of time poring over industry materials that included a wine bible, *The World Atlas of Wine*, and *The Ultimate Guide to Spirits and Cocktails*.

"How much longer before you're ready?"

One of the few people who showed more than a cursory interest in her studies was Jackie, who also helped her with her study drills. But Esteban appeared genuinely interested.

"Soon, I hope." The cost of the materials and the exam were all mitigating factors.

Maybe it was the wine or just the quiet comfort of the house, but Sonia relaxed into an enjoyable conversation with Esteban as they finished the meal. When her plate was clean, she patted her stomach.

"Thank you, that was delicious." She drained the last of the wine from her glass and stood, reluctant to leave but not wanting to over-stay her welcome.

The legs of Esteban's stool scraped the floor when he pushed it back. "Thank you for joining me." He went over to the desk, opened the top drawer, and withdrew an envelope, the same as he'd done the first time.

Sonia quietly took it. "Thank you. Good night." She turned to leave.

"What do you do when you go home at night, alone?"

Esteban's voice stopped her departure. He settled his butt on the edge of the desk and folded his arms, waiting for an answer.

"What do you mean?"

"It's a shame that you sleep alone. I sleep alone. Maybe we should sleep together."

She laughed, heart racing. "Are you drunk?"

"I'm quite sober. All night with my guests you were charming, funny, sweet. They like you. I like you. So why do you go home alone?"

She hadn't told him about Pedro, that the man whose résumé she'd handed him at the first party was her boyfriend. At the very least, he ensured she didn't spend every night alone, though that hadn't been the case for a while. They'd been drifting apart.

"Thank you for this." She held up the envelope and folded it, tucking it into the pocket of her jumpsuit. "I appreciate your generosity more than you know, but the extent of our conversation should center around business."

"There's more than business between us, *querida*. You know that as well as I do. You pretend with me, but I'm no fool. If I kissed you right now, you would kiss me back."

Her heart rate quadrupled. "If you kissed me right now, I'd slap you."

"No, you wouldn't."

The arrogant, smug way he dismissed her comment inflamed her anger. "Why do you sleep alone, Esteban?" she asked, throwing caution to the wind. "Other than the woman I saw you with after Arturo's party, is there anyone in your life? Do you have a girlfriend?"

"I don't have girlfriends. I don't need girlfriends."

"Of course you don't. You have your cars and your big house and your private plane, which makes women flock to you, I'm sure. It doesn't matter if you have a heart, because all that matters is the money."

"Having a heart is for weak fools. When you have a heart, it gets trampled on by selfish people who don't give a damn about you and your *heart*. You want to know what matters, Sonia?" He pushed off from the desk and came closer, his dark eyes glittering down at her. "Money, *querida*, is what matters. You don't want to hear that, but it's the truth. Money is more important than heart. More important than love."

"I feel sorry for you."

"Really? Is that what you *feel*, when you look at me with those big brown eyes, as if you want to tear my clothes off? When you look at me and lick your lips, as if you want to lick my skin?"

"I-I don't do that."

He let out a dark chuckle, one filled with the raw hunger of a man who'd reached the edge of restraint. "I'd have to be blind not to see how much you want me, and I've been very patient, giving you time to get used to me, but tonight, you've tested me in this outfit. You're not wearing a bra, and I can see your nipples pressing against the fabric. But you know that, don't you? That's why you wore it."

"That's not true!" Sonia's voice shook with the need to make him believe the lie. That she hadn't worn this one-shouldered jumpsuit with him in mind. That she hadn't considered how the royal-blue color looked against her skin, or spent much too much time making sure her face, hair, and makeup were perfect.

"Business?" Esteban continued with a scoff. "You weaken what's between us to business—what's been between us from the beginning."

"I don't know what you're talking about. There's nothing between us, and I'm leaving."

His hand snaked out and caught her wrist. "Admit you feel the way that I do."

She twisted her arm, but he refused to release her. "You said you were hiring me to be a wine consultant. Nothing more."

"I lied."

He gently pulled her into his body and her skin came alive. Looking down into her face, he gave her ample time to resist. When she didn't, his nostrils flared and his mouth crashed down over hers.

CHAPTER 12

S onia had suspected Esteban would be a good kisser, but this —this kiss was bone-melting and hot. He took control of her mouth, and inside her head explosions and fireworks went off.

A hand at the middle of her spine crushed her breasts into his hard chest, and she melted against him, wanting to disappear inside him. His other hand roamed her body in an exploratory fashion that made her tremble at the heat of his touch. He squeezed her breast, and she gasped when his thumb circled her nipple, and then he squeezed her breast again. All she could do was arch her back to fill more of his hand.

She felt him *everywhere*, even places where they didn't touch. Her fingers crept up his torso, past the thundering of his heart until her arms folded over each other behind his strong neck. She couldn't stop kissing him. She drowned in pleasure as he kept her pinned to him with strong arms and firm lips.

One of his hands eased downward and smoothed over the fleshy contours of her bottom. The intimate contact was unexpected but not unwanted. Moaning in the back of her throat, she shivered as the same hand contracted around her right buttock and squeezed.

In the next instance she was pushed against the edge of the desk, the hard steel of his erection wedged at her crotch as he hoisted her knee up to his hip and settled between her thighs. Slanting his head, he drove his tongue between the seam of her lips and took charge of her mouth, lapping at the sensitive interior.

His hips began a slow grind that matched the sultry music softly playing in the background. Trembling, Sonia lost control of her senses and tunneled her fingers into his soft hair, to keep his head and keep him firmly in place. She sucked on his lower lip and panted into his mouth with unchecked passion. Thirsty, hungry for more as her insides coiled tight and she joined him in a slow grind, with her leg still hoisted up, like a woman in heat.

Esteban slid a hand into her short hair and dragged a line down her neck with his lips. "This thing between us won't go away. Spend the night with me," he demanded huskily.

His teeth scraped her skin, and Sonia gasped at the heated exploration of her neck and collarbone. He was merciless. How did he instinctively know how to touch and kiss her?

"Sonia," he breathed in her ear. Goodness, the way he said her name. Every word from his lips sounded so sexy with that Spanish accent. She would gladly listen to him read the ingredients on a box of cereal. "Say yes. Spend the night with me."

Her hands dropped to his shoulders with every intention of pushing him away, but her fingers fastened around the strength they encountered.

"I can't," she said in a weak voice.

"Why not?" he asked, his voice gravelly and hungry. The arm banded around her waist held her secure as he gazed down into her face. "I'll give you anything. Name it."

"I don't want anything from you, Esteban." Sonia twisted her face away from him. "I can't stay because...because I have a boyfriend."

He stopped breathing, and the air around them stilled. "What did you say?"

"I have a boyfriend," she said, even softer than before.

His hands fell away. "A boyfriend?" Esteban stepped back. "The pastry maker?"

"Yes." Sonia nodded.

Esteban ran a hand down his face. "Why didn't you say something before?" he asked. When she didn't reply, he answered his own question. "Because then I might not have hired you."

Her head tilted up. "I'm not wrong, am I?"

"No, you're not," he admitted. He muttered a stream of Spanish, but she didn't need a translator to know he'd cursed. His angry eyes settled on her. "Did he see the flowers I sent you?"

"Yes," she said.

"And what did he say?"

"He didn't like it. He doesn't care too much for you."

"Because I appreciate his woman more than he does?"

"He appreciates me."

"No, he doesn't, or you wouldn't be here. He allowed you to come here even though he didn't like me sending you flowers—"

"He doesn't allow me to do anything. I'm my own person—"

"What kind of man is that, hmm? I'm a jealous man, and I would never allow my woman to get dressed up and go to the house of another man, especially a man I'm jealous of. Or perhaps he doesn't care because he wants you to do something for him."

She tried to move past him, but he stepped in front of her and blocked the entrance. "Get out of my way."

"I've upset you, but surely you see the truth that this man is not worthy of you."

"And you are?"

"More worthy than he is. If you were mine—"

"Yours? You own things, inanimate objects, Esteban. Paintings, wine, cars. *Not* people."

A semblance of a smile lifted the corner of his mouth, but there was no humor in the depths of his eyes. "You're so angry, but who are you angry at? Me, or the pastry maker? When was the last time he took you out? Does he treat you the way a man should treat his woman?"

"What I do in my personal life is none of your business. You and I have a business arrangement." After tonight, she was certain that was at an end, if for no other reason than she couldn't come back here. Not after such an explosive kiss, not after he'd made his desire for her so clearly known, and laid bare her desire for him.

"I want more than a business arrangement with you."

"You can't have it. Please let me by."

"Your boyfriend treats you like an errand girl, asking you to deliver his résumé to me. You don't deserve that. You should be draped in diamonds and the finest clothes, taken to concerts and dinners around the world. Shown a good time. Shown off. Not sent to run errands." His eyes dragged down the length of her body, and her skin prickled under the heat of his gaze. "But you're right; you should leave now. Or I'm afraid we'll be responsible for breaking the pastry maker's heart." With a cruel twist of his mouth, he stepped aside.

Sonia rushed toward the door on legs as sturdy as overcooked noodles.

He didn't follow her like he'd done before. She stood uncertainly in the middle of the courtyard with the moonlight shining down and the Maybach parked nearby. She walked to it and pulled on the back door handle.

Locked.

Surely he wouldn't leave her stranded? Sonia glanced back at the house, but the windows at the front door were all dark, and she couldn't see inside the house to tell if Esteban was nearby or not. She didn't even have her phone to call a car service for a lift.

"Are you ready, Miss Kennedy?" She whirled around and saw Abel's kind eyes looking back at her.

"Yes," she said, relieved.

He opened the door and let her slide into the back. Sonia slumped in the seat, jittery and with her head pounding from a stress headache.

Guilt and disappointment pressed down on her shoulders. Guilt because she spent time with Esteban, knowing full well that she was attracted to him while she had a man in her life. Tempting danger. Teasing her senses with the irresistibleness of his presence. Disappointment because of her lack of control when he kissed her.

It was only a kiss, but earth-altering—as if a monumental shift had taken place inside of her. Her belly trembled and her nipple ached from when he touched her breast. Biting the corner of her mouth, she recalled the sensual tug of his lips, the gentle pressure of his teeth, and how perfectly she fit in his strong arms.

A soft moan escaped her throat, and her eyes flicked to the front. Abel didn't seem to hear, and if he did, he ignored the sound.

Sonia rested her temple against the cool glass and closed her eyes.

She needed the money, but at least now the achy hunger she experienced with Esteban might finally be over. Because she'd never see him again.

* * *

ESTEBAN SAT out on the dark patio, legs stretched out before him in the pool chair. Smoke from a cigar swirled up into the night.

After his guests had left, dinner had been a ruse to keep Sonia around longer. All night he'd barely been able to keep his hands to himself, aching to undo the clasp on her shoulder and pull down the front of her jumpsuit to find out what color those perfect little nipples were. Brown? Dark brown? He was dying to know the answer.

He shook his head on a humorless laugh. A boyfriend.

She'd never said a word, so he assumed she didn't have one.

Damn.

CHAPTER 13

*N*o. Way.

Standing inside the gate of her apartment building, Sonia stared in disbelief at the approaching couple across the street. Moments before, she'd walked home from Azul, but the sound of a woman's loud laughter caused her to turn around out of sheer curiosity. She wouldn't have seen them otherwise, she was so deep in thought about Esteban and their kiss a few days ago.

Pedro was outside his building, hugged up with a giggling redhead wearing a short, tight skirt and stilettos. Apparently, he'd found a way to occupy himself while unemployed.

As Sonia watched, the woman flung her arms around his neck, and he dipped her over his arm, fitting his mouth over hers in an amorous kiss. When they finally came up for air, Pedro slipped his arm around the young woman's waist, and they sauntered toward his building.

What the hell?

Three nights ago she'd left Esteban feeling guilty about her enthusiastic response to his advances, and here was Pedro about to go upstairs with another woman. Inflamed with anger, Sonia charged across the street. The couple moved slowly because they were so busy groping and kissing each other.

They didn't hear or see her coming until she was right up on them, steps from the door of Pedro's building. His eyes widened, and the redhead twisted her head to see what had caused his change in expression. Whatever she saw in Sonia's face made her scramble behind Pedro for safety.

"You son of a b—"

"Hold up!" Pedro grabbed her wrists before her hands could connect, and shoved her away. Sonia stumbled backward, losing a shoe in the process.

She yanked off the other one and tossed them both at him. He deftly sidestepped the weapons, his face darkening, fists clenched at his sides.

"I suspected you were cheating, but...how could you do this to me!" Sonia screamed.

The redhead cowered near a bush at the door.

He stared at Sonia with an arrogant set to his jaw. "What the hell do you want from me, Sonia? Huh? I'm a man. I have needs. And let's be real, you weren't satisfying them."

"Are you kidding me? Are you saying I was bad in bed?"

"I'm saying you checked out of this relationship a long time ago. I've been doing this by myself, while you act like you're doing me a favor by being with me. You're fine and everything, but ain't a man alive who wants to be with a woman who acts like he should be grateful she's having sex with him."

"That's bullshit! I have never treated you that way. You're making excuses for your own disgusting behavior. I've been your supporter and your champion from the beginning. You're the one who checked out. I've given you all of me."

He pointed at her. "See, that's exactly what I'm talking about. You act like you're better at relationships than I am. And then you act like when you fuck me, you're doing me a favor."

Sonia's mouth fell open. How could they have such divergent opinions of the same relationship? "You acted like you weren't even interested in sex anymore."

"Nah, don't put that on me. I wanted you, but the only time you were interested in sex was probably when you got tired of your toys."

"We haven't had sex in months, because of you!" She jabbed a finger at him.

"Me? Because of you! My needs haven't changed. Yours did. Guess you thought you were too good for me, that I somehow fell short. And don't deny it, because I see it in your face every time I try to have a real conversation with you about my dreams. You think I'm impatient because I didn't want to wait my turn like you, right? You're complacent, Sonia."

"Complacent?" she repeated, appalled.

"You have no drive, *mami*. You still haven't gotten your certification, and then you take a job doing private parties for some rich dude —for what?"

"To make money, you moron. It takes time to get certified, and I've been working. Hard. But it takes money, too, and you know my hours were cut at the restaurant."

Pedro sucked his teeth and waved a dismissive hand. "You think I'm stupid, don't you? There's something going on between you and that guy, and whether you admit it or not is irrelevant to me. You've been withdrawn from our relationship for a long time, and it's gotten worse since you started working for him."

"You are such a jerk."

"Yeah, whatever. I'm not trying to hear any of this right now. I'm busy."

"We are done!" Sonia yelled at his back.

"No kidding." He didn't even bother to turn around.

"Give me my keys."

He stopped and took a deep breath. Waited, as if he was counting to ten, and then turned around. "You want your keys?" He jerked her keys off his bundle and tossed them at her.

They fell onto the grass.

"You're such a jerk!" Sonia easily found the silver keys and snatched them from between the blades of grass. "You'll be sorry!"

Pedro and his date paused at the door of his apartment building, and he looked back at her.

Humiliated, Sonia grabbed her shoes and half ran across the street barefoot. Pebbles dug into the soles of her feet as she stomped across the yard, but she ignored the pain and raced up the stairs to her apartment.

"To think I was trying to be a good girlfriend," she muttered, slamming the door when she got inside.

Shaking, she stormed into her bedroom and yanked up the window, letting in the warm night air. Pedro, perhaps suspecting what she was up to, came tearing out the door of his building.

"Don't do it!" he hollered, his voice echoing in the empty street.

"*Fuck. You. Papi*," she hollered back.

She jerked open the drawer in her dresser that contained all of his belongings, grabbed an armful of shirts and underwear, and tossed them through the window.

"Bitch!" she heard him yell.

"I got your bitch," Sonia muttered to herself.

She hauled another armful of clothes against her chest and tossed them out, too. The articles of clothing rained down on Pedro's bent head as he scurried to pick up the first set.

"Does this make you feel better? You feel good now?" he yelled up at her.

"Yes!"

"You know what, I was trying to spare your feelings earlier. You're a beautiful woman, but you can't fuck. You *are* bad in bed. That's why I've been fucking Mandy and Kristin at Azul for months now."

Mandy and Kristin were waitresses at Azul. Low blow.

"Hey!" The neighbor below her poked his head out the window. "Do the two of you mind having this argument during reasonable hours? Some of us are trying to get some sleep!"

Sonia didn't respond, but Pedro yelled at the man in Spanish.

While they argued, she tackled the closet next, yanking the few items that belonged to him off the hangers and picking up his two pairs of shoes from the floor. She tossed everything through the window. When she looked down, the neighbor had disappeared, but the redhead had joined Pedro in gathering up his belongings.

His electric razor, toothpaste, lotion, deodorant, and toothbrush were next, flung hard and fast. The toothbrush bounced off the top of a car in the street, and the razor tangled in a tree limb by the cord.

Pedro yelled in Spanish and shook a threatening fist up at her.

"You can have him," Sonia screamed so loud at the other woman that her throat hurt. She slammed the window hard, and for a split second panicked when she thought it would shatter. That would be just her luck.

Shaking, this time not from anger but frustration, she dropped to the floor beside the bed. Relationships were not her strength. She couldn't get them right. Men had been disappointing her all her life, starting with her own father.

She'd known her relationship with Pedro was finished, but to have it end this way was crushing. She felt dismissed and unimportant.

Sonia pressed her face to her bent knees.

She'd lost so much in the past few days. Her side gig. Her man. Most importantly, her optimism.

She felt like she had nothing left.

* * *

ESTEBAN HEARD movement behind him and swiveled in the chair to see Abena enter the office with his lunch on a tray, a light meal of lobster bisque and a mixed green salad. She set the food and a glass of water with half a lemon on the table at one end of the office.

Tucking the tray under her arm, she tilted her head to the side and frowned, looking at him with concern. "You haven't been yourself today."

"You're imagining things." Esteban stood and walked over to the table.

Abena pressed her lips together into a thoughtful pout. "That I doubt. By the way, the *Miami Herald* called. They want to do a story on you and your contributions to the food bank."

"No."

Abena sighed. "Mr. Galiano—"

"Abena, you know how I feel about that kind of press, so why even ask? If the paper wants to do a story on food donations, there are plenty of other restaurant owners they can interview."

"But they want to do a story on you, the mysterious owner of Patagonia, Nonna, and many other restaurants."

"My food and service speak for itself."

"They're interested in you, the person. Even more so because you refuse to do press."

"And I refuse to do press because I want to keep my private life private."

"But your philanthropic work—"

"Is none of their business. I don't do any of it for publicity. The answer is no."

Esteban didn't want to add to the twenty percent of food waste contributed by full-service restaurants nationwide, so for years his establishments donated the extra food to feeding programs. Volunteers came by several times a week to collect the extra food, which was neatly packed and labeled by designated staff. This project was important because it gave him a chance to give back, and it offered personal satisfaction.

Before he was adopted, Esteban had an intimate relationship with hunger in an orphanage that was understaffed and underfunded. As such, he'd been so unprepared for the abundance and variety of choices at his new home that he'd hidden food under his bed for weeks before his father discovered the stash and gently assured him there would always be plenty to eat.

As much as he could, Esteban wanted to ensure no other children suffered the same anxiety.

Realizing she was fighting a losing battle, Abena sighed heavily again. "All right, I'll leave you alone, but I did take the liberty of canceling your two o'clock appointment and scheduling a massage at the spa. I suspect you need it. Abel will pick you up at one forty."

That idea sounded excellent. Already the tension eased out of his shoulders. Esteban shook his head. "How do you manage to always anticipate my needs?"

"Isn't that what a good assistant does?" Abena asked.

"You're more than an assistant, and you know that."

"Does that mean I get a bigger office?"

He allowed a smile. Her office was right next door and second in size only to his. "You can have anything you want; just don't leave me. We're supposed to grow old together."

She laughed, her dark features lighting up with amusement. "I won't leave you, but not because you give me a bigger office." She paused on the way to the door. "Maybe I like working for you."

"And you like the salary I pay you."

Abena shook her head. "You're too cynical, Mr. Galiano. It's not always about money, you know. By the way, that situation has been handled. The funds were deposited into Andrea's account this morning, as you instructed." She knew better than to ask any questions and left, closing the door quietly behind her.

Esteban pushed up from the chair and walked over to the window. Two floors below, cars passed by while tourists and residents moved along the sidewalk at a leisurely pace.

Abena might be right, he was cynical, but she was wrong on the other point. It was *always* about money. Money made the world go around. With it, one could buy anything—the necessities of life, justice, respect, and even the opportunity to prove the unworthiness of one's competition.

Now that phase one of his plan was complete, time for phase two.

Esteban picked up the phone and called Adam at Premium Staffing.

"Hello, Esteban. How can I help you?"

"I need you to find a job for an assistant pastry chef."

Quiet.

"You mean you want me to fill an assistant pastry chef position in one of your restaurants?"

"No. As a matter of fact, I want you to stay far away from my restaurants and find this person a position with some other establishment. Preferably on the West Coast. I'll pay the placement fees. I want him out of Miami."

"What's his name?"

"Pedro Loisseau. I'll send over his résumé in a few minutes, and Adam, I need this taken care of swiftly. I'll pay for expedited service."

"How good does he look on paper?" Adam asked.

"Pretty good."

"Shouldn't be a problem, then."

"Can you have this done by the time I get back from Argentina next month?"

"I'll make it happen."

Adam's response was exactly what Esteban wanted to hear.

He hung up, feeling even more tension leave his body. He hadn't reached out to Sonia since the night of that heated kiss at his house, but he wasn't interested in any other woman.

He still felt her soft body and shapely curves, and hadn't been able to get her out of his mind. Quite simply, he wanted Sonia Kennedy. And he was going to have her.

CHAPTER 14

Sonia stared at the ringing phone. It was Esteban, and she hadn't seen or heard from him in weeks.

After the third ring, she answered and pressed the phone to her ear. "Hello, Esteban."

"Hello, Sonia. How are you?"

"Fine. You?"

"Surprised you answered."

"I have no reason not to answer. You're the one who kicked me out of your house."

She walked over to the window and looked down into the yard, waiting for him to respond. She didn't know why he'd called, but she'd let him lead the conversation.

Her gaze followed the man who lived in the apartment below as he walked down the street.

"As you well know, I had my reasons," Esteban finally said. "How is your boyfriend?"

"Excellent. He got a job in Southern California as a pastry chef at a farm-to-table restaurant. But you already know that because you arranged for him to be gone."

Quiet.

"What makes you say that?"

"He never signed up with Premium Staffing, and that job in California came out of nowhere. He flew out yesterday, and today you're calling me. It's not that hard to put two and two together."

Pedro had called to tell her the news, his voice pitched higher in excitement. Up until that point, he'd been begging for her forgiveness and promised to change—a complete one-eighty from his behavior the night they split. When she told him to stop calling, he resorted to following her to work. He seemed truly sorry, saying the woman was a one-night stand, someone who'd approached him at a bar.

Despite his contrition, and no matter how much he begged, she couldn't forget the insults he'd hurled at her, and couldn't look at him the same way after he admitted cheating with their coworkers in addition to spending the night with the redhead.

At least the pain didn't last forever. It had been replaced by disappointment, and she didn't love or want Pedro back in her life, no matter how hard he tried.

She'd answered the phone that day with every intention of telling him off, but then he'd excitedly shared the news about the job offer he'd received after a telephone interview. She didn't know why he'd called to tell her about the position. She'd congratulated him and cut the conversation short, but not before he promised to call her from California. He said she could move out there with him and it would be a chance for them to start fresh. She told him not to bother, and when she hung up, she knew she'd never hear from him again.

"You wasted your time. He and I had already broken up."

"What caused your breakup?"

"He cheated on me."

"I'm sorry to hear that, but I'm not surprised. He was no good for you. I told you that. Don't waste your love or time on people who don't matter."

"Thanks so much for your wonderful advice. What do you want?"

"I want to see you."

"Why?"

"Because I can't get you out of my mind."

The intimate tone of his voice sent shivers scurrying over her nipples. He did things to her body without even trying.

His voice dropped lower. "This isn't a job offer, Sonia. I'll be back in the country this weekend and have a party and the reopening of Nonna, my Italian restaurant, to attend. I want you to be my guest."

"Sounds very tempting."

"Then yield to temptation."

The soft command had her crossing her legs and biting her lip. "There's no one else you'd rather take? No girlfriend?" she asked.

"If I had a girlfriend, I would take her, but I don't have a girlfriend and you don't have a boyfriend."

"Maybe I'm pining for my boyfriend."

"You're not. You're pining for me."

He sounded so sure of himself that she wanted to slap him through the phone.

"All you want is for me to attend those events with you?"

"I want you naked in my bed. I want to spread you wide, lick every inch of your skin, and do everything imaginable to you. But for now, I'll settle for attendance at those events."

Sonia swallowed past her bone-dry throat. "The things you say..." she said shakily.

"I prefer to speak the truth. I'll cover the cost of your clothes and accessories and anything else you need. So, can I count on you?" He sounded distracted, as if something else were pulling at his attention now. Either that, or he'd grown tired of her holding out.

She was free, so why not? Pedro was gone, and it couldn't hurt, could it, to enjoy herself a little—indulge in the excess Esteban offered? "I'll be available."

"*Perfecto.*"

* * *

ESTEBAN PICKED her up in the Maybach, and she felt woefully under-dressed in jeans and a loose-fitting blouse, but the hungry way his gaze traveled over her body as she slid into the vehicle made her feel as if she were dressed in haute couture. He'd told her to have her hair done and bring along any other necessities she'd need, which she kept in the large purse at her side.

As usual, he looked impeccable in a suit, this one navy blue with white stripes and a colorful pocket square. A neatly groomed five o'clock shadow covered his chin and jaw. He reached for her hand and kissed the palm, sending tingles throughout her body, before instructing Abel to head out.

"The boutique I'm taking you to is in the Design District, near Nonna. It's not open for a few more days, but I know the owner from another shop she opened in another part of town. She's agreed to meet us there." He still hadn't released her hand, rubbing his thumb back and forth across her knuckles.

"If the shop is closed…"

"Trust me. She doesn't mind." His head turned in her direction, but the expression in his eyes was hidden from her in the dark car. "Let me do this."

He took out his phone and made a call. He spoke in Spanish for a few minutes, laughing at one point. She was enthralled by his laugh— it was so rare for her to see. His Adam's apple bobbed up and down, and his head tilted back slightly as he spoke to the person on the other end.

When they arrived at the Miami Design District, a high-end shopping mecca known for its art galleries, antique dealers, and haute couture boutiques, they passed by Nonna and turned down another street. Abel cruised to a stop in front of a store named Bella Boutique.

They only waited a few minutes before a stylishly dressed Latina woman with long, dark hair arrived to open the door. They exited the car and approached her.

"*Hola*, Esteban," she said, tilting up her lips to kiss the air beside his cheek.

"*Hola*, Linn. This is Sonia." He placed a hand at the small of her back. "She needs two outfits—one for Nonna's opening tonight and the other for a party afterward. I told her you can help."

Linn eyed Sonia with a smile, her gaze traveling up and down the length of her body. "I think I can find something you'll like," she said, the remark directed more at Esteban than Sonia, which made Sonia wonder if she'd dressed his dates before.

Inside Bella, they were greeted by stark white walls surrounding one-of-a-kind dresses and other clothes. Esteban remained at the front of the store, seated on a white leather couch, while Sonia and Linn browsed for the perfect outfit. The store's selections were geared toward women who were confident and didn't have reservations about showing skin. Backless dresses, pants with wide legs and long slits, and sheer materials dominated the selections.

They chose several items, and with help from Linn, Sonia tried each outfit, the first of which was a burnished gold dress with spaghetti straps. Although she liked it, in the end she settled on an orange sleeveless dress with a plunging neckline for the party at the Blue Top Hotel, and a carmine-colored strapless dress with an open bodice and a thigh-high split for dinner at Nonna. The dark red looked great against her light complexion and showed off her figure. Linn brought her a pair of gold strappy sandals and a gold clutch that worked for both outfits.

Sonia shifted her lipstick and some cash into the new purse and handed the old one to Linn, who stuffed Sonia's belongings into one of the store's shopping bags and hung the orange outfit over her forearm.

"He's going to love you in this," Linn said with a wicked smile.

Sonia had no doubt that he would. She applied red lipstick and dropped the tube into her new purse.

"Ready?" Linn asked.

"All set," Sonia confirmed.

They exited the dressing room and met Esteban on the sales floor. The moment he turned and saw her, he stilled. Sonia knew the picture she made in the red dress with her red lips. Her mood elevated, she posed with one hand on her hip and one leg jutted out.

"What do you think?" she asked.

Slowly, Esteban walked over and stood so close that she had to tilt her head back to look up at him. She held her breath. A cloud of lust bloomed in his eyes, and she experienced a sense of unbridled power in that moment.

"It's a shame we have to go to these parties tonight," Esteban replied.

He handed over his card without even looking at the tag, and it was then that Sonia realized she didn't know how much the items cost. None of them had price tags attached. When she saw the total, her eyes widened.

Over five thousand dollars! No wonder Linn hadn't hesitated to meet them.

Sonia gulped.

Esteban signed the receipt, and seconds later they sat in the back of the car with her belongings stowed in the trunk.

Sonia turned to him. "Esteban, I'm not sure about this purchase," she said.

"Why not?"

"The cost. I feel as if…" Her stomach knotted.

"You don't think you're worth it?"

"It's just…everything is so expensive."

"I want you to have everything you bought. Isn't that enough?"

She shook her head, staring out the window. "No, it's not. Let's go back." She regretted staying silent in the store. She'd been so shocked and hadn't wanted to appear gauche. Now she wished she'd spoken up sooner.

Esteban took her chin between his fingers and gently turned her head back to face him. "Do you like the dresses?"

"Of course. They're beautiful."

"And the shoes and the bag?"

"Yes. They're beautiful, too."

"Then there is no problem." His thumb brushed gently along the side of her chin. "Accept my gifts, without regret."

His hand slipped behind her neck and he edged her forward and kissed her. It felt natural, as if they should be kissing. The desire she'd felt before stirred to life again, and she leaned across the console to indulge in a deeper kiss, parting her lips for the entry of his tongue.

Her body came alive as his fingertip trailed down her jaw line and along the side of her throat, stopping at her cleavage. "You deserve it," he said softly. Delicate kisses followed the path his fingers trod.

Sonia didn't pull back. Instead, she leaned into the gentle caress of his mouth and hands, heart racing at a reckless speed.

He sucked her collarbone and flicked his tongue against her skin. The flesh between her legs throbbed, awakened by the persistent, seductive touch of his lips and tongue and the gentle abrasion of his hair-roughened face. If he pushed, even a little bit, he could have her in the back of this car. She was so aroused by him, so hungry for more.

But he didn't push. Instead, he withdrew, his dark eyes glittering with hunger. "It's a gift. Nothing more." He kissed her hand and then sat back.

But he didn't release her. He continued to hold her hand as they pulled up to the restaurant, and she didn't want to let him go, either.

Leaving Sonia to wonder what the hell she'd gotten herself into.

CHAPTER 15

They spent two hours at Nonna. Everyone in attendance had purchased tickets, which entitled them to a selection of wines and a multicourse tasting menu created solely for opening night.

After Nonna, she and Esteban went to Patagonia, where Sonia changed into the orange dress in a private suite. When she exited the room to rejoin Esteban, he'd ditched his tie and opened the top buttons of his white shirt to reveal the tanned column of his neck. He immediately took her hand and escorted her down to the waiting vehicle.

On the ride to the Blue Top Hotel, Esteban explained he was meeting with a couple of potential celebrity investors. The party was in full swing when they arrived. A mixed group of different nationalities and ethnicities crowded into the main room and spilled onto the rooftop around a glass-bottomed wading pool in the center that allowed guests to look down into the lobby. A deejay stood on a mini-stage pumping house music as strobe lights crisscrossed the dark sky.

Sonia stayed close to Esteban, who let one hand rest on her hip with a possessive touch as he introduced her to the celebrities and movers and shakers in attendance, including some of the Miami Heat players partying with bottles of top-shelf liquor after a winning home game that put them in the playoffs. In the past, this would have been a party she worked, but tonight, she was a guest, and the difference sent adrenalin pumping through her veins.

They'd been there an hour when Sonia excused herself from Esteban's side. He was in a conversation with one of the basketball players, but before she walked away, he caught her wrist and leaned in.

"Are you all right?" he asked.

"Fine. I'm going outside to get some fresh air."

She stepped out onto the rooftop and passed by a woman twerking while her friends cheered her on, recording every movement with their phones. She stopped a waiter on his way inside.

"I'll take one of those." She chose a multicolored Miami Vice, a drink she'd grown to appreciate ever since moving to the city. Resting her butt against the railing, she scanned the crowd and saw a familiar face coming toward her.

"Well, hello," the man said.

"Hello. Craig, right?" At the first party she hosted for Esteban, Craig, an American, attended with his wife, Ivana, a Russian designer. He was clean-shaven, in his late thirties, and had dark hair.

"You remember." His blue eyes filled with interest. "Damn, you look incredible."

Sonia blinked. Taken by surprise, she laughed uneasily. "Thank you."

"What are you doing here?" he asked.

"I came with Esteban," she said.

"He's here? Where?" He looked around.

"Inside, talking business. Is your wife here?"

"It's not her scene. Every now and again, she gives me a long leash and lets me out of her sight." He bit his bottom lip and settled his gaze on her cleavage. "I don't think that's a good idea for Esteban where you're concerned, though. Someone might swoop in and steal you away from him."

Sonia suddenly felt terribly exposed. Craig hadn't behaved like this at the party, but of course his wife had been there, and Esteban had been nearby. He certainly wasn't acting like a married man right now.

Craig leaned against the railing. "So, you and Esteban, huh? I figured something was up when he introduced you as his wine consultant." He laughed and shook his head. "I didn't believe for one minute that you were at his house to talk about wine."

"I was," Sonia said, her cheeks heating.

"Maybe you were, but I know Esteban. He can't resist a pretty face."

Sonia sipped from her glass, curious about Craig's relationship with Esteban, but hesitant to prolong the conversation. "How long have you known him?" she finally asked.

"A long, long time. Before I married Ivana, I lived in Argentina, doing club promotions mostly. That's how Esteban and I met. We used to party together all over South America. Before Ivana, of course. The good old days." Regret entered his voice.

"Craig!" a man called from across the room and motioned with his hand. A trio of women stood beside him, all dressed in designer minis and stilettos, their faces caked in makeup and fake eyelashes.

"I better go see what he wants." Craig rolled his eyes, as if he didn't want to leave but the guy was twisting his arm. "Good seeing you again. I hope to see much more of you." He slipped an arm around her waist and pulled her in for a kiss on the cheek.

Sonia stiffened in the loose embrace, and inhaled in shock when his hand brushed her bottom. Another smile, which looked innocent—but not so innocent considering how he'd copped a feel—before Craig sauntered away.

What the heck was that about? If he and Esteban were really friends, why would he do that?

Feeling a little dirty, Sonia decided it was time to find Esteban. She searched inside and outside, but he was nowhere to be found. She sauntered back to the rooftop, resisting the overtures of a couple of men who approached her, and leaned over the railing. She was ready to go. Hopefully, he'd return soon.

* * *

ESTEBAN SLIPPED BACK into the party after stepping out for few minutes to call Abena and give her the names of a couple of contacts to start researching first thing on Monday morning. When he reentered the room, he searched for Sonia. The deejay was now playing reggaeton, which kept people dancing and gyrating.

He finally saw her outside, swaying to the music while sipping on her drink as she leaned over the railing. He fixated on her, his body responding to the fluid, gentle motion of her hips. He walked out on the rooftop and came up behind her, snaking an arm around her waist.

She tensed at first, but when she realized it was him, she willingly leaned back, her soft body conforming to his. Esteban pressed his nose to her neck and splayed a hand over her stomach, drawing her even closer so she could feel how much he wanted her.

"I'm the envy of every man here," he murmured in her ear.

"You're exaggerating," she said, with a light blush.

"It's true." He kissed her bare shoulder, inhaling her perfumed skin. He wanted to wake up to that scent on his sheets. He trailed his fingertips down the length of her arm and watched in fascination as goose pimples popped up in the wake of his touch.

Sonia turned in his arms and ran a hand down his chest, stroking to his lean waist. The muscles there trembled from the gentle contact. She seduced him with her eyes, looking up at him with an expression that suggested she wanted to devour him.

He pressed her back against the cement wall and slid a knee between her legs. Resting his forearm atop the metal part of the railing, he kissed her cheek and neck, and even beneath the music he heard her gasp. He kissed her ear, and she rubbed her cheek against his hair-roughened jaw.

"So, Sonia, are you sleeping alone tonight?"

Her hand came up between them, and he thought she was about to push him away, but instead, her fingers latched on to the front of his shirt, and she looked up at him with that same sultry look of desire he'd grown accustomed to seeing.

"No," she said softly.

He wanted to take her against the wall right now. His body was so tight and hard, he felt like one big tension ball. "Let's go," he said.

Slipping an arm around her waist, he guided her through the crowd, which had gotten thicker as the hour grew later. On the way out, they ran into Craig. Esteban said a few words and then ushered her out of the hotel into the Maybach.

The ride to the house was made in complete silence. The walk to the door was made in complete silence.

"Lights on," Esteban said, once they'd entered.

He muttered a Spanish curse and pressed her back against the wall, impatience overtaking him. He'd never been this desperate to make love to a woman before. He could hardly breathe, his lungs tight and constricted as he strained to hold back from tearing off her clothes and burying himself balls deep between her legs.

Their lips meshed together and his tongue slipped over hers, taking command of her mouth. She sucked gently, as if to imitate what she would do to him at another time, to another part of his anatomy. The thought had him growling in his throat, planting both hands on her ass cheeks and grinding his hips into hers, lifting one of her legs off the floor to cradle his erection against her warm core.

He slipped his hand under her dress, pushed aside her panties, and stroked her swollen flesh. She was already wet and hot, which made him want to drop to the floor and lick between her legs.

Dragging aside her bodice, he exposed her breasts. Finally. Bending his head, he sucked on a reddish-brown nipple and it puckered in his mouth. With her moaning softly, he squeezed her breasts and lifted his head to see the soft flesh meshed together, before dipping his head to taste them again, one by one, sucking and savoring. Her eager moans turned him hard as granite.

She stroked his length through his pants. *Jesús Cristo.* He was trembling, he wanted her so badly. But he didn't want to take her against the wall. He wanted to strip her naked and make love to her properly, and learn every inch of her delectable flesh.

Sweeping her up into his arms, Esteban said, "Lights off," and the space plunged into darkness.

He covered her mouth again, and she clung to him, wrapping her arms tightly around his neck and kissing him back with the same fervor and enthusiasm. Her soft mouth inflamed his hunger, and the pulsating ache that hovered in his gut every time she was near became sharper.

Using pure instinct, he walked through the house to the master suite on the first floor. And when he entered the bedroom, he kicked the door shut—ready for the long night ahead.

CHAPTER 16

S onia couldn't see Esteban standing behind her in the dimly lit room, but he stood close and she anticipated his touch. When he finally reached out, he gathered the folds of her dress and eased the chiffon over her head until she stood almost naked, wearing only a lace thong and gold heels.

"You're a beautiful woman, Sonia." She'd heard those words numerous times before, but coming from Esteban they sounded more meaningful and impactful.

One warm hand covered her right butt cheek, and the other traced a line down her hip. Then they converged over her abdomen and her breath stilled as they glided in slow motion up her torso to cup her bosom. He filled his palms, squeezing and kneading the soft flesh until her head fell back to his shoulder in a helpless, needy moan.

Behind her, the length of his erection pressed against the cleft of her ass through his pants. As he massaged her aching breasts, rolling the nipples between his fingertips, his mouth lowered to her neck. Sucking gently, he tasted the skin along the side of her throat and the underside of her jaw. Her lips parted, the sensations he evoked making her thrust her body into an arch and reach back to hook an arm around his neck. Her fingers tunneled into his soft hair and gripped the back of his head to hold him fast. She could happily stay like this for hours.

"Yes," she whispered, angling her neck to give him more.

Yes, to whatever he wanted. Yes, to bringing closure to the pounding hunger that existed between them. She'd give him everything, offer total access to all of her body.

Esteban hooked his thumbs in the fabric at her hips and lowered the underwear to her ankles. On his way back up, he kissed her bottom and squeezed each cheek, moaning in his throat.

Sonia stepped out of her panties and turned around to watch him dispose of his jacket. It dropped with a soft thud to the floor. Next, he started on the dress shirt. Like her own private striptease, he slowly unveiled his body with the opening of each button. When he finished, he tossed that garment to the floor too, and she had the pleasure of seeing his bare chest for the first time. His pants and briefs went next, and when he was naked, all she could do was stand at stare. She'd known he'd be a beautiful man and wasn't disappointed.

"You're a beautiful man, Esteban," she whispered.

The complexion of his skin was an even, tanned color. Driven by the excitement of seeing him naked at last, she explored his hard body —squeezing his biceps, running a hand over the ridges of his abdomen, and smoothing her palms over his hard, hair-sprinkled chest. His pecs twitched when she touched, confirming that she stimulated him as much as he stimulated her. Lean, muscular thighs flanked the rigid thrust of his erection between them. He was incredible to look at—perfect in symmetry and form.

Esteban lowered her onto the bed and, lifting each leg, removed her shoes one by one. He planted kisses on each ankle and followed them with nips up to the curve of her calves.

"When I saw you in the first dress at Bella, all I could think about was getting you naked. You looked delicious. Good enough to eat."

Heat flared in his eyes, and carnal promise weighted those words.

Esteban came down on top of her, his hard flesh pressed long the inside of her thighs. She stroked between his legs, gently touching his shaft and balls. Then his fingers found the spot between her legs. He stroked her wet sex, forcing her hips to strain upward, and listened to his deep groan in response.

He pushed aside her massaging hands and lowered his mouth to her breasts. He teased the taut nipples with delicate tugs of his lips and swipes of his tongue, forcing her to lift her torso higher in a silent plea for more. With a guttural groan, Sonia pressed her hands to the back of his neck, and begged him to suck harder, urged him to be rougher.

His mouth enveloped more of her breast. His tongue flicked across the nipple, even as his hands ran over her bare thighs, abdomen, and hips. Her entire body—her entire being—trembled beneath him.

She wanted him. Now. Waiting become untenable.

"Now, please," she whispered, uncaring how desperate she sounded. She ached for him and couldn't take the prolonged torture.

"Not yet."

He kissed the tips of her breasts, and she thought she'd go mad from the exquisite agony caused by his restraint.

"I want to know every inch of you," he whispered.

He slid down her body. Her skin, a sensitive live wire of heightened nerves, sparked under the touch of his hard frame dragging over hers. A smile of satisfaction crossed his lips as he moved lower, and his dark eyes filled with lust right before he lifted an ankle over his shoulder and claimed the cleft between her legs with his mouth.

She knew his intention, yet the shock of his lips in such an intimate caress left her breathless. The deliberate slide of his tongue made her gasp. As he worked his mouth across her drenched folds, her ragged breathing and helpless whimpers filled the room.

She writhed on the bed as his mouth inflicted unbearable pleasure, so much that she begged him to stop, while pleading with him to continue. When she thought she couldn't possibly take any more without splitting in two, Esteban kissed his way back up her body. He sucked the curve in her waist and licked the underside of her breast. Everything he did drove her insane. He was brutal in his attack on her senses, uncaring that he'd reduced her to a whimpering, begging bundle of nerves.

"Now," he murmured, his own breathing sounding broken.

He moved swiftly and took a condom from the drawer of the bedside table. Groaning, he pulled a nipple into his mouth one more time, as if he couldn't help himself. He sucked the puckered flesh as his hands parted her thighs.

Gripping his manhood, Esteban rubbed the tip against her wet core and teased her with the silky firmness. The hard nudge at the entrance to her body was the moment she'd been waiting for since they left the party. She willingly spread her legs for him, her insides trembling at the promise of his possession. If he didn't take her soon, she was certain she'd explode from too much want.

At that first sweet thrust, Sonia gasped and lifted her pelvis higher. They fit perfectly together, and *oh god*, he felt exquisite. The fullness. The demand of his delicious stretching. He groaned and sank deeper into the silken glove of her body.

Then he went still. "Sonia." The husky sound was whispered into her neck with his fists clenched on either side of her head.

Sonia kissed his jaw and neckline and ran her hand over his broad shoulders. Lifting an ankle to the base of his spine, she moved her hips in slow, restless circles. She needed more than he was giving.

Esteban looked down at her, his pupils dilated but barely visible behind half-closed lids. He drew a deep breath and angled his hips into a deep thrust.

Sonia cried out. "Yes, yes," she whispered breathlessly.

He rolled over and pulled her on top of him. His eyes were dark as their hips maintained a sexy rhythm that inched them closer to the peak of fulfillment. Taking advantage of his position under her, he filled his hands with her breasts, and she covered his hands and continued to enjoy the ride. She lost herself in the throes of pleasure, tilting back her head and concentrating on this moment, with this man, and the thrill of his pumping body beneath hers.

Muttering in Spanish, Esteban slid his hands down the curve of her waist to cup her hips. She moved faster, and her moans came louder as pleasure ricocheted throughout her body.

Suddenly, Esteban sat up and halted her movements. Crushing his lips over hers, he kissed her long and hard. She dived into kiss, relishing the warm taste of his mouth and welcoming the slippery thrust of his tongue.

Then he reclaimed control and, lifting them both off the bed, lowered her onto her back against the pillows. Their tongues slid against each other and their mouths clung together in eager, greedy, grasping kisses. He slanted his hips against hers, hitting with deliberate strokes. She didn't want him to stop, pause, or hesitate. She wanted him to keep moving like that because each possessive pump brought her closer to the edge.

At the first hint of her pending orgasm, he moved with more energetic drives. She jerked off the bed and thrust her hips against his, moaning with pleasure as she gripped the muscles of his solid back.

"Esteban." Her voice was a feathery plea.

His hips slammed into hers with powerful strokes that dominated her in the bed. Soft against hard. Big against small.

"Yes, Esteban. Yes!"

As she neared the pinnacle, her head arched back and his lips found her throat. The hairs of his beard and his ragged breaths tickled her sensitive skin. Hard pants joined the sounds of the bed moaning under the forceful pounding of their joined bodies.

His movements increased in speed and became almost savage, spurred on by her throaty moans and breathless pants of encouragement.

The sounds pitched higher as the explosion came. She climaxed with a shudder and a cry of relief, turning her face into his neck. She clung to him, gripping his head, panting as ecstasy tore through her body and shattered her senses, leaving her disoriented and her mind spinning out of control.

No man had ever made her feel like this. No man had ever taken such complete control of her body and emotions. They rocked in the bed as he came, too, and she felt nothing but Esteban as the universe exploded around them.

CHAPTER 17

*S*onia stretched under the covers of the blue sheets, the softest sheets she'd ever lain in. They were probably thousand-count Egyptian cotton, or something outrageous like that. Her body was sore because she'd been handled last night, by a real man who knew his way around her body, just as sure as if he'd been given GPS coordinates ahead of time.

Looking around, she didn't see any sign of Esteban, and didn't hear him, either. One wall of the bedroom was made of glass and let in sunlight. A patio with comfortable-looking chairs and a table sat outside. A mug on the table suggested Esteban had been sitting out there earlier and left it there when he came back in.

Glancing quickly at her watch, she realized it was later in the morning than she thought. No need to wonder how she'd managed to sleep so late. After coming in from the party and then spending the rest of the night under and over Esteban, she'd been understandably exhausted.

Scrambling from the bed, she dressed quickly in the same orange chiffon dress she wore the night before. She went into the en suite bathroom, but couldn't figure out which of the buttons on the wall panel was the light switch.

"Lights on," she said.

Overhead lights illuminated the modern fixtures of the cavernous, masculine space decorated in various hues of gray marble and dark gray tile. There were no windows in the room, and dual showerheads were behind an enclosed glass shower. She washed her face at one of two square porcelain sinks positioned on separate walls across from each other. Examining her features, she ran her fingers through her hair and did what she could with the short strands, taming them into a manageable mess until she could get home.

She found Esteban in the kitchen, hunched over a mug of coffee and reading the newspaper. For a moment, she quietly feasted her eyes on his exposed skin—the tight muscles of his arms, the toned belly. Without the power suit and hard set to his jaw, he appeared at ease in a way she'd never seen before. Even his hair was a little messy this morning instead of perfectly coiffed.

The memory of his touch remained in her skin, and their bedroom gymnastics came back in a rush—his head between her legs as her fingers ran through his silky hair, and his lips on her breasts. He seemed to love her breasts, and spent a lot of time getting acquainted with them. And her ass. With all the kissing, spanking, and grabbing he did, he clearly enjoyed her ass, too.

Esteban looked up, and a wave of shyness came over her, which was silly, since she hadn't been the least bit inhibited with him last night.

"Good morning," Sonia said. Her voice sounded a bit hoarse.

"Good morning." A knowing warmth filled his eyes as they flicked over her body. The low sound of his voice was a rumbling reminder of how he'd whispered into her damp flesh while they made love. "Coffee?"

"No thanks." She walked deeper into the kitchen.

"I can make breakfast," he offered.

"I'm not very hungry."

"Are you sure? Fruit or tea, perhaps?"

"I'm fine, really. I, um…think I'd better go. I need to get home and change clothes and shower. I have to work today. I go in at noon." She yearned for his touch, and hated she had to go in to work.

"*Demasiado*. Too bad. I was hoping we could spend a little more time together." He extended his hand, and she took it, letting him draw her between his legs.

Sonia ran a hand along his bicep, distracted by the beauty of his body. He was so fit, so hard.

"Did you sleep well?"

"Like a baby," Sonia whispered, focused on his lips. She wanted to kiss him, and did just that. His soft lips slid over hers, and she leaned in as he lowered his hands to her bottom and rubbed her ass.

"You're an incredible woman, you know that?" He dropped kisses to the crests of her breasts and ran his hands up and down her sides.

"And you're an incredible man."

"Are you sure you can't stay a little longer?"

Sonia shook her head. "No, I have to go and take all the hours I can." Of all the days she'd have to go in to work, why today? And while she normally welcomed any time on the schedule she could get, today it was an intrusion. She'd much rather stay here with Esteban for a few more hours, at least. Having him want her to stay increased the longing.

"Then let me get dressed and I'll come with you."

"You don't have to do that. Abel can—"

"I want to," he said firmly.

"Okay." In all honesty, she enjoyed his insistence, and while he went into the bedroom to get dressed, she took the liberty of pouring herself a glass of juice as she waited.

She glanced at the paper and saw that he'd been reading a glowing write-up of Nonna's opening. The reporter praised the selection, the location, and the efficiency of the staff. No surprise there. She suspected that Esteban was like a drill sergeant, and from what she'd seen, he'd done a good job of making sure the restaurant didn't suffer any opening night mishaps. If there were any, the staff did an excellent job of hiding them, which was a testament to his leadership.

Esteban returned dressed in a snug-fitting white T-shirt and chinos.

"I don't think I've ever seen you so casual," Sonia remarked.

"What do you prefer? Suits or this?"

She tilted her head. "Naked."

"Oh?" He came toward her and gripped her hips.

Throwing back her head in laughter, Sonia gazed up at him. "I'm sorry, Esteban, we don't have time."

"Then you shouldn't tease me like that." He kissed her neck and collarbone, and right away, her body became aroused.

"We can't." Sonia shook her head vigorously and pushed against his shoulders, stepping back to regulate her already erratic breathing.

"You're sure?'

"I'm positive." She slipped out of the circle of his arms. "We should go."

"If you didn't have to work at Azul, you would stay if I asked?"

The question sounded simple enough, but Sonia suspected a deeper meaning behind the words by the weighty way he studied her. She was almost afraid to answer. "I would," she answered.

He nodded, as if he'd learned something of value. "Let's go."

On the ride to her apartment, they didn't say much, mostly because Esteban appeared to be in deep thought behind a pair of sunglasses that didn't allow her to see his eyes. She wanted to ask what was wrong, but decided to let him have his thoughts. When they arrived at her apartment, she expected him to leave, but to her surprise, he told Abel to wait while he followed her inside.

Compared to his spacious mansion, her little apartment felt rather inadequate, and his tall, broad-shouldered body seemed to take up an exorbitant amount of space. He looked around, studying the apartment as if he were taking notes. She could only imagine what he thought of her tiny place.

"I'll wait while you get ready, and then we'll take you to work," he said.

"It's not that far. I'm used to walking," Sonia said with some amusement.

"I don't want you to walk." Esteban lowered onto the sofa and stretched an arm across the back.

Again she got the impression that there was a hidden meaning beneath the words, but she appreciated his thoughtfulness, and simply smiled. "I won't take long."

After a warm shower, Sonia brushed her hair back into straight, smooth lines, added a choker to complement the low neckline of her peach-colored blouse, and slipped on a pair of neutral-colored slacks.

She put on a pair of three-inch heels and had a couple of turns in the mirror, then joined Esteban in the living room.

He was on the phone, speaking in Spanish, and when she appeared, he wrapped up the call and stood. "Ready?"

"All set."

They exited the apartment. Sonia's neighbor, a blonde who conducted walking tours around the city, greeted them on the way into her apartment across the hall.

"Hi," Sonia said, noting how the other woman's eyes rested unnecessarily long on Esteban.

She couldn't blame her. He certainly was a sight to see—black hair, tall, and with striking bone structure under the beard. He exuded sex appeal in the fitted white tee, and the light-colored pants couldn't hide his solid legs and firm butt.

Sonia locked the door and walked ahead of Esteban down the stairs. The silence was killing her, so near the bottom of the staircase, she finally asked, "Is everything okay?"

He didn't answer right away, and after she stepped off the last stair, she turned to look at him and watched him descend.

"I want to talk to you about something, but now is not the right time."

They remained in the entrance of the building, with sunlight pouring in through the tall windows on either side of the door. He'd removed the sunglasses, so she could see his eyes and get a better sense of his emotions.

"Tell me, what is it? Is something wrong?"

"Nothing's wrong, but we can discuss it after work."

Whatever was on his mind, it was heavy, and she didn't want to wait. She wanted to know right now, or it would prey on her mind the entire time she was at Azul. "What is it?"

"Sonia—"

"Tell me. I can handle it, whatever it is." She steeled herself for bad news.

He studied her for a moment. "All right. I have a proposition for you."

The solemn tone of his voice caught her attention. "Another one?" she asked, with mild amusement.

"I think you'll enjoy this even more. At least, I hope you do."

"What is it?"

The slow lift at the corner of his mouth should have been her clue, but even she wasn't prepared for the words that left his mouth.

He placed his hands on her hips and looked down into her face. "I want you to be my mistress."

Sonia blinked and reared back, pulling loose from his roaming hands. "Excuse me?"

"I would like to spend more time with you, Sonia," he said in a calm tone.

"That's not what you said. Your exact words were, 'I want you to be my mistress.' Did I misunderstand?" Her heart thumped insistently in her chest, tightening as she awaited his response. Surely he couldn't be serious.

"You didn't misunderstand. I want to spend more time with you, and I'm willing to pay for the privilege."

CHAPTER 18

Sonia couldn't have been more shocked if Esteban had slapped her. "I don't know if I should be flattered or insulted."

"Flattered," he said. "You're everything I look for in a companion. You're smart, a great hostess, and incredibly beautiful."

She swallowed, thinking back over their interactions in the past and the way she'd sometimes find his gaze on her, a thoughtful expression in his eyes. "Were the dinner parties and last night some kind of audition?" she asked, incredulous. He'd cheapened what they'd shared.

His eyebrows snapped together over his eyes. "Of course not," he said tersely.

"Then what the hell, Esteban! How could you ask me something like that?"

"I enjoy spending time with you. There's nothing wrong with my offer."

Offer. As if he'd presented her with a job and benefits.

"You're a wealthy man. You expect me to believe you have to pay for companionship?"

With a rueful twist of his mouth, Esteban said, "I don't, but there is a certain amount of benefit I get from such an arrangement, and so will you."

"I seriously doubt that." Sonia shook her head, still in shock. "We slept together, but I slept with you because I wanted to. That doesn't mean you get to...to *buy* sex with me in the future."

"That is not what I'm suggesting. Listen to me, I'm simply looking for a companion here in the United States. Someone to spend time with and keep me company when I visit."

"And warm your bed?" Sonia added snidely.

He lifted one shoulder in an elegant shrug. "That, too."

She laughed shrilly. "God, you're very straightforward."

"I don't like to beat around the bush. You know that already." He came closer and rested his hand on the wall near her head. "I can give you a very comfortable lifestyle. You should not be rushing off to work on a Sunday afternoon, spend hours on your feet, and then walk home afterward. You shouldn't be scrounging for dollars at parties and restaurants. You should always have a car waiting for you, and you should be taken care of."

"And you're the kind of man to do that, aren't you?"

"I'm a very wealthy man. I've made it clear from the beginning how attracted I am to you, and after last night, you can't deny the chemistry between us is explosive. If you give me a chance, I'll show you a lifestyle you've never seen before. You'll be content, and the envy of all your friends."

"All I have to do is sell my soul?" Sonia said bitterly.

"I'm no devil," he replied.

But as he looked down at her, he appeared rather devilish, with his dark eyes glinting with determination, dark stubble on his face, and his black hair pushed back from his forehead in casual disarray.

"I think you deserve more," Esteban continued quietly. "I'd like to give you more."

Sonia took a deep breath and shook her head vigorously. "I'm not the kind of woman you're looking for. The lifestyle you offer doesn't interest me. You may not want my soul, but you obviously want my body, and I am *not* a prostitute."

She barely contained her anger. What was it about her that made him think she'd be open to such an arrangement?

"You assume that because I have asked you to spend time with me and I'm willing to pay for it, that makes you a prostitute?"

"That's usually the way that it works."

"Let me ask you something," Esteban said. "When you slept with your *pastry maker,* what did he give you in return?"

"Pedro didn't have to give me anything in return. That's not the way relationships work."

"They also don't work when one person cheats on the other."

That was an unnecessary twist of the knife. "Get away from me." Sonia made to move away, but he slammed his left hand on the other side of her, trapping her against the wall.

"Aren't relationships built on give and take?" Esteban tilted his head.

"Not in the way you're suggesting."

"You find offense because I'm willing to give, in a give-and-take relationship. I understand these are unusual circumstances, but it's the same. You had no problem sleeping with a man who offered you nothing in return, but you have a problem sleeping with a man who's willing to put the world at your feet because you make me feel good and I want to show you off. All I'm asking is for you to give me the pleasure of your body and your company, and I'll give you anything your heart desires."

"That's not a relationship," Sonia said.

"It's better than the one you had with the pastry maker," he said.

"His name is Pedro, and you don't know anything about me and him."

Sonia tightened her fingers around the straps of her purse. She wanted to shove him out of the way, but he was so big and broad she knew any effort she made to do so would be in vain. He was like a tree with deep roots. He wasn't going anywhere.

"I know plenty. I know he didn't give a damn about you, or he wouldn't have taken another woman to his bed, and he wouldn't have walked away so easily."

The words cut deep, slicing into her chest with the unvarnished truth. "And what about you and that model you broke up with a few months ago—Noelle? Did you give a damn about her?"

"I took care of her, like I do all my lovers. Believe me, she was satisfied."

"Was she your mistress?"

"I've had mistresses in the past, but who and when is a private matter. All you need to know is that I took care of them."

"And in exchange, they gave you sex."

He laughed softly. "You make it sound ugly. You had sex with Pedro, no?"

"Not for money! And we had sex with each other."

"And is that all you want? Sex and empty promises?"

She wanted more, but not like this. "I've entertained you long enough." She dismissed him by shifting her gaze to a point over his shoulder.

"I won't lie to you or use you the way he did. I would treat you like the gem you are. Last night was a fraction of what I can offer. Diamonds, the finest clothes, and trips around the world. Anything you want, I'll give it to you."

"We both know it's not that simple."

"It can be as simple or as complicated as we want it to be," Esteban said. "Our relationship doesn't have to be complicated. We're both adults, and we both know what we want. I'm willing to do that for you and include a monthly allowance. When I'm not in the United States, you can do as you please. I only have two stipulations: that you make yourself available to me at my request, and you don't see any other men."

Folding her arms over her chest, Sonia spoke past a tight throat. "And what about you? Will you be seeing other women?"

"This may come as a surprise to you, but I expect exclusivity from you, and I willingly offer you the same, without reservation. You satisfy me. Very much." He said the last words slowly, and when he did, his heated gaze drifted over her body.

The flame in his eyes and rigid set to his jaw suggested that he was getting aroused. The truth was, she was attracted to him—had been from the beginning. Even now, she wanted him, and if he'd approached her with a different proposition, she might have considered continuing to see him. But he'd soiled the lovely night they spent together and crushed the feelings she felt blossoming for him.

"I'm not interested," Sonia said, with a withering glare.

His jaw firmed, and for taut seconds they remained in a staring match. At last, Esteban pushed back from the wall, dropping his hands to his sides. "I think you should reconsider."

"I don't care what you think."

"Whenever I come to this country, you'll join me at events and cohost my dinner parties. Essentially, everything you've done this weekend and in the past, except with an added benefit. I cover all your personal expenses, give you a clothing allowance, and deposit twenty thousand dollars into your account every month. Could you use that kind of money?"

Sonia inhaled sharply. Who couldn't?

"That's an obscene amount of money," she said.

Even if she found a full-time position as a sommelier, she wouldn't make that much. He'd offered her a six-figure salary. She could stop working and finish studying for her exam. Hell, she could set up a nice cushion for herself, and her mind raced with other uses of the funds.

All she had to do was sell her body. The thought sickened her.

"Don't give me a final answer yet. Consider—"

"I've considered it, and the answer is no." Yes, she'd be in a better financial position, but lowering herself to be a rich man's whore wasn't worth her pride or dignity.

"You're making a hasty decision," Esteban said tersely. "I will leave my offer open to you for the entire time I'm in the country. I travel back to Argentina at the end of the month. Once I leave, I withdraw the offer."

His callous tone turned her off, like a cold splash of water being slammed into her face. Straightening her spine, Sonia said, "You can withdraw your disgusting offer now and shove it up your ass. I won't change my mind. Goodbye, Esteban. Please don't ever call me again."

She marched out of the door.

"The offer remains open until I leave the country," he reminded her.

Sonia walked past a bewildered Abel, who'd hopped out of the Maybach to open the door the minute he saw her exit the building. She crossed the street on brisk feet. The sun overhead was bright and seemed to mock the swirl of dark emotions she wrestled under.

Of course she'd be late to work now, thanks to Esteban and his ridiculous conversation, and because she had to walk when he'd offered to drop her off.

Like so many people, he didn't see her. Only the outer shell. Her looks. That was all he cared about. He'd insulted her and basically offered her a position as his whore on demand. Disappointment burned her chest, and she gritted her teeth, fighting back unexpected tears.

Blinking rapidly, she inhaled the fresh air of the early afternoon as she turned the corner onto Ocean Drive.

She wouldn't miss any of the extravagance of Esteban's lifestyle. She didn't care about it. And she definitely wouldn't miss his arrogant ass.

CHAPTER 19

The next afternoon, a Tiffany box arrived. Sonia told herself not to open it, but curiosity got the better of her. She lifted off the cover and gasped at the necklace's brilliance, consisting of a buttercup pendant in platinum and gold with a yellow diamond.

It was simple yet exquisite—a fine piece of jewelry that she could appreciate. Exactly the kind of gift she could expect during the course of her "arrangement" with Esteban if she chose to accept his offer. That was obviously what he wanted to make clear to her. The necklace was the beginning, a sample of what he had to offer and how her life would change.

Sonia shoved the jewelry into a drawer under her bras and panties, changed into running shorts and a tight tank, and slipped her Fitbit on her wrist. She hadn't been running in a while, but a good run might clear her head.

After stretching, she left the apartment and jogged south, then turned down a side street toward Ocean Drive, quieter now, hours before it turned into a place to watch and be seen when nighttime fell and flashy cars cruised up and down the strip.

She stayed on the beach side, opposite the line of art deco buildings that housed the hotels and restaurants. Running by men working out and people playing volleyball in the sand, she thought about Esteban's offer and the deeper reason she'd become so upset.

He'd hurt her. He'd insulted her with his so-called offer. After hearing so many times what he thought she deserved, she'd begun to believe the words. But desire did not mean he valued her as a person. He'd been priming and softening her for when he asked her to be his trophy, nothing but an empty-headed bimbo on his arm. As if she had no aspirations, no goals. Her job would be to please him, and look good doing it.

Sonia went from a comfortable jog to a calf-burning sprint. Gritting her teeth, she pushed her body until she came to an abrupt halt at the end of the street and collapsed onto the grass.

Few people knew the story of what she considered to be the biggest mistake of her life. She'd kept that under wraps, having left her job in shame after an affair with the owner of the restaurant where she worked.

Maybe she'd had a weird daddy complex and was seeking love from a father figure, but Stone Riverton had been twenty-five years her senior—friendly and kind. He offered her advice often, and eventually their friendship developed into a sexual relationship. He displayed confidence in her abilities by making her assistant manager of his restaurant when she was only nineteen. She'd thought she was in love, and they continued their affair for a whole year before a coworker told her about his wife, tucked away in a facility, paralyzed from the neck down after a spooked horse attacked her.

Sonia confronted him, and he admitted having a wife, and something else that hit right at the heart of her insecurities: he admitted that he wouldn't have given anyone else with her lack of experience the assistant manager position at his restaurant.

Why do you think I gave you that position?

She knew why, and it hurt. And Esteban's offer hurt. She didn't want to care, but her chest ached, and she rubbed away the pain right above her heart.

"Screw you, Esteban," she muttered, and shot to her feet. Running in the direction she'd come from, she moved at a more reasonable pace. Near her street, she jogged between cars to the opposite sidewalk and slowed to a walk.

She was out of breath, but the exercise had expended the anger she hadn't been able to get rid of since yesterday.

Inside the apartment building, she climbed the stairs and encountered a deliveryman leaving a note on her door.

"What's that?" she asked.

"Do you live here?" he asked.

"Yes."

"Package for you." Tucked under his arm was a rectangular box wrapped in lavender paper with a silver bow.

"Who's it from?" she asked, though she already knew the answer.

The man shrugged. "I don't know, ma'am. I'm just the delivery guy."

Sonia signed the electronic device in his hand and thanked him for the package. Inside, she set the box on the counter and stared at it for a spell as she drank a bottle of cool water.

Another gift from Esteban; she was certain of it.

Ignore it, she told herself.

She went into the bathroom, stripped off her clothes, and washed her hair and skin under tepid water. She decided to let her hair air dry, and wrapped her body in a fluffy robe. She returned to the living room, and the package still sat on the counter, waiting for her.

She stared at it for a long time. Finally, with a sigh, she opened the box. Enveloped in white tissue paper was the burnished gold dress from Bella Boutique, along with a pair of earrings and a matching bracelet.

Linn said you liked this dress. I want you to have it. I hope you'll let me have the pleasure of seeing you wear it one day. Esteban.

Sonia picked up her cell phone and dialed his number. When he answered, she said, "Stop sending me gifts."

"It gives me pleasure to give you gifts."

"That's not why you're doing it. You're trying to wear me down."

"Is it working?"

"No."

She hung up the phone and switched it off. She needed a breather. Time to get out of Miami for a bit.

CHAPTER 20

A trip to Atlanta was long overdue, where Sonia truly felt at home—in Uncle Rowell's house, on Sixth Street in East Point, located on the southwestern corner of Atlanta. She'd lived there from the time she was eight years old, after her mother passed away from pancreatic cancer, until she struck out on her own at eighteen.

After the airport shuttle dropped her off, Sonia stood in front of the small red-brick house sitting back from the street. Taking a deep breath, she tightened her grip on the black rolling duffel bag and trekked up the long driveway that bisected the lawn.

As she climbed the steps onto the porch, the screen door swung open from the inside, and the smiling face of Uncle Rowell greeted her. Stoop-shouldered, he didn't move as swiftly as he used to, but the sparkle remained his eyes, and the wide, welcoming grin hadn't dimmed.

"Hey, hey, baby doll," he said, in a cheerful voice that sounded as rough and coarse as tree bark.

Sonia dropped her bag and ran into his arms, gripping him around the neck and letting the hairs of his Frederick Douglass-like Afro brush her cheek and neck.

"It's so good to see you," she said, voice quivering a little.

Coming to this small house on the edge of Atlanta was a familiar comfort, one that made her feel as if she could let down her guard and be vulnerable, regressing in some ways to the young girl who had grown up there.

Rowell Melancon was the oldest of nine, her mother Deniece being the youngest. Since his last heart surgery, she'd worried that her uncle didn't have many days left. She should have come sooner. Atlanta was a two-hour plane ride away, yet she'd stayed gone for two years. She had her reasons, but that would have to change. She loved her Uncle Rowell to death, and though she stood before him now, the emotion of missing him burned in her throat.

"Come on in. What you been up to, baby doll?" Uncle Rowell had been calling Sonia by that nickname since before she moved in with him. Apparently, the first time he saw a photo of her as a baby, he said she looked like a little doll, with her round face and full cheeks.

Sonia dragged her luggage into the house, which smelled like Bengay and kerosene from the portable heater in the corner, currently turned off, since spring ushered in warmer temperatures. The house didn't have central air or heat, so growing up they'd set the kerosene heater in the hallway and left the bedroom doors open so the warm air could travel into the rooms where they slept.

Sonia sat down on the old brown couch in the living room, careful not to sit on the crack in the upholstery, which in the past had snagged her pantyhose or pinched her skin. The small space also contained a recliner that no one sat in but Uncle Rowell, an armchair, and a floor-model TV that was currently turned off.

Her uncle sank onto the recliner. Knowing him, he'd been sitting there before she arrived, fast asleep when the shuttle pulled up. The sound of the engine would have awakened him. He had the hearing of a bat.

"What you know good, baby doll?"

Just like that, Sonia felt as if the weight of the world had been lifted from her shoulders, and the pressure of thinking about Esteban's indecent proposal disappeared.

They spent the afternoon reminiscing, and she complained—but not too much—about her lack of job opportunities, and listened to his encouraging words. He'd always believed in her, and when she'd mentioned that she wanted to become a sommelier, he'd encouraged her to pursue her dream, even though he had no idea what a somme-lier was or did.

After their conversation, Sonia took her uncle to his favorite buffet, and they spent a couple more hours laughing and reminiscing and eating way too much. Several members of the wait staff, who knew him well, came by the table and chatted with them while they ate.

On the ride back to the house, Sonia was in good spirits. With her arm wrapped around her uncle's shoulders, she helped him maneuver onto the porch. As they unlocked the door, the lights from a vehicle swung across the front of the house and a black sedan pulled into the driveway.

"Val's here," Uncle Rowell said, sounding pleased.

Of course he'd be pleased to see his daughter, but Sonia immedi-ately tensed, her cousin Valencia's appearance putting a damper on the otherwise pleasant day.

Uncle Rowell shuffled inside, with Sonia guiding from behind with a hand on his lower back. Minutes later, Valencia appeared in the door-way, dressed in a black suit and white shirt—more of a uniform, since she wore the same combination every time Sonia saw her.

"Hi, Daddy, how are you?" She kissed his cheek.

"Good, now that I got a belly full of collard greens, corn bread, and country-fried steak." He grinned at Sonia.

"Don't forget the ribs and carrot pie."

"No, no, can't forget that." Shaking his head, he chuckled.

"Hey, Sonia. Daddy told me you'd be coming for a visit. I stopped by earlier but the house was empty. Would've joined the two of you for dinner if I'd known where you were." Her shrewd eyes bored into Sonia's, her intense dislike palpable by the slight wrinkling of her nose, as if she smelled a foul scent.

Sonia deflated internally but kept her feelings from displaying outwardly. "I guess we'll have to let you know where we are next time."

When they were younger and Sonia had moved into the house, they used to tell people Sonia was Valencia's younger sister. As the years wore on, Valencia became known as the smart one and Sonia as the pretty one, and their relationship fractured. Her cousin, one year older, became resentful of the attention Sonia garnered from the boys in the neighborhood and in school and at church, and eventually made sure everyone knew they were cousins, *not* sisters.

Then Tyler Stevens happened.

Sonia faked a yawn, covering her mouth with the back of her hand. "I'm going to bed. Tired from my trip. Good night. I'll see you in the morning, Uncle Rowell."

"Good night, baby doll."

Sonia went into the bedroom where she would sleep the weekend and started getting ready for bed, thinking about her relationship with Valencia.

Valencia's crush on Tyler Stevens, a high school junior who lived in their neighborhood, was no secret. What was a secret was his interest in Sonia. He spent a lot of time over at the Melancon household, doing homework with Valencia and helping Uncle Rowell around the house. Turned out he did all those things to be close to Sonia, and he acted on his feelings one day after school.

Sonia had missed the bus, and Tyler gave her a ride home. When they pulled up to the house, it looked empty. They sat in the driveway and talked for a few minutes, both apparently reluctant to separate— because the truth was, Sonia had a little crush on him, too. He was tall and cute, with light brown skin and a lean, wiry build. She'd stayed away because of Valencia.

Yet when he leaned over and kissed her, she didn't push him away. It was her first kiss, and her young heart fluttered and danced in her chest, a short-lived excitement when Valencia unexpectedly came out of the house and caught them in the act. The resulting confrontation resulted in name-calling, tears, and pleas for forgiveness, and was the final straw that broke the back of their tenuous family bond.

After that, Sonia avoided Tyler, and she and Valencia barely spoke. They didn't double-date to the prom as planned, and six years later their relationship had remained less than cordial, so it was no surprise that Sonia's invitation to Valencia's wedding had supposedly gotten lost in the mail.

Sonia didn't dwell on the slight or question her cousin's decision to exclude her. She knew Valencia's behavior was the result of resentment that had accumulated over the years. But being excluded stung. Even now, she longed to repair their relationship, but so much time had passed, she didn't know how.

At the staccato rapping on the door, she called out, "Come in."

Valencia entered, flicked her gaze over the open suitcase, and crossed her arms. "Long time no see."

"Yeah, it's been a minute." Sonia waited, wondering why Valencia had come back here to talk to her.

"Still trying to find full-time work?"

Uncle Rowell must have told her about Sonia's job situation, because she certainly hadn't. She and her cousin never spoke.

"Yes."

"That's so sad. Maybe you should try to get some...real skills. You think?" She spoke in a syrupy voice, dripping with venom.

"Is that why you came back here? To insult me?"

"I don't know what you mean."

Sonia took a deep breath to stay calm. "Don't you think this has gone on long enough? You're married now. Why are you still angry about something that happened twelve years ago, when we were kids?"

"You think I'm still angry about you and Tyler? I'm not."

"Then what? Why do you have to insult me every time I come around? You're a successful attorney, but you act like a jealous brat."

"Jealous?" Valencia's nostrils flared and her mouth twisted up. "You're so vain, it's pathetic, you know that? You want to know the truth? Here it is: I think you're ungrateful and don't appreciate the sacrifice my father made to take you in."

"That is not true."

"Oh yes, it is. When was the last time you sent him some money or offered to help him in any way, huh? You see how he's living. All he has is social security and a small pension, and I help him out whenever I can. But what do you do, Sonia?"

"I appreciate everything Uncle Rowell did for me, but I don't care what you think and whether or not you believe me."

"You're twenty-seven years old, and you work a part-time job at some raggedy restaurant in Miami. When are you going to get your shit together, Sonia? You're not a big-time sommelier. What do you have to show for all the money you spent and the time you wasted working in restaurants all these years?"

"It wasn't a waste of time. It's called paying your dues."

"And you have such a great job now, am I right?" Valencia tapped one pointy-toed shoe.

"It'll come, in due time."

"Whatever. I hate to speak ill of the dead, but you're a dreamer like your mother. You need to be smart and practical. But looking pretty is more your style, so I shouldn't expect much. You could always marry rich or hook up with some rich man who's looking for arm candy. Might want to stay away from the married ones this time," she finished with a tight smile.

"You're such a bitch."

"A bitch who speaks the truth." Her gaze flicked over the open duffel bag on the bed. "When do you leave?"

"In a couple of days."

"Perfect. I won't come back until after you're gone, and if you're feeling generous, you might want to leave a few dollars for Daddy to help with some bills. You know he'd never ask, but it's obvious he can use the help." Valencia swung on her heel and closed the door on her way out.

Sonia sank onto the edge of the bed and swallowed down her cousin's painful barbs. Valencia was right. She should be further along by now and have more to show for her efforts. She should be able to help out Uncle Rowell in his old age, after all he'd done for her.

She could accomplish all of those things if she accepted Esteban's offer. But at what cost?

She set the duffel bag on the floor, turned out the light, and crawled under the covers.

Accepting his offer would solve a multitude of problems and put her in a position to help her uncle, but could she do it? She was attracted to him, and sleeping with him would not be a chore. They had chemistry, and the night she'd spent in his arms was hands down the best night she'd spent with any man. Esteban was not only sexy, he was a skilled lover.

No one would have to know the details of their arrangement. She could request he keep the exact nature of their relationship quiet.

Was she crazy? Was she seriously considering becoming his mistress?

She swallowed as a knot emerged in the lower part of her belly.

Instead of making a decision tonight, she'd sleep on it.

CHAPTER 21

*B*runch with Jackie was one of Sonia's favorite things to do. There was nothing like sitting outside and feeling the balmy breezes off the Atlantic Ocean, listening to the rumble of the vehicles go by, as they sipped mimosas and indulged in fattening and delicious breakfast fare.

This time, however, Jackie wanted to get in some shopping after they finished the meal, so they ate at Lincoln Road Mall, which ran the length of a pedestrian street, filled with shops and plenty of places to eat. They ordered mimosas and breakfast tacos, and caught up with each other's news.

"How was your trip to Georgia?" Jackie asked.

"Good. Uncle Rowell is doing well."

"How was that awful woman you call a cousin?"

"Still awful," Sonia replied. "You're not coming back to Azul, are you?" Jackie had taken a leave of absence.

"I'm afraid not. It was fun for a while, but I'm over it." A dreamy smile crossed her lips.

"What is that smile about?"

Jackie bit her lip and looked around as if she were about to divulge a secret she couldn't afford to let anyone else hear. Leaning across the table, she whispered, "I have something to tell you."

"What?"

"I met someone." She bit her lip again.

"When? How? Tell me everything!"

Jackie giggled, covering her mouth with her hand. "His name is Evan. We met in the line at the grocery store, of all places. Can you imagine? He made a clever remark about all the snacks I had in my basket, and we started talking from there. He's a personal chef to a few celebrities and wealthy sorts, and he's absolutely brilliant. We've been on two dates already. He's blond and not my usual type, but I don't care. He makes me laugh like no one else."

"Oh, that's wonderful." Sonia reached across the table and squeezed her friend's hands.

"He's wonderful, but he not exactly the kind of man my parents would like to see me marry." She wrinkled her nose. Jackie's parents wanted her to marry someone who matched her social status. "They're going to be appalled, of course, but I'm so happy I don't care if they disown me."

"They won't disown you."

"I hope not. I've never felt this way before. He makes me so...happy."

"When do I get to meet him?"

"How about in a couple of days? I can set something up."

"Sounds perfect. I need to make sure he's good enough for you."

"You'll love him, I promise." Jackie rested her chin in her hand. "What about you, love? Have you recovered from Hurricane Pedro?"

Sonia smiled. "His cheating hurt, of course, but our relationship was already nearing the end." She shrugged.

Jackie nodded in agreement.

"I have something to tell you. A development in my personal life." Sonia took a deep breath. "It's about Esteban Galiano."

Jackie's eyes widened. "You worked for him for a spell, but that didn't work out, yeah? What about him?"

Sonia licked her lips nervously because she didn't quite know how to tell her friend she was going to accept Esteban's proposal. It wasn't exactly the kind of thing one could brag about, but Jackie was her closest friend, and Sonia had to share her decision with someone. "It turns out that he wasn't only interested in my wine knowledge. He was interested in me, too." She bit the corner of her lip and waited for Jackie's reaction.

Her friend's mouth fell open, and she leaned across the table. "What are you trying to tell me?"

"I sort of slept with him."

Jackie shrieked and clapped a hand over her mouth, eyes darting back and forth at the other diners. Everyone else was engrossed in their own conversations and didn't pay them any mind. "Are you kidding me?" she demanded in a hushed whisper. "Tell me you're kidding."

"I'm not."

"Oh my, I know a man like him must know his way around a woman's body. This is terrible, but you must tell me—how was it? I want to know all the details!"

"It was...excellent." Which was the absolute truth.

Sitting here with Jackie, Sonia wondered why she was even telling her that she was going to do this before she'd spoke to Esteban. Maybe she wanted Jackie to help her figure out the ins and outs, or perhaps even talk her out of this crazy idea. She needed a voice of reason and knew Jackie would be that voice.

"So...?" Jackie prompted, wiggling anxiously in her seat as she awaited more details.

"I'm not going to give you any specifics, Jackie. But you're right, he knows his way around a woman's body."

Jackie sighed dramatically. "I knew it. I'm not surprised." Her head tilted to one side as she observed Sonia across the table. "But I feel like there's more. Are you holding back on me?"

"There is more, but I'm not sure how you're going to react to what I say."

"Tell me. I'm dying to know now."

The waiter arrived with their mimosas. "Here you go, ladies. Your order will be up shortly."

They murmured their thanks, and Sonia took a sip of her drink to give herself a little liquid courage. "He asked me to be his mistress."

"I beg your pardon. His *what*?"

"His mistress," Sonia repeated. What she said sounded ridiculous even to her ears.

"Like a prostitute?"

"No, like a mistress. There's a difference." She'd had plenty of time to convince herself of that.

"A mistress? He's not married, is he?" Jackie sounded appalled.

"No! Stop, okay?" Sonia lifted her hands to stem the flow of panicked questions. "His mistress, as in the woman he's seeing."

Jackie slumped against the back of the chair. "I'm speechless. Has he had this kind of arrangement with other women?"

"He has, but he wouldn't say with whom. He doesn't want a girl-friend, but a mistress meets all the criteria without the demands of a committed relationship."

"It sounds dreadful."

"I think it can be mutually beneficial for both of us." Another thing she'd convinced herself of. "I get all the benefits of being a girlfriend, without having the burden of being a girlfriend. And he gets a companion." Sonia shrugged, as if this information were common knowledge.

"You make it sound so…"

"Cold? Clinical? It's better that way, so both parties don't get their feelings tangled up, don't you think?"

"And you think you can have a relationship like that with him without getting your feelings involved? You're not that type of woman, Sonia."

"Well, maybe you don't know me as well as you think you do."

Relationships were being redefined in all kinds of ways nowadays, and she could go with the flow and be that type of woman. And why not capitalize on her looks? Instead of feeling bad about it, she should play up her appearance and, as her cousin had said, be practical.

"I don't like this at all. Is he going to—to pay you?"

Sonia's face burned. That part still bothered her, but she pretended otherwise. "Don't be so judgmental."

"I'm not. I just know I could never put up with that type of lifestyle."

"You don't have to. You're rich."

"Sonia…"

"Listen, I'm sure lots of women say they couldn't, until presented with the opportunity. I felt the same way, until I was presented with the opportunity."

Jackie leaned across the table. "I don't want you to get caught up. Men like Esteban are temporary. They're not for keeps, and they discard women like old newspapers."

"I know, but I'm not playing for keeps, either. I'm going into this thing with my eyes wide open."

"I certainly hope so, or you'll end up in a world of hurt," Jackie muttered. "I'm not judging, but I could never be a kept woman. You're basically working for this bloke, and I'm not sure it's worth the money. I don't like it, Sonia. In a relationship like that, he holds all the cards."

"Does he?

"Isn't it obvious?"

"Not really. I've thought about it, and I want to see him anyway. The money is a bonus."

"All the more reason why you need to be careful not to get caught up." Jackie sighed. "You've already made up your mind," she said sadly.

Admittedly, Sonia had. Maybe what she'd really wanted was for Jackie to tell her this was a good idea. Because the more Jackie tried to talk her out of it, the more Sonia was determined go through with her plans.

"I hope you know what you're doing," Jackie said, concern in her dark eyes.

"I do. I'm pretty sure that I'll be happy. We're attracted to each other, so what's wrong with letting a man spoil me for a change? At least for the time being, for however long we want to continue in our relationship."

"And how long do you plan to continue this?"

Sonia shrugged. "A year, max. If I want to end it before then, I will. Honestly, I doubt we'll stay together that long. It's not like we're in love. This is a business arrangement. I'll collect as much money as I can and move on when it's over."

"Just like that, eh?"

"Just like that." A niggle of doubt was at the back of her mind, but she didn't let on. "I haven't been happy in my past couple of relationships. So why not try something different? He has money and likes to spend it on me." She shrugged.

"Money can't buy you happiness," Jackie warned.

"I used to think the same thing, but you know what I think now? I think people who say that just don't know where to shop," Sonia said.

CHAPTER 22

$\mathcal{S}$onia stared at her phone on the coffee table. She ran her sweaty palms down the length of her jeans and then stood abruptly. After all her bravado at brunch with Jackie, she was now acting like a big chicken, hesitant to make the call to Esteban. But he'd told her she had until he left town, so she still had time. She simply needed to pick up the phone.

Before she lost her guts, she snatched it up and dialed his number. Her jumpy nerves offered no reprieve and jumped even faster as she listened to the phone ring. After the fourth ring, she was about to hang up when Esteban answered.

"Hello?" His warm voice came through the line.

"It's me, Sonia."

"It's good to hear from you."

I don't need forever, she reminded herself. She only needed right now, and she'd be able to secure her future and help her uncle. It was a small price to pay.

Sonia closed her eyes. "I accept your offer, but with conditions."

Silence for two beats, then, "We need to talk. When are you available?"

"As soon as you're free."

"I'm free now. I'll send Abel to bring you to me."

* * *

Esteban hit the intercom button. "Abel, please pick up Miss Kennedy from her home. She's waiting for you."

The speaker clicked. "Right away, sir."

Esteban sank onto the sofa in his home office and propped his feet on the coffee table. He should be ecstatic he was about to get what he wanted. Sonia Kennedy was about to become his mistress. He hadn't planned this, but from the beginning he'd been obsessed with her.

But why? He'd dated plenty of beautiful women before. Was it because she was a challenge, when so many women were not?

Restlessly, he rose from the chair and stared out the window.

He'd only wanted to sleep with her, but from that first night, he'd known once wouldn't be enough. Twice wouldn't be enough. And even though she'd agreed to his proposal, a part of him rebelled at the thought that she was, indeed, like other women. And reminded him of a bitter truth he'd learned as a young adult: a man could have anything, if he paid the right price.

* * *

Sonia arrived at Esteban's home with a rapidly beating pulse. She was actually going to do this. And why not? Why shouldn't she capitalize on her looks? Why shouldn't she have nice things, even if only for a short time? Why continue to deprive herself out of some misplaced sense of guilt when she'd done nothing wrong? Esteban wanted her company and would pay an obscene amount to have it. She was the one in control.

Ready to negotiate, she traipsed into his home with her head held high, and he led the way into the living room. Esteban, wearing a plain white T-shirt that showed off his thick biceps, stood in front of the floor-to-ceiling glass with his arms crossed and his intense gaze resting on her face. Behind him, one of the boats that showed tourists where the stars lived chugged by.

"I'm glad you came," he said. "What changed your mind?"

"I realized you were right. We are good together. We do have chemistry. And I enjoy the lifestyle that you offer."

He nodded, studying her with perceptive eyes. "You said you have conditions."

"Before we get started, you're not married, are you?"

His eyebrows shot upward. "Of course not."

"Can't be too careful," Sonia muttered. She let out a breath. "I want the first month deposited before we begin."

"Fine."

"I don't want anyone to know the type of arrangement we have."

"No problem. My arrangements are always confidential."

"My apartment is my sanctuary. You have no right to come there unless invited."

"That's going to be a problem."

"Why?"

"That's not part of the contract." He lifted a paper from the table that she hadn't paid attention to before. It was only one page, but it took her by surprise.

"Contract?"

"I spell everything out in black and white, to ensure there's no confusion."

She took the sheet and reviewed each line, noting the agreed-upon sum would be deposited into the bank account of her choice every month. There was also a clause that stipulated they both get tested for STDs and she must agree to get on the pill.

Her eyes zeroed in on the paragraph that stipulated she move in with him. "You never said anything about me moving in with you."

"I prefer to have you here with me. In my house."

"I want to keep my place." She felt the control she was certain of slipping away.

"That won't be possible. I want you here," he said firmly.

"Why? So you can keep tabs on me?"

He smiled slowly but didn't answer the question, and he didn't need to. That was precisely why.

"You feel you can't trust me."

"I don't trust anyone."

Sonia swallowed. Having this conversation was strange, but maybe all couples should have a blatantly honest conversation before they entered into a relationship, no matter how clinical or uncomfortable.

Maybe then there would be fewer problems if relationships started with a contract that laid out each party's role and each party's expectations.

"Fine. I'll live here." It was a small price to pay, and the house was beautiful.

"Anything else?" he asked.

She glanced at the contract again. "You never mentioned I couldn't have a job, either." His stipulations were not exactly what she'd anticipated. She was moving in with him and couldn't keep her place, and now she couldn't even have a job.

"You won't need a job, and it would pose too much of a problem. From time to time you'll need to travel with me, and of course attend events while I'm here in the States. You need to be available, and that won't be possible if you have to ask permission to take time off."

He picked up a pen and extended it to her.

Sonia took the pen and stared at the sheet of paper. She was really going to do this.

She signed on the top line, and he signed below it. After folding the document in half, he set the agreement on the table.

"Now let me give you a proper tour of the place."

He took her throughout the house, introducing her to rooms that she had not seen before. He showed her the additional bedrooms, bathrooms, and living rooms upstairs. They didn't enter Delores's quarters, but Sonia knew the exact location now. A tour of the grounds followed, and she saw his pearl-gray GranTurismo, the Porsche, and the guest house where Abel resided.

They made their way back indoors and entered the living room. Moving into his mansion made her feel as if what little control she'd hoped to maintain was slipping through her fingers like water.

"Without a job, what exactly am I supposed to do all day?"

He shrugged. "I don't know what women of leisure do all day." He sat in one of the armchairs. "But I know that a job will get in the way, so it's not a good idea for you to have one."

What else could she do? Shopping, hair appointments, massages, and manicures and pedicures came to mind. After all that, she'd still have plenty of hours in the week, even worse when he was out of the country.

"You look lovely today," Esteban said. "Come here."

She swallowed. "You come here."

A smirk filtered across his lips, as if he'd heard something very amusing. He unfolded his long body from the chair and walked over to her. She held her breath the entire time. He cupped her chin in his hand and angled her head up so he could look her directly in the face. As he dipped his head close, she saw a gleam in his eyes—a ruthlessness that sent trepidation tripping through her chest.

"Make no mistake who is in control in this relationship, Sonia. You are *my* mistress. I'm the one in control."

"Are you sure, Esteban?" Sliding her mask into place, she aimed a sultry smile at him and slipped an arm around the back of his neck. His eyes narrowed as she rose onto her toes. Tugging his head down to hers, she kissed him, determined to take charge, a confident seductress about to get what she wanted.

She'd give it a year, like she'd told Jackie. No more than a year, and she'd save all her money and move on. Until then, she could pretend that this was like any other relationship.

She didn't have much time to think about anything else. Esteban angled his head and roughly slid his fingers into her short hair, tugging her closer by the belt loop in her jeans. His firm mouth was demanding as it moved over hers, and already she felt the scales tipping in his favor.

He lifted her into his arms, and her legs and arms immediately wrapped around him. She fell deeper into the kiss, savoring his mouth and the strength in his biceps as he carried her back to the bedroom that was now equally hers.

He undressed her swiftly and easily, and within minutes, his hard body pressed into hers and she was pleading with him, begging in a trembling voice as she gripped his firm backside and he thrust deep and hard. When she came, it was almost a relief.

It was frightening how quickly she had acquiesced to him, and frightening how easily she'd given in to his demands. As if in the back of her mind she'd been worried she would lose this connection with him for good.

"You'll move your things in tonight," Esteban said, bowing his head to her breasts. He sucked a nipple into his mouth, and her still-sensitive body shivered in response. He'd just given her an incredible orgasm in the middle of the day with the sun's rays slanting through the window.

And still she thirsted for him. Still she wanted more.

CHAPTER 23

Eight months later

The mild breeze blowing across the patio ruffled the curls on Sonia's head. She'd fallen in love with Argentina. Of course, it helped to have friends here.

She surveyed the expansive grounds of Esteban's estate in Nortada, a wealthy enclave on the outskirts of Buenos Aires that was essentially a city within a city, with its own schools, stores, sport center, and other amenities meant to accommodate the wealthy owners behind the gated boundaries.

Esteban lived as lavish a life here as he did in Miami. Last time they visited, he'd had a royal blue and black Bugatti Chiron delivered, bringing the total number of sports cars he owned in Argentina to eleven. The interior of the two-story mansion was decorated with beautiful sculptures and art, including bold pieces by photorealistic painter Audrey Flack, and more of the subtle beauty of his favorite artist, Benito Quinquela Martín. High-end furniture filled each room, some purchased in Argentina, other pieces imported, like the solid maple mid-century Danish chair and desk in his home office.

One of Sonia's new friends, Nadine Alesini, sat beside her on a patio chair, holding her fourteen-month-old son, Nicolás. Nico, as they called him, was playing with an old cell phone they let him have. He liked gnawing on it and punching the buttons to hear them beep.

Nadine was African-American, with a bright smile that immediately welcomed Sonia into their tight circle. She was the wife of Esteban's friend and business associate, Cortez Alesini. Sonia's bond with the other woman was cemented when she learned Nadine was also from Atlanta. They spoke in detail about familiar places and restaurants, and discovered they even knew a couple of the same people.

While the men had taken a day trip to São Paulo to meet with a real estate developer, Sonia and Nadine had not too long ago returned from a shopping trip with the baby, the couple's fourteen-year-old daughter, Antonella, and her older cousin. As it was December, the teenagers were taking advantage of the southern hemisphere's warm summer climate and splashing around in the pool.

"*Señorita.*"

Esteban's Argentine housekeeper was wringing her hands. Marta was a petite woman, with her dark hair cut in a short, tapered style.

"Yes, Marta?"

"Would you like to look at Saturday's menu? I think something is wrong, but I'm not sure. I want to make sure I have what Sr. Galiano wants."

Cortez and Esteban had planned an informal meeting for when the real estate developer and his wife came to Buenos Aires to expand their business interests in Argentina.

"Sure, I'll take a look."

Nico's eyes followed Sonia's movement as she stood, and he dropped the cell phone on his mother's lap and outstretched his hands to her.

"No, Nico, leave her alone," Nadine gently chided her son, and set the abandoned toy on the table.

"I don't mind. He can come with me," Sonia said.

"He'll get in the way," Nadine said uncertainly.

"No, he'll be fine. Won't you, sweetie?" Sonia lifted the little boy into her arms, and he grinned up at her with bright-eyed, adorable innocence. "He's got me wrapped around his little finger," she admitted. She'd fallen in love with him from the first day. He was such a friendly baby, and so full of energy.

She went into the house with Nico on her hip and reviewed the catering menu on the laptop screen on the kitchen counter. After a quick scan, she immediately identified the problem. Pointing at the item, she said, "We can't have the soy because one of the guests is allergic."

"*Ay.* I knew something was wrong, but I could not remember." Marta muttered in Spanish and shook her head.

"Wasn't there a choice of chorizo and smoked shrimp canapés?"

"Yes." Marta nodded.

"Add those to the menus, too."

"*Sí, señorita.*"

"Did you hear back from the band?" They'd tried to secure a local band Esteban liked, but didn't know if they could because of the short notice.

"Yes, I did, and they agreed to play. The *señor* will be happy."

"Perfect. Sounds like we're ready for Saturday."

"*Sí.* The wine and special glasses you ordered were delivered today, the menu is almost ready, and I will make the staff to use the new linens on Saturday."

Nico squealed and kicked his feet.

"He is happy, too." Marta smiled and pinched his cheek.

Sonia grinned and dropped a kiss to the opposite cheek. Nico smelled like babies do—sweet and as if he'd been doused in powder. She took his little fist between her fingers and wiggled his hand playfully. He giggled some more, with an adorable laugh that created a little twinge in her chest.

She had never thought of herself as the maternal type, but for a split second she got caught up in the entire scene—holding Nico on her hip and reviewing the plans for the dinner party with the housekeeper. It all felt so foreign, but at the same time, familiar. Comfortable. An achy sensation—like longing—blossomed in the pit of her stomach.

"We're all set, then, Marta?" she asked, shaking off the feeling.

"*Sí.*" Marta looked up from the email she was in the process of typing to the caterers.

"*Bueno.*" Sonia went back out to the patio, and Antonella and her cousin were now lounging poolside playing with their iPads.

"Did he behave himself?" Nadine asked.

"He was an angel." Sonia handed the baby back to her.

"Are you Mommy's good boy? Huh?"

"Mama, goo boy," Nico said.

Nadine smiled, lifting him above her head and lowering him close enough to kiss his nose. She did that repeatedly, and he loved the little game, laughing and grabbing at her face with each iteration.

"Mom, can we go back to the house to watch a movie?" Antonella asked.

"Yes, you may. Did you already call Joachim?" Nadine asked, referring to the family driver.

"Yes." Antonella hopped up from the chair with a towel wrapped around her torso, and her cousin followed suit. "Want us to take Nico with us?"

"You can, or I can keep him."

"We can take him. We don't mind." Gabriela, Antonella's cousin, crouched to eye level with Nico. "Want to come with us?" She held out her hands, and he immediately went to her.

"You all be careful," Nadine said.

"We will! Bye, Miss Sonia," Antonella said.

"Bye, girls," Sonia said to them.

They disappeared inside.

"She's always so willing to spend time with her little brother," Sonia remarked.

Nadine nodded. "I'm lucky, for sure. It gives me a break, and he absolutely adores her." A flicker of sadness entered Nadine's eyes. "I don't know if Esteban ever told you, but Cortez and I had another baby, in between those two."

"No, he didn't."

"We lost him," Nadine said quietly.

"Oh, Nadine, I'm so sorry." Sonia touched her arm. Nadine had been so kind and friendly since they met, and it hurt to think what she and her husband must have gone through.

"It was a long time ago, but it was hard."

"I can't imagine."

Sonia's phone beeped on the table between them, and she glanced at the screen. Right away, she felt a rush of excitement when she read the text. "It's Esteban. He said they'll be back around nightfall."

"He's checking in," Nadine teased.

"No, he likes to keep me informed, that's all." Esteban always kept her updated on his schedule.

A ghost of a smile hovered around Nadine's lips.

"What?" Sonia said.

The smile widened into a knowing grin. "You're good for him."

"Who? Esteban?"

She nodded.

"What do you mean?" Sonia asked.

"I'd given up hope he'd ever settle down. Now I'm not so sure."

"Not because of me," Sonia said, although her heart raced. The tightness in her chest deepened when her friend nodded.

If she was good for Esteban, he was certainly good for her, too. In a short period, she'd met so many people thanks to him—some of them acquaintances meant to be kept at arm's length, but a few select ones became genuine friendships, like her relationship with Nadine.

He'd opened her up to a whole new set of experiences, and as a result, her world view had expanded. She was taking online Spanish classes and had seen marked improvement, mostly in understanding the language. Her speech still needed quite a bit of work, but she was getting there.

While this was her third trip to Argentina, her passport had accrued stamps from other countries around the world. The weekend of her twenty-eight birthday, he'd chartered a plane for her and three girlfriends to Cabo San Lucas, where he covered all their expenses. They stayed in a private villa, partied at local clubs, and Sonia took a giant leap and even learned to scuba dive.

"Definitely because of you. It's hard to explain, but Esteban is different." Nadine bit the tip of her finger as she thought. "As far as I know, he's never brought a woman here."

Sonia didn't know that. She'd assumed she was one of many.

"And I think he's more relaxed with you," Nadine continued. "He has a full staff to take care of his needs, and Marta does a good job, but Esteban is the type of man who thinks if he tells you something once, he shouldn't have to tell you again. He can be a little…how do I put this delicately…abrupt with his staff."

Sonia smiled. She'd seen it herself. "He doesn't like the details." He was a perfectionist, and he expected perfection in the people he employed. Because of that, he tended to have a short fuse when it came to mistakes or what he considered shortcomings.

"No, he does not. I'm sure he's glad to have you around to help. Other than Abena and maybe one other person, I don't think I've seen him trust anyone else this much."

She and Abena coordinated the management of the household staffs here, in Miami, and his Caribbean property. Esteban never had to concern himself with planning meals or taking care of landscaping, or making sure the cars were properly maintained on schedule. Anything concerning his places of residence, she and Abena took care of, and it was obvious he'd gladly relinquished those responsibilities.

"So whatever you're doing, keep doing it," Nadine said.

CHAPTER 24

$\mathcal{E}$ steban walked through the house to the courtyard in the back. He'd had a long day, but already felt better walking into the house and knowing Sonia was there. He found her swimming laps in the Olympic-size pool.

Setting the snifter of brandy he'd poured himself on the patio table, he took a seat in one of the cushioned wicker chairs and stretched his legs. From here, he had a good view of her gliding through the water with graceful strokes.

She exercised regularly, jogging South Beach or Star Island, and when they traveled, she made use of the gyms at the hotels where they stayed, but she preferred to get her exercise outdoors. Sometimes they raced each other in the pool, and although she gave it her best, he always won. He was simply a better and stronger swimmer, and the one time he let her win, she'd not been pleased. It was one of the few times he ever saw her upset, because she usually kept a genial disposition.

He couldn't have picked a better woman to be his mistress. His friends liked her, and his household staff loved her—clearly preferring her to him. His mouth turned into a wry twist. Dolores spoke fondly of her, and he was pretty sure Marta would adopt her if she could. She trusted Sonia completely. Both of his drivers, Abel and the one here, visibly lit up when she appeared. "Where to, ma'am?" Abel had asked one night, completely ignoring the fact that Esteban was standing right beside her.

Sonia cruised up and stood in the pool, resting her forearms on the edge. "How was your trip?" She sounded a little out of breath, but not winded.

"Very successful." The meeting had gone surprisingly well, and the real estate developer, a man by the name of Renaldo, and his wife had agreed to come by for dinner. "I'm certain I'll be able to seal the deal of opening two restaurants in their mixed-used developments—the one in São Paulo and the one they plan for here."

"Are you coming in?"

"No. Why don't you come out? I have something for you." Esteban removed the dark, velvet-covered square box from his pocket and set it on the table.

His shaft twitched and became semi-hard as he watched her lift out of the water in a white bikini that fully covered her upper body but didn't provide much support, leaving her breasts to hang like ripe fruit above her narrow waist. Smoothing a hand over her short hair, she squeezed out the excess water and then came toward him, droplets glimmering on her amber skin like jewels. She moved in a naturally seductive way, her full hips swaying with each step. Sensual, yet subtle. Not overly done, so it was clear that was her natural walk and not put on for effect. That made her sexier. She was magnificent.

Sonia wrapped a towel around her waist. "You don't have to buy me something every time you travel."

"Maybe I want to." Esteban took her hand and tugged her onto his lap.

She squealed. "Esteban, I'm going to get you all wet!" she said, but she was smiling.

"I don't care."

He tilted her head back to his shoulder and placed his mouth over hers. God, the taste of her still lit his blood on fire. Instead of tiring of this woman, he seemed to want her more. His heart rate sped up as he cradled her in his arms, exploring the texture of her soft mouth and dragging his tongue over the curve of her bottom lip.

Her fingers moved from cupping his jaw to diving into his hair. Her short nails scraped his scalp and the nape of his neck, sending a rush of shivers down the middle of his back.

Trailing his lips down her chin to her breasts, Esteban pulled one of her erect nipples into his mouth and sucked it through the cloth. She moaned and arched up so far that he slid his hand under her bottom and got a good grab of her ass.

"I promised you something, didn't I?" he said to her cleavage.

"Huh?" She sounded disoriented, and he smiled, knowing she'd temporarily lost herself. She was such a passionate woman that watching her get aroused gave him almost as much pleasure as touching did.

"I said, I promised you something." He kissed the swell of one breast, her neck, and her cheek.

She let out a breath, obviously meant to calm herself down. "Yes, you did."

Esteban lifted the box from the table. "Here you go."

"What is it?" Sonia twisted around on his lap, and the movement rubbed against his erection.

After a bite of his lip and a quick groan, he could formulate an answer. "Open it and see."

She leaned back against his chest and flipped up the lid on the box, revealing a little black pouch and a drawstring. Inside the bag were four sleek stainless steel wine pearls.

"Thank—" She gasped when she saw the engraved symbol.

Their first and only time in Paris, he'd thought for sure she'd want to go shopping at the most exclusive designer shops and burn through his euros, the way other women he'd taken to Paris had done. Instead, they'd spent days in the wine-growing regions of Alsace and Bordeaux, touring the vineyards and sampling wine from the barrel. At one particular vineyard, she'd wanted to buy a set of engraved wine pearls from the gift shop as a souvenir of the trip, but they no longer made them. He hadn't forgotten her disappointment.

He instructed Abena to contact the winery, and they finally agreed to create a special set, just for her. They'd arrived at his Buenos Aires office earlier today, and he'd stopped on his way from the airport to pick them up.

"How did you get these?"

"It took a lot of persuading," he said.

"I can't believe you remembered," she said, a little catch in her voice.

He couldn't believe it either. In the past, he'd have Abena find the presents for his lovers. Jewelry or expensive cars always seemed like good choices. But with Sonia, he paid attention to her preferences and saved them in his memory bank for later. He took pleasure in finding the right dress, the perfect pair of earrings, or some sentimental item he knew she'd appreciate.

He kissed the damp skin of her back and then her shoulder, but she slid to her feet and set the box on the table.

"Come here," he said, burning for her.

She dropped the towel to a nearby chair and watched him with a playfully coquettish smile over her shoulder. "You have to wait. If you're not patient, you won't get what you want."

His eyes scoured the curve of her back, her lovely behind, and the lean length of her shapely legs. "And what's that?"

"Me."

He hated to wait, but at the moment she held the control. She had the power and knew it.

She stepped between his legs, and he knew better than to reach for her when she played this game. If he did, she'd withdraw, and then he'd have to wait even longer. He gripped the armrests as she undid his tie and flung it to the pavement. She slipped the first button from its hole, and one by one slowly unbuttoned his shirt and pushed the edges apart to bare his torso to the evening air.

"What would you like me to do, *señor*?" Her forefinger zigzagged from the rapid pulse at his throat, veered off to circle the flat disk of one nipple, and then continued down his hair-sprinkled chest.

Her touch held him captivated. He could hardly breathe. "Surprise me," he said huskily.

She tugged the leather belt from the loop of his pants. "You don't want to give me a little hint?" she purred.

The rasp of the zipper sounded in the stillness of the night as she dragged it down. He didn't bother to answer as she crouched before him and lifted his hardened flesh from the snug-fitting boxers. He couldn't talk. Not with his throat so tight.

At the first slide of her tongue, his body tightened like a clenched fist. In merciless slow motion, her pink tongue slid from the base to the tip. He gripped the chair to refrain from gripping her.

"I think I know what you'd like me to do," she whispered. Her gaze held his as her mouth enveloped the head.

She took him deep and, with gentle suction, brought him exquisite torture. Pleasure rolled through his body as her tongue pressed the underside of his erection. His fingers tangled in her wet hair, while she worked his length with her hands and mouth. Groaning, and at the brink of exploding, Esteban pulled her away and stood on unsteady feet, hauling Sonia up with him.

He indulged in the pleasurable task of removing the bottom half of her bikini. Tugging the strings at her hips, he watched the flimsy white covering fall away to the ground.

"Esteban." Her voice trembled with breathy need.

He lifted her onto the table and fastened his mouth to the delicate skin of her throat. Head tilted back, she let out a short gasp and clamped her arms around his neck, and a tiny shiver shook her body. His hand slid up her smooth, open thighs to thumb the taut nub between her legs. She was wet and slick and so ready for him.

He slid in with absolutely no resistance. The snug fit of her body around his made him clench his ass cheeks to keep from a premature nut.

"You're incredible, *querida*," he whispered, lifting her off the table.

"Esteban," she whispered. "Oh god. You feel so good." She clamped her limbs around his hips and began thrusting, using the muscles in her thighs and her arms around his neck to lever her hips against his. He braced one hand on the table and the other beneath her bottom, angling his hips and pumping deep between her legs.

He found her mouth again and swirled his tongue against hers. He kissed her jaw, her clavicle, her neck, her breasts. Anywhere he could reach, he inhaled her feminine scent and tasted her skin.

She was a work of art. A goddess.

As they climaxed together and their cries lifted into the night air, he considered how lucky he was to call her his.

CHAPTER 25

*S*onia sat very still on the loveseat. Then she reached for the glass and examined it from a side view as the guests waited quietly and patiently. Holding the glass up to the light, she tilted it at various angles and allowed the wine to roll toward the edges so she could see the complete color range. Then came the swirl, followed by a good sniff. A fruity bouquet with a scent of cocoa filtered into her nostrils.

She took a taste and swished it around her mouth. Almost immediately, she knew the origin but delayed the answer to build suspense.

"Full-bodied, vibrant, with notes of cinnamon and a hint of peppery spice." The complexity of flavor almost made her close her eyes and moan, but she had an audience of seven. After long seconds, where the tension thickened to the consistency of pudding, and she knew everyone hung on her every word, Sonia announced, "Syrah. Year, 2013. Torbreck winery, Barossa Valley, South Australia."

Craig, standing nearby as a sort of master of ceremonies, removed the piece of paper taped over the bottle and displayed the label to all assembled. Gasps filled the room, followed by a loud round of applause. No one clapped louder than Esteban, standing behind the opposite sofa beside his friend, Cortez Alesini, whose expression was one of amazement.

"How do you do that?" asked Cortez.

"Yes, you must tell us." Craig's wife Ivana sat across from Sonia. She spoke in a brisk voice with a thick Russian accent that was at times difficult to understand, but endearing at the same time. Her shoulder-length hair, the color of dandelion florets, was pulled back into a tight bun that seemed to stretch the skin of her face.

"A magician never reveals her secrets," Sonia said. A round of laughter went up from the group as she sat back and crossed her legs with a triumphant smile.

"It's amazing how you can do that," said Renaldo, the Brazilian in the group. He was a giant of a man. Esteban had spoken to her in the past about wanting to open a restaurant in the mixed-use development he and his wife Sabrina had built in São Paulo, but this was the first time she'd met them.

Renaldo's wife turned out to be a native of Chicago. She was an eye-catching woman—tall, with a head full of curly hair. She sat in an armchair near Cortez's wife, Nadine, their heads close together as they quietly conversed.

"Pick any bottle of wine, and she'll tell you the grapes and the region they were grown in," Esteban said with pride.

"Not *any* bottle," Sonia said, though he was pretty close.

She continued to host parties for him, but also concentrated on getting her sommelier certification. When she'd passed the sommelier exam, Esteban had been out of the country on business. But he made sure to send six dozen roses and a diamond bracelet to congratulate her. Shortly thereafter, a ticket arrived to join him in São Paulo. From there they'd zipped across the Atlantic to Europe so Esteban could check on his businesses there, before returning to Miami.

On a personal front, she used the first deposit from Esteban to install a heating and cooling system into her uncle's old house. He'd protested, but she insisted, and finally he acquiesced. And although she'd moved in with Esteban, she'd kept her apartment. The benefit being that she generated a little cash subletting the apartment to visiting tourists. Fortunately, her landlord didn't mind, as long as he received the rent on time.

"You're giving her some kind of signal," Nadine accused Esteban teasingly, a bright smile on her dark brown face.

"It's not a trick, and I have nothing to do with it," Esteban said. "I'm very lucky to have met someone who knows her wines." He winked at her.

"You two are so cute. How long have you been married?" The woman who asked was a stranger to Sonia, but a friend of the Alesinis.

Color bloomed at Sonia's throat, and a few seconds of awkward silence ensued before Esteban responded, "We've been together for eight months."

"We're not married," Sonia added. She looked at him, and he looked at her.

"Oh! I assumed..." The woman's eyes dropped to Sonia's hands resting in her lap.

"People often make that mistake. I guess because we know each other so well," Sonia said, fighting back the sting of embarrassment.

As the perfect hostess, she'd planned tonight's meal, the wine pairings, and arranged for light entertainment in the form of a band who'd packed up their instruments moments before. Her role as mistress had expanded, so she understood why people were confused about the nature of their relationship.

"You're like a married couple," Ivana said. "You know each other better than Craig and I do."

Craig snorted and sat beside Sonia, crossing his legs. "There are plenty of married couples who don't know each other very well, love."

Ivana raised one eyebrow. "Are you saying you're satisfied with barely knowing your wife? Should I be concerned?"

A trickle of laughter went through the room, and a good-natured argument erupted about how long couples should know each other before they got married, and what constituted actually knowing one's spouse. Sonia grinned and nodded accordingly, interjecting comments here and there. But as she looked around the room, it suddenly dawned on her that she and Esteban were the only unmarried couple present.

"Gentlemen, can I interest you in a cigar?"

The business part of the evening was about to begin. Esteban opened a box of thick Cubans, and right away there was a murmur of assent as the men prepared to step out onto the balcony and smoke and talk business.

Sabrina stood. "I don't smoke, but I'll join you," she said. As the person in charge of the finances, her role was a critical one in her and Renaldo's business.

"I can't make a decision without her," Renaldo said, placing an arm around his wife's waist and guiding her out the door with Cortez, Esteban, and the other male guest interested in investing in Esteban's restaurant in Brazil.

"You're not going, darling?" Ivana asked Craig.

"No. I'll stay in here and enjoy the lovely view with all you women." He grinned.

Sonia stood. "I'm going to the kitchen to get more wine. Should I bring out more snacks?"

She heard groans of "I'm full" and "No more food," but also "Yes! More wine."

"Thank goodness we're not driving," Ivana said, laughing as she looked at her husband.

He nodded in agreement.

In the kitchen, Sonia popped a chorizo and smoked shrimp canapé in her mouth and then perused the choices in the wine cooler beside the refrigerator. She chose one of her personal favorites, a fortified red made in the southern Rhône and Languedoc-Roussillon region of France. She was certain their guests would enjoy that.

Their guests. She sometimes thought in those terms, even though this was Esteban's house and, technically, she was a guest, too.

Craig sauntered into the kitchen. "Need any help?"

She'd seen Craig once since the night at the Blue Top Hotel, and that had been at another party in Miami where she made sure to steer clear of him. But he and Esteban had known each other for some time, so she couldn't avoid him altogether. She considered him a lurker, or a hanger-on. The kind of person who thought following the cool kids around made him cool, but instead, it made him look sad. Because the cool kids had moved on, while he was still living in the past.

Her skin prickled with unease when his gaze lingered an inappropriately long time on her cleavage. She'd worn the fuchsia dress because Esteban wanted to see her in it, but now she wished she'd resisted and worn something with more coverage.

"No, I'm fine."

She smiled politely, hoping her answer would be enough to shoo him back to the living room, but he didn't move. Standing in the middle of the kitchen, he watched her.

"How *do* you know your wines so well?" he asked from behind her. His voice sounded much closer, the tone pitched lower.

"Years of practice," Sonia answered shortly. She removed the cork.

"Do you still do wine consulting?" he asked.

"I haven't worked in the business for a while."

"You don't have to, I suppose. Not with a man like Esteban paying you a salary."

Her head jerked up. "Excuse me?" The nature of their relationship was private. They'd agreed not to tell anyone about their monetary arrangement.

A slow, slick smile lifted each corner of Craig's lips. "I've heard things."

Sonia's eyes flicked to the open doorway of the kitchen. The women were down the hall, and everyone else was on the balcony, and she recognized how very alone she was with Craig.

"You should go back to the living room." Sonia reached into the cabinet for a decanter.

Craig came close behind her, so close she felt the heat from his body and his breath on the back of her neck. "There was a time Esteban and I shared everything. Did he tell you that? *Everything.*"

Sonia swallowed, a sick feeling sliding into her stomach.

"But it's different with you. A lot of things are different with you. I've never known him to stay with a woman this long. I'm accustomed to seeing him date on a heavier rotation. And what's really peculiar is that he invited you here, to his house in Argentina. That's definitely new. I've never known him to do that with any of the other women he's been involved with."

Sonia's grip on the neck of the bottle tightened. She hadn't moved the entire time Craig was speaking.

"Lucky, lucky Esteban. Tell me, what does it cost to keep a woman like you in his bed, on his arm, and in his home to entertain? Can't be cheap." He trailed his fingertips down the length of her arm, and she moved away.

"Stop it," she whispered, scanning the counter for a weapon.

"Come on. Name your price." Snaking a hand around her waist, Craig tugged her back into his erection.

Sonia snatched a knife from the stand on the counter and turned quickly, pressing the tip of the blade against his throat. He froze, and his eyes went wide. The knife shifted as his Adam's apple bobbed up and down.

"Take your hands off me."

He lifted his hands up and away from her and slowly backed away.

"Don't you ever touch me again," Sonia said through her teeth. She kept the blade to his throat. "Are we clear?"

"Crystal." His jaw hardened.

She lowered the knife, and he closed his eyes briefly, letting out a relieved breath. Sonia kept her hand clenched around the handle of the knife.

Craig continued to back away, and when he was at a safe distance, he smirked, allowing his gaze to travel over her figure in a way that made her skin crawl. "What a lucky son of a bitch my friend is. He has a firecracker in his bed. But I wonder, how much longer will your relationship last before you're looking for a new sponsor?"

"Whenever that happens, I promise, I won't come looking for you."

"Don't burn your bridges. You never know what the future will bring, and I can be a very generous man."

"Generous with your wife's money?" Sonia asked.

He walked out, his robust laugh trailing behind him.

Shaking, Sonia slumped against the counter, and the knife dropped with a clatter from her hand.

That encounter with Craig was jarring and a rude, unexpected intrusion of reality. She'd been enjoying herself so much, all but forgetting the true nature of her relationship with Esteban. Craig did an excellent job of reminding her, and it took a few minutes to recover.

Taking a deep breath, she wondered who else knew. Did the Alesinis know? His other friends? The staff? Business associates?

She didn't want to go back out there, but she couldn't ignore their guests.

His guests.

CHAPTER 26

"You're awfully quiet," Esteban said.

The guests were all gone, and Sonia and Esteban were in the kitchen. She busied herself cleaning up while he watched.

"I'm glad everyone's gone." She carefully placed dishes in the dishwasher.

"I thought you were having a good time."

"I was. I'm just tired."

She saw him nod from the corner of her eye.

"It's been a long night. Come to bed. Marta can take care of all that in the morning."

That was typical of Esteban. It never occurred to him that she didn't want to leave all these dishes for his housekeeper. He may not have been born into wealth, but he certainly appreciated it.

Shrugging, Sonia said, "I don't mind, and I hate to leave a mess for her to see first thing in the morning."

She added the final dish and snapped the machine closed. Pressing the buttons on the console, she said, "Craig and Ivana are an interesting couple."

"They are," Esteban agreed. He sipped from a glass of water with lemon that she'd set out for him. Like everything else, he was very particular about the way he liked his water. Twelve ounces and half a lemon. He laughed. "To be honest, I was surprised when they married."

She glanced up. "Oh?"

He shrugged. "I've known Craig for a long time, and I never saw him as the marrying kind."

Sort of like you, Sonia thought.

"You're close to Craig, aren't you?"

"Not as close as we used to be, but we've remained in touch mainly because Ivana is my go-to designer for my restaurants. She and I have a good relationship."

"So your relationship with them is mainly business now?"

"For the most part." He drank more water and then set the glass on the counter. Folding his arms, he asked, "Why are you asking me these questions?"

Sonia shrugged, uncomfortable about the conversation she knew she needed to have about Craig. If they were no longer close, it would be easier. She continued moving around the kitchen, straightening the stools around the island and tossing paper napkins and other trash in the bin.

"He and I were talking, and he made it sound as if the two of you were a lot closer. According to him, there was a time you shared everything."

"There was a time…"

Sonia was at the other end of the kitchen, and she turned when his voice trailed off. "Is it true?"

"We were young."

"You shared women?"

"Sonia—"

"Did you?" She stared at him in dismay.

"It was after a particularly painful breakup, and I was in a bad place. Some women will do anything for money."

Her face burned.

"That came out wrong."

"Of course it did." She swallowed back the foul taste in her mouth.

"We were all young once and made mistakes." He ran a hand over his hair. "I have a hard time understanding why Craig would say something like that you," Esteban said slowly. "When did the two of you have this conversation?"

"He mentioned it when we were in here," Sonia said, feeling numb.

His body became unnaturally still. "The two of you were in the kitchen alone?"

"Yes, earlier."

Esteban's face hardened. "When I went out to the balcony?"

"Yes," Sonia answered slowly.

"He came in here after you?" His face darkened with anger.

She swallowed. "Yes."

A pause. He watched her closely. "Did he touch you?"

Sonia swallowed again and saw the anger in the hard set of Esteban's jaw. While that was the type of reaction she'd wanted, she suddenly worried his fury would bubble up to a dangerous level. Then she remembered her first impression of him, that of ruthlessness beneath the polished exterior.

Her heart kick-started to a faster pace. "There's nothing for you to worry about. He said some things I didn't like, but I handled it."

"And one of the things he said to you was that we share everything?" he asked tersely.

He prowled closer, his footsteps measured and the sharpness of his penetrating gaze boring into her as he searched for the truth. He stopped directly in front of her and asked again, "Did he touch you?"

There was no mistaking the rage now. It practically seeped from his pores, barely restrained as he spoke through gritted teeth.

"He... What he did was—"

Esteban swung away with such quickness that it took Sonia by surprise. He was halfway to the door before she thought to run after him.

"Wait!" She grabbed his arm, but he jerked away.

"He had no right to put his hands on you. You should have told me immediately!" His brown eyes flashed with anger.

"I didn't want to cause a scene with guests here. I'm telling you now, and I'm telling you that I'm fine. There's no reason for you to go after him."

"That's where you're mistaken. I can't let him get away with that. Yes, there was a time when we did share everything, but that time is long gone, and it certainly does not apply to you. I need to make it clear he has no claim to you at all."

"So you're only going to talk to him?"

His mouth twisted into a caustic smile. "I can't promise you that all I'll do is talk."

He charged out of the kitchen, and Sonia followed, watching helplessly as he slammed the door and hopped into a white Jaguar XKR-S GT. The electronic gate opened, and the car tires squealed on his way out.

Esteban was on his way to confront Craig, and she was worried about what the ramifications of that confrontation would be.

* * *

OVER AN HOUR LATER, Esteban entered the house and went to the kitchen.

He sensed her presence before he saw her, and turned. She'd changed into a white silk negligée, one that he had given her over a month ago. She looked particularly lovely in it this evening, but she looked lovely in everything that she wore. Perhaps that was part of the problem. She was so beautiful, so desirable, that it was no wonder other men found her attractive and would try to take her away from him.

He thought about it constantly. How to keep her happy; how to keep her satisfied. Knowing that someone who had come into his house and disrespected him in that way enraged him. But what had also enraged him was his own lack of control.

It was inexplicable the power she had over him. He'd lost it. Lost his *goddamn* control over this woman. All he'd wanted to do was fight —what his younger self hadn't done when another man had stolen away his woman.

"What happened?" she asked.

"We talked," he said.

"That looks like you did more than talk." Her gaze lowered to his bruised knuckles.

He clenched and unclenched the fingers of his right hand to relieve the ache. "I'm beginning to wonder why you're so concerned about him," he said in a hard tone.

"I'm not concerned about him, Esteban. I'm concerned about you and what you did."

She walked to the refrigerator and dropped ice into a plastic bag. "Your knuckles are swelling."

"I don't care." He examined the throbbing, inflamed skin. "He deserved every blow."

Sonia came over and took his hand. She placed the icy bag atop his knuckles, but Esteban tossed it in the sink and backed her against the counter.

"Esteban—"

"He had no right to touch you," he grated. "No one gets to put their *fucking* hands on you but me." His voice sounded harsh even to his own ears, as if he were angry with her. But in reality, he was angry at Craig and angry at himself for his lack of control. He and Craig had shared women in the past, treating them like objects, mere possessions to his lifestyle that he discarded when he finished.

Normally that didn't take very long, but here he was, eight months later and unable to shake the obsessive, out-of-control need for Sonia. And while he'd fully expected to be getting tired of her by now, the opposite had occurred.

This thing between them had started out purely physical, solely a convenience for him. But he felt it evolving into something more. Something uncontrollable that he hadn't seen coming.

He insisted she travel everywhere with him. At first he told himself it was to keep an eye on her, but as time wore on it became clear that he wanted to keep her close—needed to. She'd become a necessity. He needed to hear her voice every day and know she lay beside him in bed every night. He needed to wake up next to her in the morning to get his day started.

While he craved her like oxygen, she was with him because he delivered a five-figure sum into her bank account every month.

He hoisted the hem of the negligée.

"You're hurting, Esteban." Sonia looked up at him.

"I'm fine."

She wore nothing under her clothes, and he groaned at her nakedness. He smoothed his hands over the soft skin of her thighs, sliding between her legs to stroke the dampness already emerging between them.

Her breathing became labored and she moaned, tilting back her head.

Esteban kissed her neck gently and then nibbled with more vigor. Her arms climbed around his neck and held on. Gripping her bottom, he lifted her onto the counter. His kisses became more ardent as they traveled over her collarbone and down to her silk-covered breasts.

His mouth moved up her chin to her lower lip, and he sucked on it. Capturing the back of her head, he slid his tongue between her lips and kissed her properly.

She grasped his neck, sinking her fingers into his hair and allowing him to kiss her even deeper.

Her hand slid between them to the front of his pants. He swelled against her palm, and soon they were both moaning as they kissed and sucked on each other's lips.

She easily unbuttoned and unzipped his pants, and he entered her with a deep groan. Her body was so wet and warm that he shuddered at the pleasure of it. That anyone would try to take this—take *her*—from him was out of the question.

Her arms and legs tightened around him, and with each thrust he staked his claim. Burying his face in her neck, he breathed in the scent of her skin. Still thrusting. Making sure that she knew that she was his.

They orgasmed within seconds of each other, and afterward breathed heavily in an effort to catch their breaths.

Esteban pulled up his pants and helped Sonia from the counter. They climbed the stairs to the bedroom, where she got into bed and fell asleep right away. He, on the other hand, remained wide awake and restless.

He lit a cigar and stood in the open doorway that led onto the balcony, staring out into the darkness. His hand throbbed, but he ignored the pain. He'd taken great pleasure in slamming his fist repeatedly into his ex-friend's face.

Sonia moaned, and he twisted his head to watch her sleep. The ambient light coming from the lamps embedded in the walls cast a yellow haze over her golden skin and the white sheets. She was an enigma. A woman who'd agreed to be his mistress while at the same time not quite adhering to the role. She'd taken over aspects of his life no other woman had been involved in, and while she took whatever he offered, she never asked for anything extra.

He stared at her for a long time, letting the cigar burn down.

How well do you know her? Craig had taunted as Esteban walked away. The words had been unintelligible at first, garbled because of his busted, bleeding mouth. *How well do you know your precious Sonia? You're not the first man she's done pay for play with.*

Had he said that to mess with him, or did Craig know something Esteban didn't?

CHAPTER 27

*J*ackie's male housekeeper led Sonia into the great room. Traditional antiques, floral patterns, and staid, solid furniture filled the decor. The furnishings were in complete contrast to Jackie's personality, because her parents had paid for the house and interior design.

"What was so important that you needed me to come over right away?" Sonia asked by way of greeting.

Jackie bounced up and down with a broad smile on her face. All of a sudden, she thrust her hand forward and splayed her fingers for Sonia to see the emerald-cut diamond.

Sonia's mouth fell open. "You're…you're engaged?"

"Yes!" Jackie squealed.

"Ohmigod! Congratulations!" Sonia pulled her in for a hug.

At the same moment she became excited, Sonia realized Jackie was now engaged to a man she'd been dating for approximately the same length of time Sonia had been involved with Esteban. Unexpected envy snatched at her chest and squeezed, but she brushed it aside.

"Of course I want you to be my maid of honor. Will you?" Jackie asked.

"Absolutely! I'd be hurt if you asked anyone else."

She pulled Sonia down onto the settee. "I must warn you, though, you'll have your work cut out for you. I talked to Mother, and she mentioned we must have two of everything." She rolled her eyes. "Two engagement parties and two wedding ceremonies. My parents want to do the traditional Chinese thing." She rolled her eyes again.

"Why do you always make your parents sound like tyrants?" Sonia laughed.

"Because they are."

"I don't believe you." Sonia had met Jackie's parents once and found them to be polite.

Jackie was silent, staring down at her hands.

"What's wrong?" Sonia asked.

"My parents think it's time for me to come home and participate in the business."

Sonia gasped. "So you're moving back to London?"

"I will have to. Eventually. I've had a spot of fun the past few years, but now I suppose it's time to act like a grown-up. I am getting married, after all, and my parents won't be around forever."

"Is that what you want to do?"

"I don't know. I've been away from the company for so long, I'm not sure. But I do feel a bit as if…I need to do *something* besides fritter my days away." Jackie shrugged.

They sat in silence for a while. Jackie was Sonia's best friend, and had been for the entire time she lived in Miami. She'd miss her terribly. "Whenever you decide to leave, we'll still keep in touch."

"Of course! You're not getting rid of me that easily." Jackie grinned, looking more like her typical lively self.

"Okay, now tell me everything. How did he ask?"

Jackie beamed as she prepared to recount the story. "I could tell something was up, though I didn't know what. He'd been acting strange all day and made me promise I would be on time for dinner at a little Italian place we like to go to. We met, and at the end of the meal, he asked if I wanted dessert. But I was full, so I said no. He kept insisting, so finally, I said yes, and he asked the waitress for the cannoli sampler. Apparently, he asked her to hide the ring in one of the cannoli but didn't know which one. So he started smushing each one on the plate."

Jackie started laughing, and Sonia joined her.

"By then I realized what was happening, but I didn't want to spoil the surprise, so I patiently waited, and of course it was stuck in the last one. He picked up the ring and got down on one knee, but he was so nervous that he wasn't paying attention, and ended up tripping a waiter holding a tray of drinks behind him."

"Oh no!" Sonia covered her mouth.

Tears were streaming down Jackie's face now. She swiped them away. "Luckily, the waiter must've been a juggler or something, because he managed to right himself and barely spilled a drop of water from one of the glasses onto the floor. Poor Evan was sweating. So much his hair was stuck to his face around the forehead. Then he opened his mouth, and I think he asked me to marry him."

"What do you mean, you *think*?"

"Because he asked me in Cantonese, and I didn't have the heart to tell him I don't speak Cantonese. I speak Mandarin, so I didn't know what he was saying, but whatever it was, it must have been lovely, because he spoke for a solid minute. In the end, I said yes. I went by the visual and assumed he was asking me to marry him."

They fell out laughing.

"At least he tried," Sonia said, wiping tears of laughter from her cheeks.

"Yes, my darling fiancé gets an A for effort."

"And your parents are on board."

"They are surprisingly excited, even though my future husband is not wealthy. I think they're happy I'm finally settling down." Jackie pinched her own arm. "Can you believe it? I'm getting married." She stared at the ring on her finger.

"I am so happy for you." Sonia sounded like a robot, but Jackie didn't notice. She was too busy twisting her hand one way and then the other to let the light catch the diamond at different angles, while the knife of jealousy twisted another quarter turn.

"Oh my goodness! I've been talking about me, me, me. What about you? We haven't talked about your trip."

"You're getting married, so that's big news." Sonia took a deep breath. "There's nothing going on with me right now. We had a great time in Argentina. Esteban's back to work, and I...I'm taking Spanish classes and getting better all the time."

"Good. I'm sure he appreciates it."

"He does, and we practice sometimes."

"What about your somm certification? How are you going to use it?"

"I won't right now."

"Why not, for goodness' sake? Because you're with Esteban? You didn't go through all that trouble to sit on your certification, did you?"

"No, I didn't, but..." Sonia couldn't bring herself to tell Jackie that part of her agreement with Esteban was that she wouldn't work, so that she would be available to him at all times. She figured she'd get back to work *after* her relationship with him ended. Whenever that was.

"There's no harm in staying busy. Maybe you could do something part-time," Jackie suggested.

"Maybe," Sonia murmured.

The more she thought about it, the more appealing the idea became. Now that she had her certification, so many more doors would be opened to her. Working nights at a restaurant was problematic, and she had no desire to restart her wine consulting business, which even during the best of times had been fledgling at best.

The best option, for now, was to find a company interested in contracting her services. She knew of one based out of California called the Sommelier Group. They had offices around the country, including one in the Miami area. She'd spoken to a rep in their recruitment office before, and though he was impressed by her knowledge, he'd suggested she come back when she had earned her certification.

"You know what, you just gave me an idea," Sonia said.

"I did?"

"Yes. I'll start floating my résumé around."

"Brilliant idea."

If they could use her part-time, Esteban shouldn't mind.

* * *

EVER SINCE THEY returned from Argentina, things hadn't been quite right between them. Sonia couldn't put her finger on precisely where the problem lay, and she wasn't certain whose fault it was, hers or Esteban's. All she knew was that something felt a little...off. So tonight's event was an opportunity for them to reset.

Esteban received invitations to all kinds of events, not only in the Miami area, but around the country. Most often, he attended parties that doubled as opportunities for networking, but tonight was not the case.

While some of the residents of Star Island kept a low profile, others took full advantage of their celebrity status and competed against each other to throw the biggest and best shindig that would be talked about in the press and lauded for its excess on social media. Tonight promised to be one of those events.

Italian billionaire Cesar Bertolli lived on Star Island and was throwing a thirtieth birthday party for his wife, French actress Veronique, thirty-three years his junior. Guests were flying in from all over the United States and Europe, with limousines commissioned to ferry them from the airport, to their hotels, and eventually to Cesar's palatial waterfront home.

Because of the black-and-white theme of the party, Sonia wore a black jumpsuit with three-quarter-length sleeves and a plunging neckline. The white in her outfit would be the pair of Harry Winston diamond drop earrings from the jeweler's New York collection.

After a quick assessment of her appearance, she went in search of Esteban, and found him in the living room with the phone to his ear, speaking to someone in what sounded like Italian. The white shirt and black slacks were the perfect uniform for a man of his complexion and physique. He managed to look casual, yet elegant, his skin glowing from a healthy tan.

She'd grown accustomed to his moods, and could tell by the knit in his brow and the way he paced the floor that this was not a personal call.

He worked too hard. Days, nights, weekdays, weekends—he seldom took time off. She understood the need for him to stay on top of his business affairs but wondered at times if something else drove him. Not the need for success or to accumulate more wealth, but another, more deeply rooted reason for his ambition and obsession with perfection.

Esteban's gaze landed on her, and he stopped pacing. Immediately, the crease in his brow smoothed out, and he looked at her with what she deemed to be genuine affection, letting his gaze trail down her attire in appreciation. Keeping his eyes on her, he said a few words in Italian and then hung up.

"Maybe we should stay in. You're going to take all the attention from Veronique," he said.

"I won't do that, and we're not staying in."

He stepped up from the living room and towered over her. The warmth in his eyes coiled heat low in her belly.

"Then we should plan to leave early, because I don't see how I could possibly keep my hands off you for very long." Esteban slid an arm around her waist and dropped a kiss to her breastbone.

"I'll consider it," Sonia whispered.

He chuckled. His breath fanned lightly over her skin, and her nipples puckered in response.

After another quick kiss to her jaw line, he steered her toward the door, but she stopped him with a hand on his arm. "Let's just have fun tonight, okay?"

He studied her for a moment. "Okay."

"So no business and no phones."

His eyebrow arched. "Sonia, you know—"

"Yes, I know, you're a very busy man. But we'll probably only be there for a couple of hours, and whatever happens, I'm sure you can have Abena or someone else on your staff handle it." She extended her hand for the phone and held her breath.

He didn't move. "You really want me to do this?"

"Yes. Please."

A small smile lifted the corner of his mouth, and he handed over his phone without another word.

"I'm going to send Abena a quick message and let her know you're not available for the rest of the evening unless it's an emergency." Sonia tapped out the text as Esteban looked on, then she tucked the phone into her black wristlet. "There. Now we're ready." She grinned at him.

Esteban took her hand and started toward the door. "If my empire falls apart tonight, we know whose fault it is."

"Your empire won't fall apart," Sonia said, leaning into him. Her mood had elevated already.

Outside, thunder rolled and a flash of lighting zigzagged across the sky.

Walking briskly to the car, they stared at the dark clouds overhead.

"A storm is coming," Esteban murmured.

CHAPTER 28

The glitterati were out in force when Esteban's Porsche pulled up in the long line of cars outside Cesar's mansion. Valets whisked away the vehicles, and attendants in solar-powered golf carts carried guests from the gated entrance to the front door.

Sonia had attended her fair share of parties since becoming Esteban's "lady friend," as some people referred to her, but this had to be one of the most outrageous ones. Inside, her mouth fell open at the topless women wearing glittery black booty shorts and performing an amazing feat of acrobatics on swings suspended from the three-story ceiling.

Black and white balloons decorated the wide-open space, which led into a great hall packed with guests clad in black-and-white attire, some of them dancing in front of the live band on a stage near the back of the room. Other performers circulated among the throng—a fire breather, a sword swallower, and a woman in a thong bikini juggling on stilts.

Familiar faces, acquaintances and friends, approached or waved when she and Esteban entered the room. She still marveled at how Esteban managed to keep a low profile among all the revelry and excess he was exposed to. Though friendly, he stayed aloof enough that no one tried to rope him into selfies or other types of candid shots.

Sonia jumped when she heard a high-pitched scream, but grinned when she saw Veronique rushing toward her in a sparkling red strapless gown, with arms outstretched. The actress pulled her into an exuberant hug.

"Darlings, you made it." Veronique's puckered red lips delivered air kisses on either side of Sonia's cheeks.

"*Feliz cumpleaños,*" Esteban said. With a loose arm around Veronique's waist, he leaned in to give her a proper kiss on the cheek.

"*Merci beaucoup, mon amour.*" Veronique batted her eyelashes, but Sonia paid her flirtations no mind. Veronique enjoyed playing the role of French temptress, but she was as devoted to her husband as he was to her.

"We wouldn't have missed this for the world," Sonia said. "You went all out, I see."

Orchids rumored to cost in the neighborhood of forty thousand dollars, and more black and white balloons, filled the party room.

"Oh, this." Flamboyant and theatrical, Veronique spoke with her hands. Her normally dirty blonde hair was dyed black this month for a role in a period film. "You know Cesar. This is all his doing. Everything must be big and bold and extravagant! It's too much, but I know it makes him happy."

Sonia barely managed to not burst out laughing at the blatant lie. Esteban lifted a hand to his mouth and cleared his throat, hiding his laughter, but Sonia was certain Veronique didn't notice.

The actress looped her arm through Esteban's. "I must steal you away. I know you're not here on business, but I have a friend who's interested in opening a restaurant and wanted some advice. I told her I know just the person to offer guidance. Do you mind terribly, darling, helping my friend?"

He turned to Sonia with a gleam in his eye. "You have to ask Sonia. I was given strict instructions to refrain from doing any business tonight."

"I'll make an exception for the birthday girl," Sonia said.

"Oh thank you, darling. I promise to only borrow him for five minutes." Veronique snapped her fingers at one of the servers. "Please see to my guest," she said, pointing at Sonia.

The server hurried over as Veronique and Esteban walked away arm in arm. Sonia took one of the flutes of sparkling champagne and, searching the crowd, saw a trio of women she recognized and navigated over to them. They immediately greeted her with one-armed hugs and air kisses, and they all caught up on each other's news since the last event. Inger's daughter had started preschool, and a week ago Jasslyn had returned from a trip to Rome with her Italian boyfriend.

Ten minutes into the conversation, Sonia excused herself to go in search of something to eat. There were plenty of food stations with a variety of choices, but she ended up perusing a tray of crudités, when she heard a familiar, gravelly voice.

"Sonia?"

Eyes wide, she twisted around. Eight years had passed since she last saw this person.

His eyes lit up. "I thought that was you."

Stone Riverton was the owner of Stone River restaurants, and twenty-five years older than Sonia. At nineteen, her love for him had been absolute when she worked at his restaurant in Atlanta. He'd left an indelible impression on her life and introduced her to heartbreak.

"Hello, Stone. It's been a long time."

Lines of maturity creased the corners of his eyes, and gray hair, absent during their affair, dusted his temples. He was dressed the same as Esteban in a white shirt and black pants, but carried a little more weight around the midsection. Overall he looked like a dignified fifty-three-year-old, not unlike the person she'd known him to be—her first lover and the man she thought she couldn't live without until she learned the truth.

"It has been a long time, and you look great." His gaze swept her from head to toe. "You've matured, and travel in different circles now, I see."

"A little."

She could guess what he saw. Back then, she'd been young and raw —now she was older, polished, wearing designer clothes, and partying with billionaires, movie stars, and music moguls.

"So, are you here alone?" he asked.

"No, I'm not. I'm here with someone."

"Of course you are," he said, with a rueful twist to his mouth. "Lucky man."

"Stone..."

He smiled. "I know. Very inappropriate, but it's true. He's a lucky man, and I'm an old fool."

"We shouldn't have gotten together. You lied to me."

He acknowledged her statement with a nod.

"I trusted you." She'd been crushed when she learned about his wife.

Regret filled his eyes. "And I abused that trust. I took advantage of your naiveté."

Having him acknowledge his sins came as a surprise. "You did," Sonia said quietly.

"I've changed."

Her gaze shifted to the gold wedding ring on his finger, something he'd omitted when they first started their affair. "Because you're wearing a ring now?"

He stared at his finger, as if seeing the jewelry for the first time. "Yes, but I'm also a little older, a little wiser. Different."

"But still married."

"Yes. Although...there hasn't been anyone else since you."

Sonia gave a short, humorless laugh. "I'm not sure that's a compliment."

"It is, but I understand if you don't take it as one."

Sonia was fiddling with her wristlet, thinking about how to extricate herself from the conversation, when Stone asked, "So what have you been doing since you left Atlanta?"

A man came over to the table, and they edged out of the way, which caused them to stand closer together.

"Still working in the restaurant industry," Sonia replied. "I'm a certified somm now."

"That's wonderful!" Stone looked shocked but pleased. "Where do you work?"

The little pride she felt suddenly deflated. "I'm not exactly *working* at the moment."

Stone's eyebrows rose. "Why not?"

"I...I plan to get back into it eventually, but I've been busy with other things."

"Oh." Stone frowned. "Would you like to work as a sommelier?"

"Eventually, definitely."

A thoughtful look came into his eyes. "I'd like to help, if I can."

"Help how?"

"I could find you job."

She laughed.

"I'm serious," Stone said.

"Why would you do that?"

"Why not?"

The smile fell off her face when she saw how serious he was. "Because you don't have to do that."

"I feel likc I do."

"You don't owe me anything, Stone."

"I do." Briefly, he looked away and shook his head. "I took your innocence. I lied to you and didn't tell you I was married. I owe you plenty." He pulled out a gold business card holder and extended a card. "Take my card."

"Stone, you don't have to do this."

"Take it. It's the least I can do. I have a few connections here in Miami. Give me a call sometime, and I'll see what I can set up for you. Matter of fact, I know a couple of people over at the Sommelier Group, if you're interested in doing workshops and such. They're always looking for good somms."

"I was thinking about reaching out to them the other day."

"Good, you should. Give me a call. Better yet, send me your résumé, and I'll put in a good word for you."

She smiled at him. "I appreciate that."

"Like I said, it's the least I could do." He looked at her with fondness and hesitated, as if he wanted to say more or lean in for a hug.

Not wanting to encourage him, Sonia stood in place and ended the awkward moment by saying, "I'll be in touch."

"Do that."

He walked away and she looked after him for a moment. Stone had taught her a lot. She hadn't left the relationship with a broken heart alone. She'd left with a love of wine, and he had taught her so much about grapes, the winemaking process, and the complexity of flavors in each vintage.

She stared down at the business card and realized she wouldn't call. Not because she hated him, but because she was no longer the naive nineteen-year-old who'd believed his lies, or the broken twenty-year-old who'd summoned the strength to walk away. They no longer knew each other. They were strangers with a common past that was better left…in the past.

"Who was that?"

Sonia jumped and looked up at Esteban. She'd been so focused on her memories that she didn't see him walk up.

"Oh, um…an old friend. Stone Riverton. He owns a chain of restaurants in Georgia and Tennessee."

Esteban looked at the card in her hand.

"He offered to help me find a job." This wasn't the way she'd hoped to broach the subject of getting a job, but it might be a good way to feel him out.

One eyebrow lifted. "Lucky for you that you don't need to work."

His expression didn't reveal much, but it was clear he wasn't open to the idea, which annoyed her. "He thought since I have my certification, I could find a position as a sommelier somewhere."

"We agreed you wouldn't work, so what he thinks doesn't matter."

He smiled, but it wasn't a real smile, and having him shut down the suggestion so swiftly and without regard to her opinion made Sonia dig in her heels.

"Well, I'll hold on to the card. Just in case." She tucked it into her purse and gave him her own fake smile. "So, how did your talk go?"

His eyes narrowed slightly on her, but he followed the change in subject and updated her on his conversation with Veronique's friend.

For the rest of the evening, Sonia focused on having a good time, whether or not Esteban was by her side. At one point in the evening, she saw him in conversation with Cesar, but his distracted gaze rested on the back of Stone's head as he chatted with a guest standing in front of the musicians on stage.

They left the party three hours later, and by then the pending storm had arrived, dousing the landscape in a torrent of raindrops.

CHAPTER 29

*E*steban should have left it alone, but Sonia's answer about Stone Riverton being a friend didn't appear completely truthful, and their body language as he'd watched from across the room made him suspicious there was much more between them.

He'd done some digging and now knew more about Sonia's relationship with Stone Riverton than he ever needed to know. Stone was a married man, with a disabled wife, and during his affair with Sonia gave her perks, including a car and a promotion to assistant manager with very little prior experience.

He entered the house, and the aroma of a baked cake greeted his nostrils. He stopped in the foyer and listened to feminine laughter coming from the direction of the kitchen. Heading that way on quiet feet, he found Sonia and Delores at the island, jazz filtering through the invisible speakers in the room.

Delores was smoothing buttercream icing on a two-layer cake on a pedestal, while Sonia perched on one of the stools in a floral print kimono, watching with her body angled over the island. Her short hair was brushed back from her face so he could clearly see her smooth, round cheeks and plump lips.

As though she suddenly sensed his scrutiny, she looked up, eyebrows rising in surprise. "Oh, you're here!"

Instead of the tension leaving him like always, it increased. Esteban rolled his shoulders. "What's the reason for the cake?"

"No reason. It's my uncle's recipe for what he calls the best darn red velvet cake in the country. I had told Delores that people love it, and he gives them out at Christmas, and she demanded the recipe."

"I did not demand, *señorita*." Delores smiled at her.

Sonia giggled. "Anyway, I called up Uncle Rowell for the recipe, and we decided to give it a try."

"Tell him your news," Delores said, continuing to smooth the icing.

The smile on Sonia's face wavered a bit, but then she perked up. "Nothing's definite yet, but I contacted the Sommelier Group, and it turns out they're interested in hiring me and think I would be a good fit for a few hotel projects they have planned. They want me to come in for an interview." She looked at him expectantly.

"So you applied for a job?" Esteban asked.

"It's only part-time."

"You're wasting your time and theirs, because if they offer you a job, you won't be able to take it."

Except for the wail of a saxophone from the stereo, silence filled the room, and the soft glow disappeared from Sonia's brown eyes.

Delores slowly set down the spatula. "Thank you for the recipe. I'm going upstairs now. Good night." She walked out of the room with her eyes averted.

Sonia cleared her throat and straightened on the stool. "I know we agreed I wouldn't work, but this gig won't take a lot of my time, and it'll give me something to do. There are only so many times I can go to the salon and eat lunch with my girlfriends."

"That's not part of our agreement. You agreed to be available to me, and I agreed I would take care of all your expenses. If you want to work, you can come work for me so that there's no conflict with your schedule."

"I already work for you."

Her mouth set in an obstinate line, and Esteban gritted his teeth. "Then get a hobby. Maybe you could take up baking."

She glared at him. "You're being unreasonable," she said quietly.

"Am I? Or are you?" he asked.

"So I'm never going to work?"

"I just offered you a job, and you turned it down."

"I want something separate from you."

"Since when?"

A chilling tension filled the room.

"Are you telling me none of your other mistresses worked?"

His other lovers worked, but he'd never cared. In fact, he'd welcomed the occasional break. Everything changed with Sonia. Their liaison was the longest to date and involved different parameters. He had moved her into his home, and she traveled everywhere with him —something he'd never done before.

"Our arrangement is different," he said.

"There's not termination clause in our agreement, so how much longer is our *arrangement* supposed to continue, Esteban?"

The hairs on the back of his neck stood on end. "Why?"

She shot daggers at him. "I'm asking so I can do some planning. We never discussed an end date, and this has to end sometime, doesn't it?"

Her voice dropped at the end, and his stomach did the same— plunging with unexpected swiftness.

"It ends when I say it ends."

"There's the arrogant ass I remember." She got down from the stool. "I guess you're back to showing your true colors."

"And when do you show yours?" he asked.

Her startled gaze met his. "What is that supposed to mean?"

"It means, you like to pretend this is the first time you've ever done this, but I should have known better. You're much too good at it." She blanched, and he heard a stricken sound emit from her throat. He stalked past her. "We have a cocktail party to attend. I'm going to take a shower."

Esteban turned on the lights in the bathroom and tore off his clothes as angry tension invaded every corner of his body. Why was he so angry? Jealousy, perhaps, at knowing that Stone Riverton had established a similar relationship with Sonia? Upset, because she'd duped him into believing that this was the first time she'd been a kept woman, yet every time she gave him a sweet smile, rubbed his back, or showed concern, she was simply playing a part because he paid her to do it and had done so before.

Now he understood Craig's snide remarks in Argentina. He must have found out about Sonia's relationship with Stone.

Esteban and Sonia's agreement had been laid out in black and white, but now it soured his stomach—especially when he considered that she'd been the same way with Stone. Esteban paid handsomely for her company and loyalty, and if he lost everything, she would be gone, like his ex, Elsa. Maybe she was ready to go now. She'd certainly implied as much by her comment in the kitchen.

He stepped into the frameless glass shower enclosure, which doubled as a sauna, complete with a bench for sitting—a fixture he hadn't used once since he moved in. He turned on the water and lifted his face to the overhead nozzle, letting the spray from the square fixture pelt his face. Rolling his shoulders, he braced his hands against the cool wall and let the warm water drop in soothing beats onto his neck and back.

He sensed, rather than heard, Sonia come into the room. Glancing sideways, he looked at her looking at him.

"Whatever you think you know, you're wrong. I have never done this before." Her lips firmed, and she marched out with her back ramrod straight.

Esteban gritted his teeth and stared at the wall. He hurried through the rest of his shower and left the bathroom. Sonia sat on the bed, flipping through a magazine.

"Aren't you getting dressed?" he asked.

"I'm not going." She flipped a page hard.

"Don't be ridiculous, Sonia. They're expecting us."

"I'm not going, unless you plan to drag me kicking and screaming against my will. Otherwise, feel free to dock my pay." Their eyes locked in a battle of wills before she returned her attention to the pages of the magazine.

Fuming, Esteban went into his dressing room and after a while came out fully dressed in a dark suit. "What should I tell Annabelle?" he asked, referring to the evening's hostess.

"Tell her I'm sick."

He stalked to the door.

"Why don't you ask me what you want to know, Esteban? Or would you rather guess and silently judge me?"

He stopped. "And what do I want to know, Sonia?"

"You want to know if I was Stone Riverton's mistress."

His dark gaze bored through her. "Were you?"

Sonia shut the magazine and stood. "No, I wasn't. I was nineteen years old, and he was my boss, and I had an affair with him. I considered him my boyfriend. But I was not his mistress."

"Do you deny the car and the promotion?"

"My, my, you did your homework already, didn't you?" she said with a snide grin.

His lips tightened into a thin line.

"The car was a used Nissan I accepted as a birthday gift. I gave it back when I quit. I thought the assistant manager position was merit-based, but obviously there were other factors, such as my great ability to suck him off in the parking lot after the restaurant closed."

Esteban winced.

"I was young and didn't consider that he was rewarding me. I was good at my job, or maybe I just didn't care. It took me a while to figure out that men would just give me things because of the way I looked. I didn't even have to ask. But believe me, I learned."

"He's married."

"We'd been together a year when I found out he was married. Last night was the first time I've seen him wear his wedding ring." She placed both hands on her hips. "But let me ask you a question: whatever happened to we were all young once and make mistakes? Does that apply to you alone? Because it bothers you that I had a relationship with Stone. Why is that? Being your mistress is perfectly acceptable, but being his somehow makes me morally bankrupt? I never knew you could be such a hypocrite. I learned something new tonight."

She left him in the bedroom and went out onto the patio, to the spot where he usually sat and smoked. She pulled her feet up to her chin and stared out at the water.

Esteban watched her for a moment before heading out the door.

Another crack in their relationship. Theirs was a delicate and temporary arrangement. It didn't allow for too many cracks.

* * *

ATTENDING the cocktail party had been a waste of time because all Esteban could think about was Sonia. He'd become accustomed to having her by his side. Even if they didn't remain in the same room, knowing she was in the general vicinity was a comforting feeling, which he'd missed tonight.

Then there was the gnawing sensation that everything was falling apart. She'd been angry, but beneath the anger, he thought he might have seen hurt, too. She'd been so insulted by his initial offer that the thought of her possibly taking on the same role with another man— even if she did so before she ever met Esteban—upset him. He wasn't proud of it, but it was the truth.

Worst of all was her question about terminating their arrangement. Her question played in a tireless loop in his head, taunting him with the possibility of her leaving, a situation he staunchly objected to.

The house was quiet when he entered. Oddly quiet, as if no one else was within.

"Lights on."

Esteban went to the bedroom. The bed was empty.

A wave of panic seized him. Taking long strides, he yanked open the door of her dressing room, his heart racing. All of her clothes were there. His shoulders slumped in relief, and he clutched his head.

She wouldn't leave without a word, and not because of a stupid fight. So where was she?

He walked through the house, listening for sounds of her. Could she be upstairs?

As he passed by the living room, movement on the other side of the glass caught his eye. He hadn't noticed before because she was way in one corner, sitting on the patio with only a few of the outdoor lights on. And she wasn't alone.

Esteban stepped out, and both Jackie and Sonia stopped laughing and looked up at him. A half-drunk bottle of wine and a platter of sausages and cheeses sat on the glass table between them.

"Hello, Esteban!" Jackie waved. "Back so soon? Sonia invited me over because she thought you'd be out late."

"I have a headache, so I came back early." He rubbed a hand across his forehead, but Sonia paid no attention like she had in the past. She didn't ask if he was okay or needed an aspirin. She sipped her wine, staring at the dark water of the bay, as if he hadn't even spoken.

"I'll leave you ladies alone to get back to your conversation."

Jackie didn't appear to know about their argument earlier, otherwise he was certain she would not have been so friendly.

He went back inside the house. He truly did have a headache from that split second when he thought she'd left. The throbbing lessened to a low throb when he saw her, but it was a headache nonetheless.

Instead of going to bed, he went to his home office to work. There was a portfolio he needed to evaluate, and maybe while he was in there, he'd think of a way to make things up to Sonia.

CHAPTER 30

*S*onia was early for dinner with Esteban, but decided to have Abel drop her at Patagonia anyway. They didn't have a social engagement tonight. He was taking her to dinner and had promised a surprise.

After her morning workout in the home gym, one of Linn's personal shoppers came by with a host of garments. Bella Boutique stocked the types of clothes that showed off her figure and made her look good on Esteban's arm, and after this morning's session, her closet contained five more dresses, two pantsuits, and accessories to complement each outfit.

Following her personal shopping experience, she went to the spa for a full afternoon of pampering—a facial and body scrub, a Brazilian wax, followed by a relaxing Vichy shower and massage. During the mani-pedi, they painted her nails a creamy, light color, and then she went to the hair station. Esteban preferred her hair short, and after a deep conditioning, the stylist brushed her hair away from her face and added lift and body with a large-barrel curling iron.

She chose her clothes with Esteban in mind. Today she'd opted for a long yellow dress with sheer sleeves, belted with a yellow sash, with an open front that allowed her to show off her legs if she wanted to.

Nestled between her breasts was the gold and platinum Tiffany necklace Esteban had given her months ago.

She walked down the hall and waved at Abena through the open door of her office next to his. "Hey there." She breezed by.

"He's in a meeting," Abena called.

Sonia stopped and turned around. "I'm early," she said, standing in the door.

"Come in and sit down."

"I don't want to bother you."

"It's no bother. Would you like something to drink?" Abena rose from her desk, chic in a cream pantsuit.

"Sure. Water would be fine."

"I'll be right back."

Abena left the office, and Sonia settled into one of the guest chairs.

She heard Esteban's office door open and then voices—his and the distinct sound of a woman's softer tone. Then laughter and movement outside the hallway. Out of curiosity, she glanced through the open doorway and saw a flash of red hair and a confident strut in high heels. Sonia looked away but did a double take. Her heart raced as the vaguely familiar figure disappeared from view.

She jumped up from the chair and stood in the middle of the hallway, watching the woman walk to the elevator.

Turn around, Sonia thought. She held her breath.

The redhead pushed the down button and turned her head in Sonia's direction. Time stood still. There was no mistaking that face. The last time she'd seen her, she'd been staring up at Sonia, helping Pedro pick up his discarded clothes from the yard in front of her apartment building.

The woman gave her a friendly smile in greeting—an automatic gesture that immediately transformed into a frozen expression of recognition. Her eyes widened and her lips parted in surprise, and as the elevator doors eased open, she lowered her gaze and ducked inside.

What in the world?

Sonia could hardly breathe.

Abena came around the corner holding a bottle of water and cast a cursory glance at the closing elevator before bestowing a smile on

Sonia. "Here you go." She extended the water, but Sonia ignored her hand.

"Who was that woman?" She pointed. "The one in the elevator."

"Why?" Abena's brow wrinkled.

"I know her."

"Oh." Abena frowned. "Her name is Andrea. She works for Mr. Galiano."

"In what capacity?"

"I-I don't know."

"You don't know or you don't want to tell me?" Sonia snapped.

Abena's eyes widened at the harsh tone. "I don't understand—"

Sonia swung around and marched toward Esteban's office. Without knocking, she shoved open the door.

He stood at the desk, his finger on a desktop calendar, as if making a note of a particular date.

He preferred when she wore dresses and skirts, and his gaze ate her up. She'd grown accustomed to that look in his eyes whenever he wanted her, and anything could trigger his lust.

"What perfume are you wearing?" he'd once asked, pressing his nose to the skin of her neck.

"Something new," she'd whispered, already getting aroused by the husky sound of his voice.

Within a few minutes, they'd been naked on the bed with a type of frantic hunger that never seemed to grow old.

But she didn't care about any of that right now. She needed answers.

"How do you know that woman?" she asked.

An eyebrow winged toward the ceiling. "What woman?"

"The woman who left your office seconds ago. Andrea, the redhead. How do you know her?"

From the corner of her eye, she saw Abena standing awkwardly just inside the office.

"Please excuse us, Abena," Esteban said quietly, keeping his eyes on Sonia.

His assistant left the room and quietly closed the door.

"Andrea works for me," Esteban said.

"How? What does she do?" Her heart raced so fast that she became unsteady on her feet.

"She helps me get rid of problems."

"*She's* the one I caught Pedro with. Was he a problem, and you used her to get rid of him through entrapment?"

"Entrapment?" Esteban chuckled and sank into the leather chair behind his desk. He surveyed Sonia like a king on a throne, resting an elbow on the armrest and rubbing a finger across his upper lip. "What exactly do you think I did, *querida*?"

Sonia took angry strides across the room to stand on the other side of the desk. "You hired her to sleep with him."

"I hired her to place him in a compromising position. If she decided to go the extra mile, that was her decision, and not part of my instructions."

"So you admit you set him up?" Her head was spinning. "Why?"

"Because I needed you to see that he was no good for you. It didn't take much, from what I understand. She bought him a drink, flirted a little, and she was on her way home with him."

"How did she know when I'd be home so that I could see them?"

"She didn't. It was purely coincidence that you arrived at the same time. It couldn't have worked any better if she'd planned it herself." He sounded smug and satisfied with the outcome. No regret in his voice at all.

"So you bought her services to get rid of my boyfriend." She leaned on her hands over the desk, analyzing his features. She didn't know what she expected to find—some softness, perhaps. But there was none. He gazed back at her with amused indifference, as if daring her to ask more questions, daring her to find a soul beneath the Armani suit.

"You use your money as a weapon," she said, straightening.

"And you hate it, don't you?" he said. "You hate all the things my money buys. The clothes you wear, the shoes on your feet, the diamond around your neck. This must all be very difficult for you."

The veracity of the words stung. She had no reason to complain. In the short time they'd been lovers, she'd become obsessed with the best of everything, buying high-end brands, organic foods, and all-natural beauty products.

"You think everything is about money. There are more important issues, like honesty and integrity and—"

"*Everything* is about money. Money buys affection, respect, and loyalty. If money is so unimportant, then why are you here?" he asked.

She didn't have an answer—at least not one she could give truthfully. In the beginning, her role in his life had been about the money and what she could obtain from the relationship. But slowly, her feelings had changed. She had started to feel affection for him. She had started to care, but those were dangerous emotions. Ones she'd promised herself not to experience again, and yet here she was—her stomach tangled in knots because while her heart ached for a normal relationship, she knew she could never have one with a man who paid her to be by his side.

"I'm not hungry anymore. I'm going home."

"No, you're not," he said.

She silently fumed. "Yes, I am."

"No, Sonia. You're not. Come here."

Their eyes challenged each other in a battle of wills.

"I said, come here." He spoke slowly and quietly, but his voice was no less lethal and the words no less demanding. His eyes narrowed on her, and all she saw was raw possessiveness in his angry gaze. "*Now.*"

He'd been demanding before, but never like this.

Esteban watched the battle that waged internally play out across her face.

Should she or shouldn't she? For long seconds she couldn't decide, but at the exact moment he knew she consented, her head tilted a little higher. She approached him with a taut jaw, and he tugged her down onto his lap, her luscious bottom resting right at the apex of his thighs.

Bringing his mouth close to her ear, he hauled rough air into his lungs and smelled the sweet scent of a new perfume. She smelled like a field of flowers in bloom, and already, he felt his body hardening. "You're upset I got rid of a man who didn't deserve you?"

She stared out the window, refusing to look at him. "You don't get to make the decision about who should remain in my life and who should go."

He found the split in the dress and pushed it apart. Sliding his hand between her legs, he caressed her soft thigh and listened with satisfaction as her breathing became less steady. "I don't regret what I did, and you don't get to refuse my dinner invitation because you're upset."

All day he'd been looking forward to their evening out. They weren't only going to eat. He'd planned a big surprise. He'd instructed Abena to purchase tickets to the Jill Scott concert in New York, and they were taking his private plane on the trip after dinner.

Sonia might not understand the relevance, but in the past, his mistresses had attended events *he* liked. Tonight he'd made a conscious effort to participate in an activity just for her, to make up for his behavior about Stone a couple of weeks ago. He'd even arranged for Sonia to meet with the singer backstage after the show. To have her shove his invitation in his face, over a man he'd disposed of months ago, infuriated him.

"Whatever you say, Esteban. You pay the bills. You pay. I obey."

Any other woman and he wouldn't have cared if she'd reduced their relationship to an exchange of currency for companionship, but Sonia's response enraged him. He gripped the fine material of her dress.

He stood abruptly, and she hopped off his lap, staring at him with defiance.

"That's right," Esteban said.

"And I'm oh so appreciative of your generosity."

He clenched his teeth, almost grinding them to dust. "As you should be. Do you know how many women would kill to be in your shoes?"

"Too many to count, I'm sure."

Esteban sat down in the chair. "Take off your shoes."

The animosity on her face wavered. "Why?"

"Because I said so."

She stared at him for a few seconds, then slipped her feet from the pair of sexy gold sandals and left them beside the desk.

"Sit," he said.

"Where?"

"Here." He pointed to the desktop.

Sonia eyed him warily and then moved onto the furniture. She looked concerned, licking her lips nervously. They became moist and kissable, but he tamped down the urge to drag her close and have a taste.

"Lift up your dress, and let me see your panties."

Her eyes widened, and she glanced out the window. The sun was still high in the sky, and even on this less busy section of Ocean Drive, people and cars passed back and forth at a regular pace.

Slowly, with heightened color in her cheeks, she pulled the parted edges of her dress apart and eased the folds higher. She wore a black lace thong, the one he'd requested.

"Take them off," Esteban commanded, his voice hoarse. He positioned the chair directly in front of her to block the view from the road.

"You've proven—"

"Take them. Off."

"Esteban—"

"I pay. You obey," he snarled.

Her mouth clamped shut. The animosity returned to her face, but she hooked her thumbs in the strings at her hips, and watching her wiggle out of the tiny scrap of lace had to be one of the sexiest things he'd ever seen. She dropped the undergarment onto his desk and waited.

"Put your feet here." He patted the armrests.

Her gaze flew to the window again before returning to him. "Someone will see us." She gripped the edge of the desk as if preparing for a rough ride.

"Let them. I don't care."

Beneath the dismay, he saw excitement and the anticipation in the uptick in her breathing.

She set her feet on the rests, and his eyes dropped to the exposed area between her thighs and the strip of hair at their apex. He rolled closer, as if pulling up to the dinner table, and the angle of her knees deepened. Tracing a finger over her almost bare folds, he listened to her whimper. He knew she'd be extra sensitive there after her waxing today.

She'd waxed for him. She'd worn that thong and the yellow dress for him.

He continued to work his hand between her legs. He inserted one finger, then another into the slick channel. Another whimper dragged from her throat, this time thicker and louder. She rested on her hands, and her head fell backward. Laid bare to him and open in such a raw, uninhibited way.

Dios, she was so passionate. So aroused and ready.

"Please," she whispered brokenly.

He circled her wet clit, and she breathed his name like a prayer, her body arching into a sexy curve. He continued to massage her flesh, kneading the sensitive spot with his entire hand. The scent of her arousal inflamed his lust and turned the organ in his pants into a rod of iron.

He had to get a taste. Esteban flicked his tongue across the swollen folds of her sex, and she shuddered, spreading her legs even wider, wanting him to do more.

Gripping his hair, she held him in place. Not that he was going anywhere. This was exactly where he wanted to be. Right here, between her thighs. She pushed her hips closer and lifted one leg over his shoulder. She pressed closer to his gentle kisses, demanding a more aggressive approach, urging his mouth tighter to her drenched flesh.

It seemed to take only seconds before she came, her pink toes dangling over his shoulder as the sun's rays slanted across their bodies in full view of the street. She bit down on her lip and let out a body-shuddering moan as her body rocked through the climax.

Esteban refused to stop kissing and licking. He wanted to give her another orgasm. He wanted her to drench his tongue with proof of her desire. And he wanted her to be fully aware of who was in charge.

When the second orgasm broke free, she twisted on the wooden surface of the desk. Once again she bit into her bottom lip and stifled a cry that he suspected, if let loose, would be heard all the way to the restaurant on the first floor.

Spent, she panted on her back on the desk while Esteban wiped his mouth with a tissue.

Then he stood and unzipped his pants. He took her on top of the desk with her legs latched around his waist. Keeping her arms pinned above her head, he thrust into her and wrung another orgasm from her body as though it was his due.

* * *

SONIA DIDN'T LEAVE Esteban's private bathroom right away after she finished cleaning up. She stared at her reflection in the mirror for so long that her vision blurred and she lost track of time.

A loud rap on the door made her jump and jolted her from the trancelike state.

Esteban's commanding voice came through. "Sonia, we have dinner reservations."

She took a deep breath and said, "I'll be right there." Thankfully, her voice didn't reveal the turmoil within.

She reapplied her lipstick without looking in the mirror again. She couldn't. She couldn't bear to see the truth. The confusing emotions, the hurt from his judgment about Stone, the desperate need to hold on to normalcy in a relationship that was anything but normal meant she'd done something so foolhardy she couldn't look at herself right now.

Their relationship started out as an arm's-length transaction with no emotions and no feelings. But she wanted more. *Needed* more, from a man who'd entrapped her ex-boyfriend and got rid of him, to get her. To *win*.

She'd fallen in love with Esteban, but he paid for her to be by his side. He saw her as a possession—like one of his cars, or a painting.

After dropping the lipstick into her purse, she snapped it closed and faced the door, gearing up to get back out there and face him.

That he'd agreed to her cynical definition of their relationship hurt more than she could have imagined, and yet she couldn't stop him from taking her on top of the desk. Didn't even want to. She was so damn weak for him.

I pay. You obey.

She swallowed down the lump in her throat. She had a job to do.

Taking another deep breath, she tucked her purse under her arm and opened the door.

CHAPTER 31

*A*nother Saturday night, another party. This one took place on a yacht in the middle of Biscayne Bay. When she and Esteban received the invitation to attend, she'd initially declined because he'd told her to. But the hosts had followed up with a personal plea because the owner of the yacht wanted to talk to him about a resort in Mexico. So here they were.

She'd enjoyed the surprise trip to New York, but ever since the encounter in his office and the acknowledgment of her feelings, Sonia hadn't been the same.

"Cheers!" The sound of laughter filtered into the night air, and she watched as a small group of friends giggled and fell all over each other. Everyone in attendance was either drunk or tipsy, except her. She'd refrained from drinking because of a queasy stomach she'd experienced earlier today.

She did the usual and chatted with the women there, dutifully circulating among the guests, smiling, and laughing. While in the past she'd enjoyed herself, tonight she wished she were at home with her feet up watching television.

The women at this event represented a mix of young ladies dating older men or mature women married to men who were CEOs and presided over the boards of charities and nonprofits. She had the pleasure of listening to the women brag about how they used to work but no longer needed to, what mistakes the nanny or housekeeper had made that they'd chastised them for, and how to make the difficult decision between vacationing in the Caribbean or the South of France this year.

She twisted away from the sight of the huddled friends and made her way to the railing, where she looked out across the sea. Inhaling deeply of the salt air, she closed her eyes as the cool breeze wafted across her bare arms and shoulders.

"Why are you standing here alone?" She heard Esteban's low voice right before he dropped a kiss on her neck and closed his warm body around hers from behind.

"Enjoying the fresh air." Sonia turned her face to him because that was what he expected. After all this time, they'd developed routines.

"You're awfully quiet."

"Am I?"

"You've been quiet a lot lately." He dropped a light kiss to her lips.

"I have a lot on my mind."

"Anything you want to talk about?"

"No." Sonia dropped her gaze to the waves below, turned navy—near black—in the diminishing light.

"Are you ready to go?" His voice had dropped even lower.

Sonia smelled the brandy on his breath and knew he'd ordered it neat. She knew a lot about him, bits and pieces trickling in during the nine months of their liaison.

He stayed fit by swimming, boxing, and bike riding. He was an early riser, needed an espresso midmorning, and often skipped lunch in favor of a large meal later in the afternoon. He'd played soccer as a teenager, well enough to make the school team but not well enough to play in a league. And she was here because he needed a companion and a woman to warm his bed, and didn't mind paying for it. She could no longer pretend that this was any deeper than that.

"I'm ready if you are," she answered. She knew better than to point out that he was a specially invited guest they expected to remain for most of the night. Esteban did whatever he wanted, bucking convention and living by his own set of rules.

His hands slid to her hips, and he nuzzled her neck, this time gently nipping the skin and pressing his swelling manhood against her bottom. "Good."

He slid his hand down her arm, laced their fingers together, and drew her along with him. They said their goodbyes to the host and left on a small boat that took them from the revelry to the shore, where Abel waited with the limo.

Sonia slid into the back seat.

"Something *is* wrong," he said, watching her.

"What do you mean?" She crossed her legs.

His hand extended across the back of the seat as he watched her. "You're sitting far away from me. You do that when you're upset."

Sonia laughed easily. "I'm not upset."

"No? Then come here."

The gentle command irked her, but she slid across the seat and settled under his arm.

Esteban had a way of staking his claim when they were together. Almost from the minute they entered any party, he stayed close to her side at first. He'd keep his hand low on her back, or become even more possessive by cupping her hip as he held her close to his side. Other times he would whisper in her ear, sending tiny shivers down her spine as his lips grazed the shell of her ear or his nose brushed her hairline.

Some nights, when they left an engagement, he'd pull her on top of him in the back of the Maybach, as if to prove that she did indeed belong to him, shoving her dress up around her hips. She'd ride him as he grabbed her ass and thrust into her, her body quivering with incomparable pleasure. In those moments, when he appeared to be as helpless as she, she looked down into his dark eyes and felt they were almost on equal footing. He could no more resist the passion between them than she could. And in those moments, she knew her own power as she gripped his hair and he gripped her ass.

Then they both erupted, she around him, he inside of her. Trembling, moaning as the city lights whizzed by the tinted windows. Once their heartbeats returned to normal, she would slide off him, but he never let her go. He held on to her hand, even once they left the car and went into the house.

Being with him like that, feeling needed, as if he couldn't let her go

—those moments were special. They were the only times in their lopsided relationship that she thought the intensity of his feelings might edge toward the intensity of hers.

Then she thought it might not be so scary to love and adore him, because during those moments, she felt like more than a mistress.

* * *

"Thank you," Sonia said to Abel as she exited the car.

She heard Esteban's footsteps behind her but continued with hurried steps to the door. She punched in the code and the lock disengaged. In the silent house, the electronic keypad in the wall beeped once, signaling that in thirty seconds a silent alarm would sound. She pressed her thumb to the screen and turned it off, and the countdown immediately stopped.

Her heels clicked on the marble tile as she walked toward the bedroom, but she heard the quiet beep as Esteban re-engaged the system. In the bedroom, she dropped her purse in the dressing room and stripped out of the sleeveless chiffon dress, replacing it with her floral print kimono.

When she walked back into the bedroom, Esteban sat in the chair near the window, looking out at the night, but his gaze angled toward her when she came out.

"You've been in a mood all night," he said. She didn't see, but sensed his eyes following her movement across the floor.

She sank down on the edge of the bed.

"Did something happen at the party to upset you?" he asked.

"What if I can't do this anymore?" She hadn't even known those words were coming, but now that they were out, she held her breath, wondering what he'd say.

Esteban paused in the middle of removing his platinum Patek Philippe watch. "Do what?"

"This. You and me," she said in a small, uncertain voice. Fear twisted her stomach.

A faint smile crossed his lips, and he resumed removing the time-piece. "Did I forget something?" he asked, walking to the dresser on the other side of the room. He placed his watch on top of it, keeping his movements calm and controlled. "An anniversary that we should be celebrating? It's not your birthday, so I can't think of any other reason why you'd feel you couldn't do this anymore."

Sonia swallowed. "I'm not sure this is working out."

He raised one black brow. "Would an increase in your allowance make things better?"

Her eyes flew to his face. "I don't want more money."

"Then what do you want? More jewelry? A car?"

He continued to speak in a calm voice while her emotions careened out of control.

"No." She paced away from the bed. "I don't want you to buy me anything."

"May I ask where this is coming from, all of a sudden?"

"It's not all of a sudden."

"*¿Verdad?* How long have you been lying in bed with me wishing you were somewhere else?"

He faced away from her as he removed his cufflinks. Cold. Indifferent.

"Would you at least pay me the respect of looking at me when I'm talking to you!" she screamed.

He swung around and stared at her as if she had lost her mind. He marched over, and she shrank back internally, expecting him to yell and scream. Instead, he spoke between his teeth, practically seething with hostility. "I give you everything you could possibly want. When is it enough, eh? Tell me, Sonia." His sharp eyes ripped her to shreds. "Diamonds, clothes, shoes, trips—what else do you want? Do you want the blood from my veins next? Will that finally be enough for you? Will that finally make you happy?" His chest heaved, his flushed face hard and angry.

She felt as if he'd slapped her. "This isn't about things, Esteban."

"Then what is it about?" His mouth crooked into a one-sided smile. "Your despicable ex-boyfriend? You should be thanking me." He started unbuttoning his shirt. "Save me the theatrics. You're not going anywhere. And do you know why?" His voice lowered. "We're a lovely pair, you and me, because we're both getting exactly what we want." He tilted up her chin. "I don't want to hear another word about you leaving."

He kissed her hard, their mouths searing together in a heated kiss. They sank onto the bed as he kissed her neck and shoulders. Her fingers curled into fists between them, and she closed her eyes, determined to freeze him out.

But then he changed tactic and started whispering to her in Spanish. Her tightly compressed lips were coaxed apart by the smooth glide of his tongue—an intimate, erotic touch that sent faint tremors of pleasure rippling in her belly. She moaned, hating the way her body betrayed her, already dampening in preparation for him. Her fists tightened even more to resist, but when he stretched her arms above her head and held her wrists together with one hand, the fragile wall she hid behind buckled and fell apart. Her resistance couldn't hold up against the seduction of the softer caresses or the gentle nudge of his kiss.

She'd never known a man like him before. The way he completely controlled her thoughts, her emotions, and her body—it thrilled at the same time it unnerved her.

Her mouth opened wider so their tongues could tangle together, and he gripped her hip and ground his pelvis against hers. She kissed him back with quiet desperation, pain swelling in her chest. She was falling apart on the inside.

She wished she could unmeet him, rewind her life and go back to the time before they met. But would it be worth it? Because then she wouldn't know this painful ache called love—which made her feel alive, even as it killed her.

He entered her with a long stroke, her hands still pinned above her head, their bodies writhing together in raw, naked desire as passion consumed them. Every virile inch of him pressed her down into the mattress, and he continued to speak in Spanish through hard bursts of air, making it difficult to parse the words and his broken sentences. But she did recognize one word that he said at the end. She'd heard it before and recalled the meaning.

Nunca.

Never.

CHAPTER 32

$\mathcal{E}$ steban employed vice presidents of operations based on location. At the moment, his head of operations in South America sat across from him in his office in the Patagonia. Santiago was a few years younger, and his promotion to vice president over a more mature employee had raised a few eyebrows, but early on he'd impressed Esteban with his sharp mind and work ethic. So far, the younger man hadn't proven him wrong. In fact, he'd exceeded expectations.

The trip to the United States was a chance for Santiago to get a better understanding of Galiano Holdings' North American operations, which Esteban considered placing under his supervision. In addition to Miami, there were plans to visit locations in California and New York.

"How did you know he'd give in?" Santiago asked.

Where Esteban was conservative in style, his employee preferred more flash. He wore a gold necklace with a cross around his neck and a gold ring on his right hand. The question he posed was regarding a supplier, whose contract Esteban had told him to cancel when the man argued about terms.

"He has two daughters getting married within the next year, and a wife who's accustomed to a certain standard of living. He needs the money, and there was no way he wasn't going to sign," Esteban replied.

Santiago chuckled. "Now I understand why you always say, 'Know the people you do business with.' It certainly helps with negotiations."

At a faint knock on the door, Esteban called out, "Come in."

Abena walked in wearing a turquoise tailored dress and carrying a stack of folders in her arms. "Good afternoon, Mr. Galiano. These are the files you wanted." She deposited them on the small round table. "Will there be anything else?"

"Good afternoon, Abena," Santiago said, without even glancing in her direction. He studied Esteban's desktop and became unusually still.

Abena visibly stiffened. "Hello, Santiago." The greeting seemed torn with difficulty from her lips. "Having a nice stay in Miami?"

Every time Abena and Santiago were in the same room, the air became rife with tension, and Esteban had long suspected something must have happened between them. Her engagement temporarily ended that speculation, but he was no longer sure.

"Better than the last time. Last time it was unbearably hot." Santiago turned his head to look at her.

There was subtext upon subtext in those words.

"If you can't stand the heat, you should stay out of the kitchen."

"Good advice. I've given up cooking. It wasn't worth the trouble," Santiago said in a low voice.

Abena took a deep breath and looked about to blast him, when Esteban interrupted.

"Excuse me." They both swung their heads in his direction. "Would the two of you prefer if I leave so you can hash out whatever the hell is going on in private? Or we could set up a boxing ring outside and see who's left standing at the end of the match."

"Excuse me, Mr. Galiano." Abena intertwined her fingers before her. "Is there anything else?"

"That will be all. Thank you."

She nodded and stalked away. Santiago tilted his head at an angle as if listening for her footfalls. When she shut the door, he relaxed in the chair and finally met Esteban's gaze.

"Anything you care to tell me?" Esteban asked.

"No."

Esteban thought about pushing the issue, but then decided it was better left alone, for now. He wasn't a counselor, and as long as their personal problems didn't affect their work, he'd let them sort it out themselves.

"Let's get to work." He rose, and Santiago followed him to the table.

* * *

LATER THAT EVENING, Esteban walked the Patagonia dining room floor, checking on customers, making sure they were satisfied with their meals and service. His general manager usually performed this task, but getting out on the floor and interacting with customers offered him a firsthand sense of what they liked and didn't like. The frankness of diners gave him information to improve in areas that were lacking, and continue in areas that operated to a satisfactory level.

He needed a focus group to tell him how to deal with Sonia. She'd been markedly different of late, all starting from when she saw Andrea in his office. He didn't regret hiring her. He'd gotten what he wanted, and he was right about Pedro from the beginning. But he didn't like the changes he saw in Sonia. It was like waiting for a pin to drop. She behaved more like someone going through the motions, with cool conversation and measured emotions—as if holding back. He wanted the woman he'd become accustomed to. The woman whose every action and every breath turned him on. From her enthusiasm about wine to the sensual way she laughed, or the way she looked at him from beneath her lashes, smiling with a warmth that filled her eyes and heated his blood. She was slowly slipping away from him.

As he finished shaking the hand of a young man who explained he and his wife celebrated their anniversary there every year, Esteban noticed a woman near the back of the restaurant. Her waist-length hair, shiny and dark, half covered her face when she rose from the table. Then she tucked it behind an ear and took the hand of a little boy with her.

He recognized her immediately as someone from the past. For a moment he was so taken aback that he didn't move, and stood in the middle of the floor staring at her. She looked different, but the same. Her body had filled out and her hair was longer, but there was no doubt it was Elsa.

She spotted him, and after her initial surprise, a smile spread across her face.

He walked over. "*Hola*, Elsa."

"I can't believe it's you. *Hola*, Esteban."

Elsa Calderón, his first love. He'd loved her with youthful desperation—completely, unconditionally, and wholeheartedly. Almost every action he'd taken from seventeen years old to twenty years old had been done with her in mind. She'd broken his heart and taught him a valuable lesson about avarice—a lesson he remembered to this day.

His gaze flicked to the little boy, who looked about five years old. He was either her child or an exceptional clone in masculine form. The sight of the two of them together was shocking and caused a faint twisting of nostalgia in his gut when he recalled how they'd lain under the stars on a blanket, holding hands and planning their future.

She'd wanted a big church wedding, and he'd promised to give her one. They'd wanted three children—two girls and a boy. She'd promised to work by his side, the way his mother did with his father, the way her parents did at the small laundromat they owned. They would conquer the world—or at the very least, the Argentina restaurant scene—together.

But those dreams only partially came to be. Esteban opened his first restaurant at nineteen, a small café that served sandwiches and pastries along a busy tourist street in Buenos Aires. Then, too fast and too eager, he launched another restaurant with a more aggressive menu. He failed miserably and learned a lesson in humility. One that taught him that good food wasn't enough. So much more went into running a restaurant: planning, advertising, financial management, negotiating—all skills he didn't have enough of at the time.

He received the ultimate blow when, hot on the heels of his failure, Elsa ditched him for an older man, someone well off who could ensure she did *not* have to work in a restaurant, or a laundromat, or anywhere she didn't want to.

"Don't tell me this is your restaurant?" She sounded casual and friendly.

"As a matter of fact, it is. The first one I opened in the United States."

"That's wonderful. We had a great meal." Her eyes softened. "You look well, Esteban."

"So do you," he replied, and meant it.

"Mommy, I'm tired." The little boy rested his forehead against her hip.

"We'll be leaving soon." Elsa gently rubbed a hand over his hair. "We arrived today," she said by way of explanation.

"How long will you be in Miami?"

"A few days, until my hus—" A stricken expression crossed her face.

"It's okay, Elsa. You can mention your husband. I know that you're married."

A guilty flush filled her cheeks, and her gaze dropped for a moment. "My...husband is meeting with clients tonight." She winced, as if it pained her to say the words. "When he wraps up his business, we're flying to New York for a short vacation and then returning home."

She finally looked at him again, and in her eyes he thought he saw the same questions that used to plague him. What would their lives have been like if they'd stayed together? What would have happened if she hadn't left him for another man?

Then he realized those questions hadn't crossed his mind in a very long time. He filled his houses with expensive, beautiful items to prove to himself, and the world, that he had arrived. All these years, much of his drive stemmed from a need to prove to her and his absentee biological father exactly how valuable he was, and how much they had missed by not being in his life. Yet as he stood looking at the woman who'd held his heart for years, he came to the realization that having those questions answered no longer mattered.

"I'd better go. It's getting late, and I should put him to bed. Take care, Esteban. It was good to see you."

"Goodbye, Elsa."

She smiled and walked away. For a spell, Esteban watched her maneuver through the tables before the activity around him penetrated his brain. While a busboy collected the dishes from Elsa's table,

Esteban returned to interacting with the customers. Shaking hands. Asking questions. Explaining meal selections. Then he checked his watch and decided to go home.

He said good night to his general manager, and on the way out saw Elsa talking to Armando, the maître d'. This time, she was alone.

Surprised, he approached. "I thought you'd left. Is everything all right?"

"Yes, everything is fine." She flushed, glanced at the maître d', and then said to Esteban, "Do you mind if I speak to you privately for a moment?"

Without touching, he guided her out the restaurant into the front lobby of the hotel. "What is it?" he asked.

"I wanted to give you this." She took a card out of her purse and handed it to him. "I thought maybe we could be friends. I don't know how you feel about that, but—sometimes I think…I don't know…I thought maybe we could talk now and again. There's nothing wrong with being friends, is there? And we used to have some great conversations. We had so much in common."

"We did," Esteban said.

She nodded, satisfied by his response. "Have a good night." She reached out and touched his arm, almost as if she couldn't help herself.

His shoulders tensed, but he didn't reach back for her. "You too."

He followed her to the door of the hotel and watched as she climbed into the back of a dark sedan.

He looked down at the black card, inscribed with silver letters. Her name and number were printed on the front, and she'd handwritten another number below them in silver ink.

Esteban took out his phone and dialed.

"Yes, Mr. Galiano," Abel answered.

"I'm finished for the evening. Meet me out front."

"Yes, sir."

Esteban hung up and took another look at the card.

He'd moved past her betrayal. The anger he'd felt in the past was gone.

If not for Elsa making the decision to leave him, he might not have buckled down and worked harder. In a strange, twisted way, he had her to thank for his success.

He tore the card in two and dropped the pieces in the gold receptacle inside the door.

CHAPTER 33

"*A*re you sure you don't want to come out here and meet me?" Esteban sounded tired over the phone, and he probably was. He and Santiago had spent the past week in New York and then traveled to California this evening, where they'd remain to visit his restaurants and meet with some of the winery owners and farmers that provided the produce. Sonia knew that because Abena had flown out to California ahead of them, and both women had spoken earlier about several events on his social calendar.

"You're busy, and I'd just get in the way."

When she traveled with him before, she'd usually found plenty to occupy her time during the day while he worked. She went sightseeing or shopping, and on occasion joined him for lunch with colleagues. He did his best to spend time with her at night, taking her to a show or dinner, and if there was a business meeting, when possible he arranged for his associates to invite their significant others so she wouldn't feel out of place.

This time, she hadn't traveled with him and had told him she didn't feel well, which wasn't exactly a lie. She hadn't been feeling well. Her back bothered her a little bit, and she didn't have the energy she usually did. She'd simply exaggerated her symptoms to get out of the trip. Except for at the very beginning, this two-week separation would make the longest period they'd been apart. But she needed this time to pack up her clothes and other items and move out.

"I know things have been strained between us lately. We need to talk," Esteban said in a grim tone.

"About what?"

"Everything."

"Everything meaning what?" Sonia drew her feet close and hugged her knees with one arm. Through the open door of her dressing room, she could see the empty hangers and shelves where her clothes, shoes, and handbags used to be.

"Everything, meaning us. You and me."

She didn't know what that meant. It could mean anything, and the uncertainty was part of what was tearing her apart and wearing her down. She didn't want to talk. Not anymore.

The other day she'd gone to lunch with Jackie and Evan. Jackie giggled constantly and looked so happy, her utter joy was almost painful to watch. Seeing them together brought home the stark reality of what was happening between Sonia and Esteban.

Nothing. Nothing was happening between her and Esteban. She was with a man she didn't have a future with. They didn't make plans or discuss activities past the next social engagement or flight. Jackie was moving on—getting married to a man who adored her and discussed a future with her in terms that included babies and growing old together, and she was planning to take over the helm of her family's business. Meanwhile, Sonia remained in a stagnant, loveless relationship and sat on a certification that she should be using to further her career in a field she loved.

"You're obviously unhappy, Sonia."

"You have enough to worry about without concerning yourself with my tantrums." She said what she thought he'd want to hear.

"We'll talk when I get back." Esteban sounded distracted.

"All right," Sonia said in a hollow voice.

No point in arguing. It didn't matter because she'd already made up her mind about what she was going to do. Her only recourse was to get away from him, or she'd keep losing herself and loving him harder when he couldn't—wouldn't—love her back.

She knew the deal going into this. She had been foolish to fall in love with him.

He remained silent for a while, but she knew he was still on the line because she heard voices in the background, engaged in a conversation he probably needed to get back to.

"You *are* going to be there when I get back?" he asked.

The jarring question made her freeze. Why would he ask that? Did he sense her intent in the listless answers she gave? Before she'd removed a single item of clothing from his house? Had Delores ratted her out?

"Yes, I'll be here," she replied.

"Promise me."

Her heart constricted and she closed her eyes. She already missed him. His smell, his taste. The way he held her close and smiled at her affectionately. As if he cared, just a little bit. For her, not because he was paying her to share his bed and look good on his arm, but because he genuinely appreciated her presence in his life.

"I promise," she said.

It got easier to lie when you no longer cared.

* * *

PHONE CALLS in the middle of the night were never a good sign.

Bleary-eyed and groggy from her sleep being interrupted, Sonia stared at the 404 area code flashing on the phone. She didn't recognize the number but knew it was an Atlanta call. She answered right away.

"Hello?"

"Sonia, it's Val." Her cousin's voice sounded thick and heavy, and she sniffled at the end of the sentence. "It's Daddy. He's in the hospital, and it doesn't look good." She sniffled again.

Sonia scrambled into a sitting position in the dark. "What happened?"

"His heart again." Valencia's voice cracked.

"He told me he recently had a checkup and everything was fine."

They spoke once a week, and she'd been back to see him two months ago. She'd made him get dressed, and taken him and Valencia to a delicious seafood dinner up on Stone Mountain. Valencia had looked suspiciously at her designer clothes and the cavalier way she dropped several hundred dollars on their meal and drinks, but Sonia had only wanted to give back a little bit of what her uncle had given her, and from everything she saw, he'd enjoyed himself immensely. Last time they talked, he mentioned their meal and how one day he was going back to get that lobster in butter sauce appetizer they'd enjoyed.

"He lied. Apparently he didn't want to worry us, but everything wasn't fine. I should've…"

"It's not your fault. He was stubborn."

"Yeah, but I should've pushed harder." Valencia let out a tremulous breath. "They've wheeled him into surgery. I don't know what the outcome will be. The doctors aren't very optimistic."

"They're not optimistic, but that doesn't mean we can't be," Sonia said in a confident voice. "Uncle Rowell is tough as nails, and you know that. He's going to get through this surgery like he did the first one." Sonia turned on the bedside lamp and squinted when the light invaded her pupils. "I'll catch the first flight out."

"You don't need to come. I just wanted you to know so that you could be aware."

"I'm on my way, and nothing you say will stop me. I'm pretty sure I can catch a flight for later this morning. He's going to be all right. We'll get through this, okay?" She spoke positively as much for herself as Valencia. They were no longer close like when they were children, but they both loved Uncle Rowell.

"Okay." Valencia's voice trembled, and Sonia had never heard her sound so fearful before.

The sound of her cousin's voice frightened her more than her uncle being in the hospital. Valencia was a tough woman, but if she was worried, that made Sonia worry. She didn't want to lose her uncle. She wasn't ready to let him go yet.

She hung up and went to sit behind the desk in Esteban's office. With a quick shake of the mouse, she brought the computer to life and searched for flights to Atlanta. She found a nonstop flight that left at four forty in the morning and booked it.

She changed into jeans and a comfortable shirt but didn't bother with an overnight bag. She left a note for Delores, tossed a few necessities in her purse, and hastened out the door to wait for the taxi she'd called.

Within fifteen minutes, she was on the way to the airport, clutching her bag and praying—praying harder than she'd ever prayed before.

CHAPTER 34

*S*onia hated hospitals. Life-saving treatments and surgeries were performed in them, but having to be there meant she was ill, or someone she loved was ill.

Valencia hadn't answered her phone when Sonia called, so she didn't know exactly where Uncle Rowell was. She walked to the enclosed reception desk on shaky legs and with a stomach rolling with dread. After a brief exchange, the woman behind the glass directed her to the elevators down the hall.

Sonia found her cousin slumped in a chair on the fourth floor. As she approached, the sense of dread she'd experienced since boarding her flight intensified. Her head throbbed, and the hand gripping her purse tightened hard enough to crush rocks.

As she neared, Valencia looked up, her eyes puffy, her cheeks red and damp with tears. Her shoulders drooped so low they seemed to carry the weight and fears of every patient and their family members in the hospital.

Their eyes remained on each other, and it was then that Sonia knew. She didn't need to ask, because she saw the grief on her cousin's face. Valencia shook her head slowly in answer to the unspoken question, and Sonia stopped moving.

She was transported back to the day of her mother's funeral. Her eight-year-old brain hadn't been able to accept what was happening, and when she saw her mother lying in the casket, she fainted. She wasn't eight anymore, and Rowell was not her mother, but the anguish was no less acute.

The room spun and she slumped against the wall, never taking her gaze from her cousin.

"No," Sonia croaked.

Valencia burst into tears, doubling over and burying her head in her hands. Sonia wanted to reach out and offer comfort, but her feet wouldn't move. Her knees gave way, and she slid down the wall into a crouched position. She let out a gut-wrenching bawl, comprised of both anguish and anger.

Why him? Why did he have to be taken when there were so many terrible people in the world? Why couldn't it be someone else but this kind, gentle, loving man who had always been her support system? Why?

She thought of Nelson Kennedy, her father, and the last time she'd seen him. She'd clung to her uncle's hand on the porch because the sight of her father scared her. Drugs had completely consumed him.

He'd come by after her mother's funeral. The stench on his soiled clothes had been almost intolerable. His stringy, dirty hair clearly hadn't been cut in a very long time. His teeth were what scared her the most. They were half gone from rotting, and the few that remained looked so caked with filth that she wondered how he managed to close his mouth.

Nelson stayed for a few minutes, called her "baby doll" like her uncle, and tried his best to look and sound normal. But he fidgeted, and he gulped, and after those few minutes, she knew by the look in this eyes that she'd never see him again.

He walked down the long driveway and into the street with his head bent. He never looked back at them on the porch. At eight years old, she'd wanted to run after him. Beg him to clean up. Beg him to change. Beg him to be her daddy. She must have made an unconscious motion to do so, because her uncle's hands tightened around her fingers.

She never saw her father again. He died two years later.

But Uncle Rowell was always there, a solid presence in her life. Her rock. Keeping her out of trouble. Holding her hand. Now he was gone, and she didn't get to say goodbye.

As much as she wanted to wallow in her pain, she couldn't let grief overtake her.

She rose with difficulty and walked to where her cousin sat doubled over. Sonia put her arms around her and, without hesitating, Valencia rested her head on her shoulder.

With tears streaming down their cheeks, they cried, and they held on tight.

To each other.

* * *

THERE HAD BEEN an impressive turnout for the funeral. The number of people that attended from church, Uncle Rowell's old job, and the neighborhood was overwhelming and indicative of the character of the man who had passed away. He'd touched a lot of lives. Family members and people from all walks of life, in all aspects of the community, knew her uncle and came out to pay their respects. Sonia was grateful for the outpouring of love.

"I wish you'd called me before," Esteban said over the phone.

"There's nothing you could have done."

"Your uncle is dead, Sonia. I could have done more than send a wreath. I could have been there for you." He sounded exasperated.

It was the second time they'd spoken since her arrival in Atlanta. When she'd called to tell him about her uncle's death, he'd wanted to come right away, but she'd insisted he stay in California, pointing out that he'd arrive too late for the funeral. She'd purposely waited until the day of the service to tell him because she knew he'd want to come.

He knew about her uncle and their close relationship, but both men had never met, something she realized she'd subconsciously made sure never happened to keep both parts of her life separate. A self-preservation technique, for when her affair with Esteban ended.

"How much longer will you be there?" Esteban asked.

"Three, four days at the most, to help my cousin tie up a few things," she lied. She'd be back in Miami by early afternoon.

Sonia and Valencia had already packed up Uncle Rowell's personal affairs and prepped the house for sale. They had bonded over Chinese food, deep dish pizza, laughter, and tears while they sorted his belongings into Keep, Discard, and Donate boxes.

Valencia allowed Sonia to take a few mementos, for which she was grateful. Among them was a well-worn book of poetry he kept beside his bed with notes written in the margins, his glasses, which he seldom wore but desperately needed, and a laminated recipe card that contained the handwritten instructions for the best darn red velvet cake in the country.

She and Valencia were in the lobby of Buchanan, Rothstein, and Hoyt, a boutique firm in Midtown. They had an appointment for the reading of the will. While her cousin sat texting, Sonia stood at the window speaking quietly into the phone.

They had been surprised to learn her uncle had a will. He didn't have much, and Valencia had access to his bank account, and her name was listed on the deed of the house, allowing her to take full possession in the event of his death. Sonia was even more surprised to learn that *she* was mentioned in his will. While he did raise her, she was not his daughter.

"Are you sure there's nothing I can do?" Esteban asked.

He sounded so concerned that her resolve wavered. Then she reminded herself to be strong and continue her plans to walk away. Only heartbreak would come from loving a man who didn't love you back.

"I'm sure."

"Ladies, you can go in now," the receptionist said.

"It's time for me to go," Sonia said. "I'll talk to you later."

"All right." Esteban's voice held a note of resignation.

Sonia hung up and followed her cousin down the hallway to Sterling Buchanan's office. He stood in the open doorway, younger than expected, a light-skinned brother with blue eyes and a goatee.

She and Valencia entered his office, sat down in front of him, and waited.

"Before we begin," he said, "I'm sorry for your loss. Mr. Melancon was a wonderful man. He was kind and generous in spirit. I owe much of my success to him." His mouth twisted into a wry smile. "He sent so many referrals our way it helped us build our business. Not to mention, he made the best dang red velvet cake I've ever had. I looked forward to his delivery every Christmas."

They all laughed—bittersweet, but a much-needed easing of tension in the room.

"As you know, your father, and your uncle, lived a very modest lifestyle. Some would say frugal, and one of the amazing things about him was that he managed to hide much of his assets from the rest of the world. I was surprised when I looked at the totality of the estate he left behind."

"Estate?" Valencia said. "I wouldn't call his meager savings and that old house on Sixth Street an estate."

The leather chair creaked when Sterling settled back into it. "Well, the house is worth quite a bit. As you know, there's a lot of construction in the area, and your father was wise not to sell. He's sitting on a premium property that's worth a hefty sum. But that's only part of it. His entire estate is worth, with savings and life insurance policies, the house, and his mutual funds, almost seven million."

Valencia's eyes went wide and they both gasped.

"Excuse me? I think I misheard you," Sonia said.

Valencia sat up and forward. "S-seven million dollars? You must be mistaken."

Sterling shook his head. "I'm not. I've never seen anything like it."

Valencia's mouth fell open. "But, but he lived as if..."

"Seven million?" Sonia said again.

Sterling nodded and smiled. "Now let me tell you how he wanted everything to be divided up."

The bulk of her uncle's $6.85 million estate would be split between Sonia and Valencia. After disbursements to other entities, three million went to Valencia and two million to Sonia.

Even now, she couldn't believe the sum. He'd lived his life so simply, never buying anything nice for himself, and seldom purchased anything new. All his possessions—furniture, clothes, car, everything —he'd purchased secondhand. He'd lived in that drafty old house until she hired a company to install the central heating and air system for him. She'd thought he'd done all of that out of necessity. She'd thought he was poor, but he wasn't. Far from it, in fact. He was rich. Rich in money, rich in love, and rich in compassion. She had no doubt he'd scrimped and saved all those years to leave something behind for her and Valencia.

In death he continued to look out for her and convinced her that she was making the right decision to leave Esteban. All the pieces were falling into place perfectly.

She wouldn't live the same luxurious lifestyle she'd become accustomed to as Esteban's mistress, but thanks to Uncle Rowell, she'd be comfortable.

Her eyes welled with tears.

Unbelievable.

CHAPTER 35

$\mathcal{B}$efore Esteban landed at the Miami International Airport, he knew something was wrong. He knew it both times he'd spoken to Sonia while she was in Atlanta. She'd sounded odd on the phone—apathetic and unengaged. That was why he'd wrapped up his business in California and flown to Atlanta this morning—the day after he spoke to her, only to be told by her cousin, Valencia, that she'd gone back to Miami the day before. The unsettling feeling increased when he called and got her voicemail.

When he arrived in Miami and reached a disconnected number, the sense of foreboding grew. He called Jackie, but she claimed she didn't know Sonia's whereabouts—not that he believed her.

The Maybach glided down the causeway, but the picturesque view of Biscayne Bay sparkling on either side couldn't hold his attention. He'd seen this view thousands of times before, but it didn't matter to him because all he cared to see was Sonia waiting at the house.

By the time he walked through the front door and dropped his briefcase in the foyer, his head hurt from the stress. The cold fingers of dread fisted in his chest as he noted the eerie silence. Standing in the foyer, he listened for sounds of life.

Someone was in the kitchen.

He hurried in that direction and found Delores standing over the stove, stirring a pot of fragrant meat in preparation for the evening meal.

"Have you seen Sonia?" he asked.

"No, *señor*." She looked up briefly, and he wondered if she was hiding something.

Coiled tension gripped his body as he charged through the house like an Iberian bull, shoving open doors on the way to the bedroom they shared. He did that to every room, bellowing her name, because no matter what the knot in his stomach suggested, he refused to believe she had really left him. She must be here somewhere.

A quick sweep of the bedroom showed that it was empty, and the en suite bathroom held no trace of her. All of her lotions, gels, and splashes were gone.

No. No.

She wouldn't have left him like this.

He yanked open the door to her dressing room with such force it slammed against the outer wall and bounced. Empty hangers mocked him in silent disdain.

He yanked open a dresser drawer.

Empty.

He pulled open another.

Empty.

And another.

Empty.

And another.

He slammed the last one closed, panic seizing his muscles. Where the hell could she be? Why would she leave? He'd told her he wanted to talk. She'd promised to be here.

Back in the bedroom, his eyes landed on a white envelope propped against the stack of pillows on the bed. He'd missed it when he entered, but rushed over and tore it open.

Esteban, I'm no longer happy with our arrangement. I think a clean break is best. Don't call, because I've disconnected my phone. Don't try to find me, because you won't. Thank you for everything.

Goodbye,

Sonia

He muttered every curse word he knew as he crushed the hand-written note.

Thank you for everything?

Tossing the crumpled paper onto the bed, he bellowed, "Delores!"

Long strides took him back down the hall and past the sunken living room with its wall of windows.

Before he asked Delores a word, he could tell from her demeanor and the way her eyes didn't meet his that she was guilty. She stared down at the island, her hands loosely clenched on its stone surface.

"Yes, Mr. Galiano?"

"Do you know where she is?" he asked slowly, in a quiet voice.

"No." Her voice quivered.

"Do you know where Sonia is?"

"No." She shook her head vigorously this time. She ventured a look at him.

"Did you know that she was leaving and not tell me?"

"Yes," she replied in a distinctly smaller voice. Her eyes widened with fright.

"Why did you do that?"

"Sh-she begged me not to."

Esteban stalked over to her. "Who do you work for?"

She trembled, her gaze dropping and her hands on the surface of the island clenching tighter.

"Who do you *fucking* work for!"

Her face crumpled, and she clutched her hands to her chest. "You, Mr. Galiano," she whispered.

"That's right. You work for me." He got in her face, and she flinched. "This is the first and last time you make the mistake of betraying me. *You work for me,* Delores. Don't you ever forget that again!"

He swung around and marched to the intercom. Slamming his fist to the button, he yelled into the speaker, "Abel!"

"Yes, Mr. Galiano."

"Bring the Porsche from the garage. I'm going out."

"Yes, Mr. Galiano." Abel didn't hesitate. He recognized that Esteban was not in the mood for bullshit.

With one last glower at his cowering housekeeper, who looked like she wanted to dissolve into the floor, Esteban went back to the bedroom and changed into a pair of jeans and a black T-shirt.

He found the black Porsche in the driveway with the keys on the seat. Donning a pair of sunglasses, he hopped in and gunned the engine, driving off with a squeal of tires and smoke toward South Beach.

He arrived at Sonia's old apartment in record time. She didn't know this, but he knew she'd held on to it and sublet it for extra income. He climbed the stairs two at a time, reached the third floor, and knocked on her door.

No answer.

He pounded harder.

The door remained closed. He pounded again and again, the sound of his knocks booming in the hallway as he slammed the side of his fist over and over into the wood.

Behind him, a door cracked open, and Sonia's neighbor poked out her head. Today her blonde hair looked frizzy and she was bleary-eyed, as if she'd just woken up. Pulling a ratty robe closer around her body, she looked him up and down with definite interest in her eyes.

"She's not here," she said.

"Have you seen her lately?" Esteban asked.

"Haven't seen her in a long time."

"How long?" He studied her face. She seemed to be telling the truth.

She shrugged and pulled the robe tighter. "Few weeks, at least. Not since the last person she let use the place left. Anyway, you're wasting your time."

"Why do you say that?"

"Her lease must be up, because the landlord ripped out the carpet today. He's getting ready to put the place up for rent again."

An invisible noose tightened around his neck.

"Thank you."

"No problem." The door clicked shut.

Esteban rushed back down the stairs to his car and stood outside on the sidewalk. His gaze traversed the length of the street, as if he'd see her there somewhere, but all he saw were strangers. A little girl skipped ahead of her mother. A man rode his bike down the middle of the street with one hand, while he hugged a bag of groceries to his chest with the other. Joggers taking a leisurely run followed behind each other in an evenly spaced line of three.

He ran an agitated hand over his hair and harnessed the panic that consumed him. *Cálmate*, he told himself.

He had to find her. He loved—

Shock resounded through his skull like a sonic boom. Esteban stopped moving. He was losing the woman he loved.

This woman whom he'd simply wanted to bed had become entrenched in his life in a way he never imagined. Sonia was stubborn but kindhearted, goal-oriented and thoughtful, and completely indispensable to him.

He opened the car door and sank into the driver's seat. He had to get her back. That was the only way to get rid of this crushing, heavy weight—as if a boulder sat on his chest.

Gripping the steering wheel, he resolved to do whatever it took to make her return. He'd give her whatever she wanted.

He loved her. He *needed* her.

Esteban took a deep breath and, bending his head, closed his eyes.

Think. Where would she go?

His head jerked up. Jackie.

Jackie must have lied to him, which meant she knew where Sonia was—was probably even hiding her in her house. Esteban started the car and spun in a U-turn back down the street.

Wherever Sonia was, he'd find her. He'd tear the whole goddamn city apart if he had to.

* * *

SONIA STEPPED out of the cool shower and dried her skin in the fluffy towel she pulled from the stainless steel bar. Even though flush with money, she hadn't gone on a crazy spending spree. She'd paid cash for a used Camry and rented this two-bedroom, two-bath townhouse in a quiet community, away from the craziness of South Beach.

An older Cuban couple owned the place and lived next door. They were kind and friendly, and their son flirted whenever they ran into each other, but not so much that she became uncomfortable.

In the mornings, she walked to the park nearby and ran laps around the small track to stay in shape. At night, she kept mostly to herself. No more parties on South Beach or mixing with celebrities or the uber-wealthy. The last time she'd seen a movie, she went to the matinee. There was no private screening after a special invite from the director, or lounging in the theater room of Esteban's mansion.

A lot had changed in the past couple of weeks. Including *this*.

She stepped over to the vanity and looked down at the home pregnancy test.

Despite taking precautions, she'd gotten pregnant.

She stared at the results.

Pregnant.

She bit her lip and smiled.

"I'm going to be a mother," she whispered.

She stared at her naked image in the mirror and placed a hand on her flat stomach, imagining her widening waistline in the months ahead. There were no discernible physical changes yet, but the tiredness, mild cramping, and backaches she'd experienced now made sense.

What would it be like to be someone's mother?

She already had a good example of the patience and nurturing necessary for the role. Like her Uncle Rowell did for her, she'd give her son or daughter plenty of love and attention. And they'd learn to make the best darn red velvet cake in the country, even if Mommy didn't want to eat any.

She laughed to herself, but sobered when she thought about Esteban.

God, she missed him. Ached for him physically and mentally. She wanted to feel his strength, hear the soft rumble of his chuckle again.

Closing her eyes, she imagined his arrogant face. She needed to tell him, but would he want this child?

She spread her fingers over her belly.

It didn't matter if he wanted this baby or not. She wanted it and could afford to take care of the child by herself. She'd saved tens of thousands of dollars living with Esteban, and that didn't include the finer, more expensive pieces of jewelry locked away in a safe deposit box for a rainy future. The check from her uncle's estate had already arrived, and a meeting with a financial advisor in a few days would help her determine how best to make the money last and multiply.

"A baby."

Sonia couldn't stop touching her belly. Or grinning. She should be terrified, but wasn't. She was at peace, and could hardly contain her anticipation.

CHAPTER 36

Sonia couldn't stay at home and bask in all those emotions. Jackie's first engagement party was taking place tonight on the yacht of a wealthy developer named Daniel Baker. Her fiancé was his private chef, and because of their good relationship, Daniel had agreed they could use his property and the yacht moored in front of his house on Hibiscus Island.

Guests had permission to use the house, but the party was taking place on the yacht. The second engagement party, scheduled two weeks away in London, was a way for Jackie's parents to meet and approve of her fiancé, and begin the aspects of the traditional Chinese wedding they expected Jackie to adhere to.

Sonia was leaning against the railing of the boat and watched two leisure crafts anchored in the dark water a distance away. Guests' laughter floated on the night air as the sound of waves lapped against the hull.

"You are a doll."

Jackie threw her thin arms around Sonia's neck in a side hug.

Tonight she wore her long black hair over one shoulder and looked radiant in a sleeveless dress with spaghetti straps that skimmed her slender body. The red color, chosen because it symbolized good fortune in Chinese culture, made the diamond necklace around her neck shine with a brilliance that matched the ring on her finger.

"Why am I a doll?" Sonia grinned at her friend.

"Because you'd obviously rather be anywhere else but here, but you came anyway."

"That's not true."

Jackie cocked an eyebrow.

"You know I'm happy for you," Sonia said.

"I do. And I'm glad you came instead of moping at home."

"I wasn't moping." Sonia elbowed her friend, but Jackie cocked her brow again. "I *wasn't*."

"If you say so. Anyway, I have someone for you to meet," Jackie added in a conspiratorial tone.

Sonia sighed. "I don't think that's a good idea. I'm not ready to start dating."

"It doesn't have to be serious, love, but you need someone to take your mind off him." She leveled a concerned look at Sonia.

"Stop looking at me like that. I'm not going to fall to pieces. I managed to survive twenty-seven years before I met Esteban, and I'll be fine without him."

Jackie had been her rock and hadn't once reminded her that she'd warned Sonia against getting involved in a mistress-benefactor relationship with Esteban. She simply listened and hugged and soothed with words of comfort.

"Of course you will, but we could speed along your progress by helping you find a nice-looking, eligible bachelor among the lot here tonight." She twisted Sonia away from the water to face the people on the yacht. "As far as the eye can see, there are plenty of men available."

"I don't need a matchmaker," Sonia said. Nor did she want a man, especially since she had a child growing inside of her, her primary focus for a long time to come.

"The one over there, talking to my darling fiancé, is looking for a wife." Jackie inclined her head to a dark-haired man sipping a martini while in conversation with Evan. Evan was blond, with blue eyes and pale skin. Jackie stood two inches taller than him in flats, but it was clear that she saw him as a giant among men.

"He's a friend of Evan's, and he's dying to meet you. I promised him an introduction."

"You did what?"

Jackie shrugged. "I thought it would be good for you."

"Jackie…"

"Don't make me out to be a liar." Jackie pouted.

That face might work on her fiancé, but not on Sonia.

"*No.*"

Jackie's brow wrinkled. "You're sure?"

"Positive."

"Very well." Jackie sighed dramatically. She scanned her friend's face. "I must say, you look better tonight. Better than I've seen you in a while. You have a bit of color in your cheeks."

"I'm feeling a little better, and getting out socially is good for me."

"I agree."

They stood quietly in companionable silence before Evan caught Jackie's eyes and motioned for her to come over.

"Duty calls," she groaned, although she obviously loved it. "You'll be all right?"

"I'll be fine. Go." Sonia gave her a gentle shove. She watched as Jackie, after a brief hesitation, floated away to her fiancé's side. She said a few words to Evan's friend, who then turned in Sonia's direction. She immediately looked away, not wanting to offer any encouragement.

From the corner of her eye, she saw the trio walk farther away on the deck, and let her gaze wander around to the other guests.

Across the way, a voluptuous woman wearing a body-hugging jumpsuit that left little to the imagination drifted away and revealed two men seated on deck chairs, one of them the last person she expected to see.

Sonia's heart juddered to a stop and her breath caught in sudden panic. What was Esteban doing at Jackie's engagement party?

Entranced, she watched him bring a crystal tumbler to his lips and nod at something the other man said. His appearance reminded her of the first time she'd seen him. He looked arrogant, rich, and bored.

Then he spotted her, and his gaze lanced through her from that distance. Guests crisscrossed in front of their line of vision but couldn't break the magnetic connection that kept their gazes locked on each other. Very slowly, Esteban placed his glass on the nearby table and rose from the chair.

Sonia's eyes darted around for an escape, but instead of running, she pressed her back against the boat and gripped the edges of her maxi dress, desperate for something to hold on to.

Esteban stopped a few feet away, and his dark eyes took her in, scouring from her face to the length of her body.

"You look delicious," he said.

She knew what was coming next and didn't want to hear it. "Esteban "

"Good enough to eat."

He'd done it on purpose, of course, because the words had always precluded him doing just that. His lips would kiss and tug the flesh between her legs, and his tongue would lap at the moisture her body emitted at the sound of those words.

He looked like a predator ready to pounce, and she tried not to fidget under his scrutiny.

"You shouldn't be here," she said.

"I was invited."

"By who?"

"Daniel Baker. The man who owns this yacht."

"In other words, you used your connection to crash my friend's engagement party."

He ignored the jab. "You look well. Being apart from me has been good for you, it seems."

The back of his fingers brushed Sonia's neck, wreaking havoc with her nerve endings before she edged away from his touch.

"I miss you," he said grimly.

"Don't." It was hard enough seeing him. Hearing those words was an unbearable torture.

He walked closer, and his big body cast a shadow across her and blocked the light. "Don't tell you the truth?"

"You're not being fair."

"You turned Delores against me and moved out of our home like a thief in the night. Do you think that was fair? Especially coming from a woman who spoke to me about trust and blatantly lied to me after she promised she'd be here when I returned."

She wasn't proud of what she'd done, but she'd been right to sneak away. Seeing him and hearing the determination in his voice confirmed he would have definitely tried to hold on to her, and she wouldn't have been strong enough to leave if he tried to stop her.

"I had to leave that way, or I might…might not have gone through with it."

"Then you didn't really want to leave," he said smoothly.

"You're wrong."

"I'm never wrong."

"Maybe you are this time," she said fiercely.

He laughed softly. "What was I wrong about? That you enjoyed my gifts and enjoyed my touch. Don't tell me you faked everything. Those cries of Esteban, Esteban, please…oh god…were *fake*?"

Her cheeks burned.

He came even closer, and only a finger's width of air remained between them. "Or when you said, right there, yes—my goodness, right there. That was fake, too?"

"Mocking me is not the way to establish any type of cordial relationship between us."

"Cordial relationship?" He snorted. "I want my lover back."

"That won't happen."

"So what will it take?"

"I don't want to fight with you."

"What will it take, Sonia?" he demanded in a harsher voice. "As my mistress, I gave you everything you could possibly need."

"*You* had everything you needed." She glared at him.

"And now you're gone, and I need you to come back to me."

"Because you say so?"

"Yes, because I say so," he said, shaking with some type of emotion. She thought she recognized anger, but it seemed like something else.

His jaw hardened. "What do you want? Tell me. More money?"

"I don't need or want your money."

"You expect me to believe that?" Esteban asked.

She remained silent and stared at the mansion on the shore. Every window was lit up with lights, and guests traveled the stone path that led from the dock to the back door.

"All right, I see you're playing hardball." He chuckled, but tension radiated from him. His hand fisted at his side. "I'll double your allowance if you come back to me."

Her eyes flew to his face. "I'm not trying to negotiate with you. I don't want anything."

"Sonia—"

"God, Esteban, don't you understand? It's not about the money."

"Then what is it?" Resting one hand on the railing, he bent his head to her ear.

Night after night she'd slept in his bed. He'd given her his body, but she wanted his heart. Placing a hand on his chest, she felt the blood-pumping organ thump beneath her fingertips.

She could walk away now because she didn't need him or his money, yet...she'd missed him, and here he was, having come for her in his own way. Not the way she wanted, but all she could expect.

She inhaled silently. The scent of his skin and cologne were achingly familiar. Staying away from him had been *so hard*. An hour felt like a day, and a day like a week. She loved him. Wholeheartedly. Recklessly. And wanted him to love her, too.

"Sonia?" His voice was low, with an odd catch to it.

He'd raised the bar, and not because of the expensive gifts and trips. Those were wonderful, she couldn't deny. But it was because of how considerate he was. His thoughtfulness. He seldom paid attention to details, except when it came to her, and did so in a way other men didn't.

And she missed the intimacy between them. She longed for the weight of him between her legs, the way he worshiped her body with his mouth, sucking on her nipples, kissing every inch of skin while he whispered in husky tones about how much he desired her and how beautiful she was. He was full of compliments, yet they never sounded clichéd or fake the way they did from other men. They sounded real and sexy, and made her ache for closer contact. From the first night at Patagonia, he'd seduced her with his words, and she'd slowly started falling in love with him. If she'd bothered to pay attention, she would have seen it.

"Anything you want, you know I'll give it to you. Tell me what you want, *querida*."

Sonia swallowed past the lump in her throat. "I want a Rolls-Royce Phantom," she whispered. This was what he understood. This was what he expected.

A few seconds elapsed, and she could hear him breathing over the sound of the lapping water and the cheerful, laughing guests.

"Color?" he asked in a dull voice.

"Metallic blue," Sonia whispered, dying inside.

He kept his head bent to hers, and his breath brushed the side of her neck. "Done. What else?"

"That's it."

"You want something else. I can hear it in your voice. Tell me."

I want you to love me.

Tears crept to the corners of her eyes. "The new Hermès bag. Jackie has one, and I want it."

"Done. What else?"

She shook her head because it was too difficult to speak.

"I want you to move back in right away."

"Of course," she said in a thick voice.

He tilted up her chin with his fist. His dark eyes gazed into hers, as if they were the only two people on the yacht. No one else existed as she got lost in his eyes.

"Is it so terrible for you to be with me?"

Her breath caught. "No."

He let out a breath and kissed her temple.

"Esteban?"

"Yes?"

"I have something to tell you."

His eyes found hers. "What is it?"

She took a deep breath. "I'm pregnant."

CHAPTER 37

*E*steban sat on the patio outside his bedroom smoking a cigar and kept an eye on Sonia fast asleep on the bed, back where she belonged. He watched as she tossed under the dark sheets and then resettled, curling onto her side.

Had it only been two weeks since she left him? Add in the weeks before when he'd been traveling on business, and they'd been apart much too long.

His investigator had found her within days of leaving him, but he'd wanted to give her space and had curbed his inclination to go get her, drag her back to the mansion, and lock her away so she could never leave him again. Now that she was here, he no longer felt incomplete, splintered. He felt whole, and for the first time in weeks, his mind was at rest.

Except for one new detail. They were having a baby.

Her declaration shocked him at first. Then he'd been worried as he let her words digest. Except in very rare circumstances, abortion was illegal in his country. In the U.S., it was a different story. He'd have no rights. He'd have no say. But then Sonia said three words that put his mind at ease.

I'm keeping it.

After that, he'd whisked her away from the yacht and brought her back to the house. She slept in one of his white T-shirts, but tomorrow he'd send someone to get her clothes. For now, he wanted her —*them*—near.

He'd be a better father than his ever was. His child would never go hungry. His child would want for nothing, and he'd shower him or her with all the love and attention he never received. And Sonia would want for nothing, too. He'd get a ring and ask her to marry him. Any woman would be happy for marriage, wouldn't she? Even a woman he had to bribe to come back to him.

His jaw tightened. He never wanted to experience that type of desperation again, unable to imagine one more day without her but not knowing what it would take to win her back. He'd never wanted a woman—anything, really—so much. His love for her was all-consuming.

Esteban took a drag on the cigar and let the smoke ooze from the corner of his mouth. Marriage was the best way to make sure he could hold on to her, and they could raise their child together.

He extinguished the cigar and went back into the house through the glass door. Climbing into bed, he pulled Sonia into his arms. She murmured and her eyes opened into slits.

"Esteban?"

"Go back to sleep," he said softly.

He brushed strands of hair from her forehead and watched as she settled back into slumber. Tenderly, he kissed her brow and the bridge of her nose.

A baby. Sonia was having his baby.

He'd talk to his jeweler and start working on an engagement ring. Then he'd ask her to marry him.

* * *

"I KNEW there was something different about you at the engagement party," Jackie said. She sat across from Sonia as they ate beneath the umbrellas at their favorite brunch spot on South Beach.

"You didn't know squat," Sonia said.

"Remember, I said you looked better."

Sonia grinned. She'd been doing that a lot lately—grinning. Ever since she and Esteban reconciled.

Their relationship wasn't ideal, but he was different in subtle ways because of the baby. He was more attentive and extremely gentle.

"So when is your doctor's appointment?"

"Not until next week."

"Why so far away?"

"He's one of the best obstetricians in the city and is booked solid for weeks. The reason I got an appointment is because of a cancellation. I've been reading up online, and during the first ultrasound, we'll be able to hear the baby's heartbeat." She couldn't wait for that moment.

"So Esteban is going with you?" Jackie asked.

"I don't think I could keep him away with a bomb threat."

Jackie snorted and covered her mouth as she laughed. When she caught her breath, she studied Sonia's face. "You love him, don't you?" she asked quietly.

The question took Sonia by surprise, and she felt tears prick her eyes. She blinked rapidly to dispel them. "Is it that obvious?"

"It wasn't at first. I guessed you had feelings for Esteban, but seeing you pregnant and back together with him, I know it's more than... having feelings. You're in love him."

No point in lying to her best friend. She let out a heavy breath of resignation. "Yeah."

"Does he know?" Jackie asked gently.

Sonia shook her head and dabbed at the corner of her eye with a napkin. "How am I supposed to tell him? Hey, I'm in love with you."

"Sonia."

"No, really. What should I say? 'Yes, I know that you don't love me and feelings weren't part of our agreement, but I love you. What do you say we try to make a go of this for real? For the baby's sake.'" She let out a laugh and dabbed the corner of her eye again when another tear escaped.

Jackie reached across the table and took her hand. "Maybe you won't use those exact words, but you could certainly talk to him about your feelings."

"No, I can't."

"Yes, you can. You're having his baby, for heaven's sake. He must care about you a little bit. He tracked you down at my engagement party, and before that, when he showed up at my house, he looked like he wanted to kill someone. Namely me, because I wouldn't tell him where you were."

Sonia smiled despite herself. "He wouldn't have killed you."

"I'm not so sure," Jackie muttered. She squeezed Sonia's hand and then withdrew. "Maybe if the two of you could talk, you'll see he might have feelings for you, too."

"Honestly, I don't want to risk it. I've been disappointed enough times to know that I should accept this is the best things will get for me."

"So you're settling?"

"Yes and no. I'm back with Esteban, and he wants me, in his own way. And we're having a baby, which he obviously wants. That he can't hide."

She shouldn't have doubted he'd want this baby. Having been orphaned, he was determined to have an active role in their child's life and provide any and everything their little one could want or need.

He'd already started making plans, discussing how they could move their bedroom upstairs to be near the baby. He'd suggested knocking out a wall between two of the bedrooms and creating a baby suite, which Sonia thought was a bit much. But in true Esteban fashion, he'd already scheduled contractors and interior designers to come out and propose possibilities.

"The other day, a giant stuffed giraffe he'd bought online was delivered to the house. When I asked him about it, he said he thought our child would enjoy it when he or she arrived."

"Wait a minute, *he* bought it? Not Abena?" Jackie asked.

"He did. Can you believe it?" Sonia sipped her orange juice.

"He's really excited, isn't he? But why a giant giraffe?"

"He saw a commercial or something and thought it would be perfect."

"Oh dear, you'll have to keep an eye on him or your child will end up very spoiled, with all sorts of toys, and who knows what else. Perhaps a diamond studded stroller and Chanel diapers?"

They giggled. If those items existed, she wouldn't be a bit surprised if Esteban purchased them.

"Do you forgive him for the Pedro nonsense?"

Sonia nodded. "I do. I was disappointed by what he'd done, but he was right. If Pedro had cared about me, he wouldn't have been tempted away by that woman. Maybe that's what hurt, too, you know? I already knew Pedro was no good for me, but I didn't want to have to face that, and Esteban proved it without question."

"We have to face our mistakes head-on. We get hit hardest when we try to avoid them."

Sonia nodded. "You're right."

"So, where to?" Jackie picked up the bill.

"I should get that. It's my turn, isn't it?"

Jackie waved her off. "Next time. Besides, you're coming all the way to London for my party, and you get to meet my very traditional Chinese parents." She wrinkled her nose.

"They're not that bad."

"They're terrible." Jackie took out her wallet and dropped a credit card on the bill.

"Well, tell me all about your traditions so I get it right. I want to be the perfect maid of honor."

A slice of pain cut across Sonia's lower abdomen, and she grunted, clutching her midsection.

Jackie's brow furrowed. "What's wrong?"

"I don't know." Sonia rubbed the area where the pain stemmed from. "I've experienced cramping before, but this is worse."

"Cramping?"

Sonia nodded. "From everything I've read, it's normal when you're pregnant. Mild cramping, backaches. It's all part of my body getting ready for the pregnancy."

"When did you first experience the pain?"

"It wasn't pain. Just a little discomfort." Sonia tried to remember. "A couple of weeks ago, I think."

"Should we take you to the doctor?"

"No, I—*oh!*" Sonia doubled over and clutched her stomach. That pain was sharper. The severity cut through to her spine like period cramps on steroids.

"Sonia, what's wrong?" Jackie shot from her chair and rushed to her side.

Sonia gripped the table and breathed through her mouth. "Okay, this is more than mild cramping."

"We're taking you to the doctor right now. Come along."

Jackie helped her from the chair, and when she stood, Sonia felt moisture between her legs.

"Sonia," Jackie said from behind her.

The sound of her friend's voice worried her. "What is it?"

"There's a bit of blood on your trousers."

"What?"

"It's all right, sweetheart. It's all right. Come along." Holding on to Sonia's elbow, Jackie guided her down the side street to the Aston Martin. She helped her into the passenger seat and strapped her in.

"You forgot your credit card." Sonia focused on everything else around her to keep from panicking. The man walking his dog. The mother and daughter strolling arm in arm.

"I'll come back for it later." Jackie ran around the front of the car and hopped into the driver's seat.

Leaning against the door, Sonia clutched her stomach—not because she was in so much pain, but because she needed to protect the life inside her. "Please, no," she whispered.

Jackie reached over and took her hand. "It's okay, love. We're on the way to the hospital. Everything will be fine."

She pulled out of the parking space and sped off down the street.

CHAPTER 38

*E*steban launched from the chair when Dr. Morgan entered the private room. Lines of fatigue draped across the doctor's face, and his tall, reedlike frame seemed too narrow for the white lab coat that hung loosely on his body.

The hospital had conducted an ultrasound and run a battery of tests, and by the doctor's grave expression, Esteban knew the results were not good.

The doctor shook his head, confirming the worst. "I wish I had better news." His gaze shifted to Sonia lying on the bed. Her skin looked pale, and Esteban hadn't seen her cry since he arrived, but her red-rimmed eyes indicated she had.

"I'm sorry, but you lost the baby."

The words rocked Esteban on his feet, but he managed to remain upright despite the ferocious blow.

Sonia didn't say a word. She turned onto her side and faced away from them both.

"How?" Esteban croaked. He ran agitated fingers through his hair. He needed to understand how this could happen when they'd been looking forward to hearing their child's heartbeat in less than a week.

"She lost the baby about ten days ago."

"No." He shook his head. The doctor had to be mistaken. "She took a pregnancy test a few days ago. It was positive."

The doctor tented his fingertips together. "A home pregnancy test depends on a hormone called hCG being present in the urine. After a miscarriage, the hormone doesn't disappear completely. It can remain in the body for days, or even weeks."

He spoke softly and with compassion, but the words still grated like sandpaper on raw skin, and they angered Esteban. None of this made any sense.

"We have an appointment for next week. We were going to hear our child's heartbeat," he said, as if that made a difference.

"I understand, Mr.—"

"No, you do not understand." Esteban spoke in a firm but shaky voice. "You have made a mistake. Do more tests. Do different tests."

Dr. Morgan's face transformed into a sympathetic mask. "There are no more tests to be done, Mr. Galiano," he said quietly.

Before Esteban could rage against him, the doctor glanced at Sonia's curled-up figure on the bed. Without saying a word, he reminded Esteban there was someone else in the room in just as much pain as he was. He was disoriented and discombobulated. Dizzy with sorrow. But he couldn't imagine how much Sonia must be hurting, and here he was—arguing and thinking about himself instead of comforting her.

He needed to be strong, even though being strong was the last thing he felt like being right now. He felt weak. Helpless. Impotent. He couldn't save his unborn child, and he didn't know how to comfort Sonia.

"I'd like her to stay overnight so we can keep an eye on her," the doctor said. "I want to ensure all the fetal tissue has expelled from her body and make sure there's no chance of infection. She also lost quite a bit of blood. I'm sure she'll be okay, but I want to take this extra precaution."

Esteban nodded in agreement.

"I'll leave the two of you alone." Dr. Morgan walked quietly to the door. Seconds later, Esteban heard it close behind him.

"Sonia?"

She didn't respond. She faced the window, and he couldn't see her expression.

Esteban walked around the foot of the bed to the other side. Sonia was staring out the window, clutching a wad of tissue as fresh tears left a wet trail over the bridge of her nose.

Her silent grief gutted him. Sinking onto the mattress, he reached for her hand, but she tightened her body and shrank away. In response to her rejection, his fingers curled into a ball on the sheets. He wasn't upset. He knew she was hurting. He was hurting.

"I don't know what to say," he whispered.

Trite platitudes that promised everything would be okay were the last thing he wanted to hear, so he knew she didn't want to hear them either.

Sonia sniffled and held tight to the tissue in her hand.

"The doctor wants you to stay overnight."

She continued to stare out the window, as if he wasn't talking. As if he wasn't there.

"I know you don't feel like talking right now, but when you're ready, I'm here. We can talk whenever you want."

Still nothing. Only an empty gaze.

Esteban remained in the same position for a few minutes, contemplating what he should do or what he should say. He'd never felt so helpless in his life.

"Go." She spoke in a soft voice.

"No." He couldn't leave. Not now. Not when she needed him.

She swallowed, and a fresh tear leaked from the corner of her eye and bled over her nose onto the pillow. "Please."

Her hoarse plea tore him apart. Not wanting to leave but wanting to give her the space she needed, Esteban chose to put distance between them.

He returned to the chair he'd left when the doctor came in. Taking a seat, he watched her back. He sat there for a long time, without thinking, numb. Shadows overtook the room when the sun gave way to evening.

A nurse came in to check on Sonia, and Esteban awoke from his comatose state and shifted position. Sonia still hadn't moved. She remained curled up on her side, like someone afraid to move because movement brought too much pain.

The nurse ran through a series of checks, gave Sonia pain medicine, and spoke quietly to her for a few seconds.

On her way out the door, the nurse paused and looked at him with compassionate eyes. "Can I get you anything, Mr. Galiano?"

"I'm fine, thank you."

She left, and he shut down again. Became numb and empty inside.

Night fell, casting the room in dark shadows.

A different nurse came in, checked on Sonia, and cast a pitying look at him as she walked through the door.

How much time had passed? He wasn't sure and couldn't keep track.

This time, he didn't fall back into a numbed state. This time, he remained conscious, and his thoughts tormented him. That was when the pain started. The pain he'd been avoiding by shutting down. Disappointment and loss filled his chest and bulldozed their way into his gut and neck and brain.

His head dropped forward under the weight of the crushing emotions. Their child was gone, and there was not a single thing his wealth and power could have done to save their baby.

A line of tears scrolled down his left cheek, and Esteban scrubbed it away with a rough hand. Easing from the chair, he straightened and stretched his body, stiff and aching from having sat in the same position for hours.

Then he heard the whimpers. Grief had fought its way through their barriers at the same time. Sonia was crying.

Without hesitation, Esteban rushed to her side and climbed into the bed behind her.

"Shh," he whispered, gathering her close. "*Todo estara bien, querida.*"

He kissed the back of her neck and held her tight as sobs racked her body.

"*Todo estara bien, mi amor.*"

He didn't know if she heard him or understood the words he said, but right now, no matter how trite the promise that everything would be okay, it was the only way he knew to ease her pain and bring her a little bit of comfort.

CHAPTER 39

*I*t was time to go. Her frazzled nerves wouldn't last much longer in this tension-filled house.

Sonia zipped the suitcase shut and moved it from the bed to the floor. She hadn't been at Esteban's very long. The boxes and containers in the dressing room remained unopened because she hadn't yet instructed a member of the staff to unpack her clothes and other personal effects.

Casting an eye around the bedroom, she knew with certainty this would be the last time she'd ever see this place. She'd come back because she couldn't bear the thought of life without Esteban, and willingly accepted his definition of a relationship so she could have a fragment of the kind she craved.

But being a kept woman wasn't enough. It would never be enough. She loved Esteban and wanted to be his wife, and every word Jackie said at brunch was true. Sonia *was* settling, and five years from now she didn't want to mumble that she'd settled for her life. She wanted to scream out loud that she'd chosen it.

Sonia turned when she heard Esteban in the doorway. His powerful body was clothed in a charcoal-gray shirt and dark jeans, and his brow remained in what seemed to be a perpetually furrowed state.

His somber gaze flicked over the suitcase and matching bag beside it on the floor. "You're leaving."

"I told you I would."

She couldn't stay. Everything had changed. The energy and excitement of the coming child had been extinguished with abrupt finality. The contractors and interior design team had been canceled. Delores, who had three children of her own and from time to time had offered words of advice, hadn't said much except to ask what they wanted for dinner.

A hard swallow traveled the length of Esteban's throat. "I thought I could talk you out of it."

"You can't. We're past the expiration date on our affair, and after what happened…" Grief tightened her throat, but she fought through. "After what happened, I have to go. It's too much now."

Since leaving the hospital, Esteban and Sonia had barely spoken. Neither knew what to say. They slept in the same bed but never touched. The invisible chasm between them was as deep and wide as the Grand Canyon.

Silence filled the room. Neither of them looked at each other.

"I feel like I could have done more," Esteban said.

"There's nothing either of us could have done."

Dr. Morgan had been very explicit, giving her statistics on how many pregnancies ended in miscarriage and explaining there was nothing she could have done to prevent it. His words didn't make the cross of losing her baby any easier to bear, and nothing he said assuaged the guilt of acknowledging her baby had died, and she hadn't even known. She felt extra empty inside, even though she'd never once felt the flutter of life inside her womb.

"There's nothing more for you to do. You're off the hook," Sonia said.

Esteban's brows snapped together. "How could you say that? Do you think I'm some kind of unfeeling brute who doesn't care about the loss of his own child?"

"No. I didn't mean…" Sonia took a shaky breath. "My words came out wrong. I know you cared about the baby. I meant that you don't have to worry about me. I'm fine." She pulled up the retractable handle on her suitcase and slung the bag over her shoulder. "I'll get the rest of my things later." She walked to the door, but he didn't move.

"Where are you going?" he asked.

"I'm checking into a hotel for a few days." She'd given up her townhouse. Jackie had suggested she come stay with her, but Sonia wanted to be alone for a while. She had a lot of planning to do and considered moving back to Georgia. Per capita, Atlanta had more restaurants than most cities in the country, and with her sommelier certification, she could probably find a job there. If not there, she could start over fresh somewhere else. She only knew she needed to leave Miami and its memories of Esteban behind. New York. Texas. The options were limitless.

"Why waste money on a hotel when you could stay here?" Esteban asked.

"I'm not going to stay here."

He ran an unsteady hand through his hair. "There's plenty of room. Make use of the house, save your money—"

"No."

"Why not?"

"Because, goddammit, money isn't everything, okay?" His eyes widened at the outburst, but she couldn't stop now that she'd let out a portion of her frustration. "You want to know the truth? I don't need to save. I've hardly put a dent in the allowance you gave me every month, and my uncle left me a small fortune."

His startled gaze studied her. "You never mentioned your uncle left you money. He can't have left you much."

"Two million dollars."

He blinked.

"That's right. Two. Million. So you see, I don't need you or your money. I have my own and will be set for a very long time to come. We had an agreement, and we both filled our roles. We didn't have anything special. You made that very clear." She laughed bitterly. "You pay. I obey. Anyone could have been a mistress to you. You never needed *me*, Esteban." Her fingers tightened on the handle of her suitcase, and she stared at the middle of his chest, waiting for him to move.

He finally stepped aside without a word, and Sonia rushed out the door and down the hall. She saw Delores on her way up a side stair-case with a basket of linens in her hands, but the housekeeper paused when she saw Sonia. Sadness filled her eyes. Sonia managed to give her a small, grateful smile, and the housekeeper smiled back before continuing the climb up the stairs.

Sonia was almost to the door when she heard Esteban's voice.

"If you have money, why did you come back?"

She stopped.

"You didn't need me," he said.

"Because I...I thought I could get more. Did you forget? I wanted the Phantom and the Hermès bag."

A slight pause. "That's not why."

The sun came through the decorative glass on either side of the door. Freedom was within reach.

"I came back because of the baby," Sonia whispered.

"I don't believe you. Stay, Sonia."

She dropped the bags and swung around. Why was he doing this? Why couldn't he stop being so selfish and let her go? "Stop it! Stop trying to hold on to me!"

He charged toward her, his pupils flaring with passionate light. "What else am I supposed to do?" he demanded. He cupped her face in his hands and stared down into eyes. "What else is a man supposed to do when the woman he loves is about to leave him, and he's desperate to hold on to her but cannot think of a single way to do that? Tell me what to do, Sonia. Tell me how to hold on to you. Because I cannot let you go."

Sonia blinked and stared up at him in shock. "Wh-what did you say?"

"I can't let you go."

"The part before that. Three sentences before."

His expression softened, raw emotion on his face as plain as day for her to see. "I love you, *querida*."

"When? How? You never said a word before."

His face filled with regret. "As soon as I realized my feelings for you, I should have."

"When did you realize you felt this way?" She couldn't believe the words he was saying. Her heart had never beat so fast before in her life.

"For a long time. When things were smooth between us, I was all right and didn't have to face my feelings. Then a couple of months ago you started slipping away from me..." His voice thickened, and his right hand clenched into a fist. "Slowly, I saw our relationship falling apart, but I didn't know how to fix it. When I came home and you weren't here, I had no choice but to accept that I was in love you, and I was willing to do anything to bring you back home. Anything to get you to stay."

Sonia bit the corner of her lip. "You have no idea how long I've wanted to hear you say those words. I love you, too. God, I love you so much."

They moved at the same time and their mouths meshed together in a hungry, passionate kiss. As Sonia clung to him, Esteban lifted her from the floor and walked slowly to the living room, nipping at her lips, sucking on her tongue.

He lowered onto the sofa and Sonia sighed, brushing her fingers through the thick softness of his hair. "Do you mean it? Please tell me you mean it." Gazing into his dark brown eyes, she held her breath, worried this was all a dream but hoping it wasn't.

"I mean every word. I love you." He kissed her hard. Then soft. Then hard again, and she drowned in the pleasure of his lips. "I should have told you right away, but our damn arrangement complicated everything. I assumed you were here because of the money and gifts."

Sonia traced a finger over the curve of his full bottom lip. "And I assumed you wanted me in your bed and as arm candy. Goodness, we made a mess of everything." She laughed a little and rested her head on his shoulder. Pure, undiluted joy filled her soul. "I'm definitely not dreaming, right?"

"This is no dream."

For a few minutes, Esteban rubbed her back, and she remained quiet and peaceful on his lap, content in a way she never imagined she would be. To think, she'd been ready to walk out the door and leave him behind—no matter how much it pained her—because she didn't think her feelings were reciprocated.

Esteban shifted on the chair and stuck his hands into his pants pocket. The next thing she knew, a small black box appeared in her line of vision.

Sonia's head popped up from his shoulder and she gasped. "Esteban…"

"When you came home with me that night from the yacht, I knew I couldn't let you go again. You make me whole. I was only half alive without you." He opened the box and revealed a brilliant Asscher-cut diamond with smaller diamonds set in the platinum band. His thumb gently brushed her cheek, and he gazed into her eyes with that intense look that had snared her from the very beginning. *Te amo. Eres mi sol. Eres mi luna.*

I love you. You're my sun. You're my moon.

"Will you marry me, Sonia?"

"Oh, Esteban," Sonia whispered. She kissed him, pressing her body as close as she could get.

Esteban eased back, and a slow smile hovered around his lips. "I take it that's a yes?"

"Yes!" Sonia giggled and extended her hand so he could put the ring on her finger, and he slipped it on with ease. "Perfect."

Esteban rubbed his thumb across her fingers and frowned as he looked down at the glowing band on her hand. "I should have done a grander, more creative proposal."

"No, this was just right. Trust me, creative proposals aren't always the best idea." At his puzzled look, Sonia laughed.

Another time she'd tell him Jackie's humorous proposal story. For now, she wanted to bask in the perfection of this moment with her fiancé, the man she'd fallen madly in love with and who, as it turned out, loved her in return.

Sonia wrapped her arms around Esteban's neck and planted another kiss on his delicious mouth.

Nothing else mattered right now. Not the mistakes of their past loves, the missteps they made in their own liaison, or the pain of their shared loss.

All that mattered was that they loved each other.

EPILOGUE

*T*heir sixteen-month-old was a little terror.

Deanna ran through the bedroom suite of their house in Argentina, laughing her little head off as Sonia tried to catch her. Which, at six months pregnant and in heels, was not an easy task. The little thief had snatched Sonia's diamond bracelet from the bed where she'd temporarily set it as she waited for Esteban to come in and fasten it around her wrist.

"Give Mommy the bracelet, Deanna."

"No!" She thought it was a game, and took off toward the sitting area, an energetic ball of wild, curly hair and chubby legs that were surprisingly fast.

Esteban came out of his dressing room, smelling good and looking elegant in a tuxedo that hugged his muscular body. They were on their way to a political function, one that included the president of Argentina and other high-ranking government officials.

Their good friends Nadine and Cortez Alesini would be there. Before Deanna snatched her jewelry, Sonia had sent a quick text to Nadine and let her know they were leaving in a few minutes. Nadine had been a godsend during the difficult period after the miscarriage, when she struggled with the loss. Her friend had encouraged her to keep an open dialogue with Esteban. She advised that hiding their emotions from each other would cause the pain to fester and create problems in their relationship.

Esteban quickly assessed the situation and snatched up his daughter.

Deanna screamed and giggled as he hoisted her in the air and nuzzled her little neck.

"Give Mommy her bracelet," he said in Spanish.

"No, Papa."

Sonia laughed as she watched her husband hold Deanna on one arm while pretending to have a hard time wrestling the jewelry from her tiny fist.

A knock sounded at the door.

"Come in," Sonia called.

The nanny they used while in the country, Lucilla, came in holding a pink stuffed bear. "Good evening, *señor, señora*." She waved the bear at Deanna, who stared at her with uncertainty because she understood if she took the bait of the stuffed toy, she'd be in the clutches of the nanny, and that meant her parents were leaving.

In typical Deanna form, she burst into tears, burying her face in Esteban's neck and wailing her little eyes out to avoid the inevitable.

"Oh, Deanna, baby, we'll only be gone for a couple of hours." Even though she knew Deanna's behavior was theatrical, it broke her heart to see her daughter so distressed. Sonia stroked the little girl's hair. "Be a good girl and go with Lucilla."

Esteban handed off their daughter to the nanny, and after one more outburst of "Mama, no," Deanna comforted herself by clenching her arms around the bear's neck in a wrestling-worthy chokehold.

"Bye, sweetheart." Sonia kissed her tear-stained cheek. "Be good for Lucilla, okay?"

Deanna sniffled and gave her best pitiful face, but when Lucilla walked away with her, she didn't utter another sound.

After they left, Sonia breathed a sigh of relief. "If our son is as rambunctious as she is, we're in trouble."

Esteban chuckled. "Here, let me put this on for you." He fastened the bracelet on her right wrist and then stood back to take a good look. Raising an eyebrow, he said, "You look delicious."

"Don't you dare," Sonia said, blushing. No wife could keep from blushing when her spouse looked at her like that.

She was wearing Esteban's favorite color. The gown was made of chiffon in the palest of yellows. The maxi design exposed her arms but fully covered her breasts, which were heavier and fuller than when she was pregnant with Deanna. The sparkling beaded waistline fit right under her breasts and gave her belly plenty of room among the folds of the dress.

Esteban smiled a devilish grin. "At least let me sneak a kiss."

"A little one," Sonia said, holding her thumb and forefinger less than an inch apart.

He dropped a soft kiss on her lips, but that wasn't enough for her. She lifted a hand to his neck and deepened the kiss, moaning when she had to reluctantly pull away.

She swiped remnants of lipstick from his mouth.

"Ready?" he asked, his smile affectionate.

"Yes." Sonia fit her hand in his, and they exited the bedroom.

The past few years had passed by in a blur of happiness. She and Esteban were married a few months after their reconciliation. Their home base was Miami, but most of the time she traveled with him back and forth to Argentina, as well as to other countries on business, and oversaw the purchase of wine and spirits for all his restaurants.

Although she knew she hadn't done anything to cause her first miscarriage, she slowed down considerably when she became pregnant with Deanna. She was careful not to overexert herself, engaging in moderate exercise, and carefully considered every morsel of food she put in her body. When her baby girl arrived, her joy was only equal in measure to the day she married her husband.

Sonia slid into the back of the limo and Esteban slid in beside her. He was on the phone, and her Spanish had improved enough that she understood every word he said. He was talking to Santiago about a burst pipe in their largest restaurant in California. They'd had to shut down for half a day, but from what she could hear of Esteban's side of the conversation, they should be back in business tomorrow.

Esteban held her hand on his thigh as he wrapped up the phone call. When he finished, she took the phone and dropped it into her purse. She nestled against his side, and he placed an arm around her shoulders and kissed her forehead.

As they rode in comfortable silence to the venue near Plaza de Mayo, the main square in central Buenos Aires, Sonia thought of all those other times, years ago, when they'd sat in the back of a limo or the Maybach, and he'd held her hand or she'd nestled against his side. Not much had changed. She still dressed the way he liked. Her hair was a little longer—long enough to cover her ears, but still short because that was the way he preferred it.

What had changed was her reason for doing those things. Before she'd fulfilled a role, one wrought with uncertainty and dictated by rules of engagement that didn't leave room for openness and honest emotion.

Now she held a more prominent role in his life, Sonia still wanted to make Esteban happy. Not because she had to, as his mistress. But because she wanted to, as his wife.

Still in Love

Read more about Cortez and Nadine Alesini, Sonia and Esteban's friends in Argentina, in Still in Love.

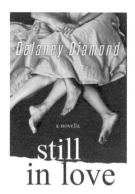

Three years ago, Nadine Alesini divorced her husband and left Buenos Aires with her daughter in tow. Now she's back and forced to spend time with the man she left behind.

Cortez Alesini long ago accepted that his music career aided in the demise of his marriage. So he didn't expect that he and Nadine would spend passionate nights together while she's back in his country, causing them to question if they gave up too soon. But the reappearance of someone from his past immediately causes friction, and may destroy any chance they have at a true reconciliation.

LATIN MEN SERIES

Check out the entire Latin Men series with heroes from Mexico, Ecuador, Brazil, and Argentina: The Arrangement, Fight for Love, Private Acts, The Ultimate Merger, Second Chances, More Than a Mistress, and Undeniable.

ALSO BY DELANEY DIAMOND

Brooks Family series

- Passion Rekindled

Love Unexpected series

- The Blind Date
- The Wrong Man
- An Unexpected Attraction
- The Right Time
- One of the Guys
- That Time in Venice

Johnson Family series

- Unforgettable
- Perfect
- Just Friends
- The Rules
- Good Behavior

Latin Men series

- The Arrangement
- Fight for Love
- Private Acts
- The Ultimate Merger
- Second Chances
- More Than a Mistress
- Undeniable
- Hot Latin Men: Vol. I (print anthology)
- Hot Latin Men: Vol. II (print anthology)

Hawthorne Family series

- The Temptation of a Good Man
- A Hard Man to Love
- Here Comes Trouble
- For Better or Worse
- Hawthorne Family Series: Vol. I (print anthology)
- Hawthorne Family Series: Vol. II (print anthology)

Bailar series (sweet / clean romance)

- Worth Waiting For

Stand Alones

- A Passionate Love
- Still in Love
- Subordinate Position
- Heartbreak in Rio (part of Endless Summer Nights)

Free Stories: www.delaneydiamond.com

ABOUT THE AUTHOR

Delaney Diamond is the USA Today Bestselling Author of sweet, sensual, passionate romance novels. Originally from the U.S. Virgin Islands, she now lives in Atlanta, Georgia. She reads romance novels, mysteries, thrillers, and a fair amount of nonfiction. When she's not busy reading or writing, she's in the kitchen trying out new recipes, dining at one of her favorite restaurants, or traveling to an interesting locale.

Enjoy free reads and the first chapter of all her novels on her website. Join her mailing list to get sneak peeks, notices of sale prices, and find out about new releases.

Join her mailing list
www.delaneydiamond.com

Made in United States
Troutdale, OR
04/21/2024

19351647R10146